CHILDREN
OF
THE WIND

Daughters of the Lamp Series

Daughters of the Lamp
Children of the Wind

CHILDREN OF THE WIND

SEQUEL TO *DAUGHTERS OF THE LAMP*

NEDDA LEWERS

G. P. Putnam's Sons

G. P. Putnam's Sons
An imprint of Penguin Random House LLC, New York

First published in the United States of America by G. P. Putnam's Sons,
an imprint of Penguin Random House LLC, 2024

Visit us online at PenguinRandomHouse.com.

Library of Congress Cataloging-in-Publication Data
Names: Lewers, Nedda, author.
Title: Children of the wind / Nedda Lewers.
Description: New York: G. P. Putnam's Sons, 2024. | Series: Daughters of the lamp series |
Summary: Upon thirteen-year-old Sahara's return to Egypt, she must learn how to wield
the power of the wind in order to stop el Ghoula from stealing Ali Baba's magic lamp.
Identifiers: LCCN 2023031457 (print) | LCCN 2023031458 (ebook) |
ISBN 9780593619339 (hardcover) | ISBN 9780593619346 (epub)
Subjects: CYAC: Magic—Fiction. | Egyptian Americans—Egypt—Cairo—Fiction. |
Fantasy. | LCGFT: Fantasy fiction. | Novels.
Classification: LCC PZ7.1.L4957 Ch 2024 (print) |
LCC PZ7.1.L4957 (ebook) |
DDC [Fic]—dc23
LC record available at https://lccn.loc.gov/2023031457
LC ebook record available at https://lccn.loc.gov/2023031458
Printed in the United States of America

ISBN 9780593619339

1st Printing

LSCH

Design by Eileen Savage | Text set in Arno Pro | Hamsa image courtesy of Shutterstock

◇—○—◇

For my husband, Scott—
It is impossible not to bloom in your light.

CONTENTS

CHILDREN
OF
THE WIND

PART ONE

Returning Home

Unexpected Magic

If last summer had taught Sahara anything, it was that when things didn't go as planned, they usually ended up working out better than she could've imagined. That didn't mean she'd given up on planning entirely—that would be absurd—she just left room for the unexpected. Because that's where the magic happened.

Never would Sahara have believed anything could trump Horace Harding Elementary's grand end-of-the-year fair. But Metropolitan Junior High's Club Clash competition on the last day of seventh grade did not disappoint. And unlike the games at the fair, they weren't rigged. A carefully selected panel, split evenly between student and teacher judges, presided over the annual contest between after-school clubs. After preparing all year for today, participating teams, ranging from drama to debate, would finally get to show off their skills onstage before the judges and an auditorium filled with their peers. But only one team would be awarded the shiny

Club Clash trophy in the shape of the school's lion mascot. Sahara was determined for it to go to hers.

She drew a deep breath and pressed her mother's hamsa necklace to her chest. There was no way, after nearly one hundred and eighty days of hard work, her robotics team could lose. That's not to say Sahara didn't sing along to the choir club's rendition of "Don't Worry Be Happy" or gasp at the gymnastics club's daring flips and splits. But they hadn't programmed a robot with a gagillion C++ codes to automatically perform the "Y.M.C.A." dance.

Halfway through the song, one of Omni's rear wheels got jammed with a rogue ball left onstage by the juggling club, tilting him forward and giving Sahara and her teammates a momentary heart attack. The audience went wild, assuming that Omni's C and A, with his back wheels hovering off the ground, had been by design. Sahara yanked his manual remote control from her shorts pocket, quickly rolling him in reverse to dislodge the ball and saving him from crashing offstage. *Crisis averted.* She smiled to herself at the lucky mishap. Omni's impromptu acrobatics ended up clinching the win of the Club Clash Championship Trophy for robotics.

After many high fives and photos with her coach and teammates, Sahara searched the auditorium for her best friend. *Where is she?* She climbed back onto the stage for a bird's-eye view, a gray cloud of worry sweeping over her victory. Vicky never missed the opportunity to show off her happy dance.

Especially when it was to celebrate one of Sahara's wins. One of *their* wins.

"Your win is my win," Vicky had often said, even when Sahara's came at the expense of her own, like at *Super Mario Bros*. Sahara always rescued Princess Peach first.

Brrriiing. The last school bell of the year brought in an uproar of cheers. Students bounced excitedly past Sahara, not wasting any time starting summer break. She plunked down in one of the aisle seats before she got run over by the crowd.

"See you at the park," Angela from her robotics team yelled as she made her way out of the auditorium.

"Meet you there. I'm just waiting for Vic," Sahara shouted back.

Heading to Flushing Meadows Park after early dismissal for an informal end-of-the-year bash was also a Metropolitan Junior High tradition. Vicky and Sahara had talked about going since September. And they would, once Vic showed up.

After a few minutes, the wave of outgoing students had slowed to a trickle, until the only people left in the auditorium were teachers guffawing over each other's summer plans. Sahara glanced at her watch—12:40 p.m. Maybe she had misunderstood and was supposed to meet Vicky at Avelino's instead of here. She'd better head over there before they ran out of pizza. Half the school was grabbing a slice on their way to the park.

Sahara threw on her backpack and hustled outside. Luckily,

the pizza parlor was only a few blocks away. She scanned the kids waiting in line at the outside takeout window, but there was no sign of her best friend. So she peeked inside, relieved to find Vicky sitting at one of the booths.

Sahara hurried in. "Vic, where've you been? I waited for you at school." She tried to tamp down the worry in her voice.

"I'm sorry. I wanted to make sure we got a table."

Sahara looked around at the empty booths. "That's not gonna be a problem today. Everyone's taking their pizza to go and heading to the park. Like we planned."

"Right. Is it okay if we have it here? I ordered us each a slice, but you can take yours to go if you want." Vicky began futzing with the cheese shaker. "After my humiliating performance today, I don't really feel like being around a crowd."

Sahara had been looking forward to celebrating her victory with the team, but there was no way she was leaving her friend alone now. "Nah. I'd rather stay here too," she said, taking a seat across from Vicky. "You know what happened during the *Wizard of Oz* performance wasn't that big of a deal. Besides, everyone's too busy celebrating summer to think about it."

"Are you kidding?" Vicky snorted. "Did you hear how the whole auditorium cracked up when I tripped on the yellow brick road?"

"Not everybody. Just Corey Burke and his birdbrain friends." Sahara could've killed jerky Corey and his goons for singing "Fall Off the Yellow Brick Road" as Vicky, dressed like Dorothy, regained her footing during the theater club's performance.

Sahara reached for Vicky's hand. "Didn't you tell me to ignore Corey after he told everyone the Merlin's Crossing amusement park pin I finally got last summer was a fake?"

"I did. And I will ignore him. Eventually." Vicky stared down at the table. "I'm okay. Really."

Sahara could tell her friend really *wasn't* okay. She'd been looking away a lot lately. Sahara wasn't sure what was going on with her. And anytime she got even close to asking, Vicky had somewhere she suddenly needed to be. There was no way anyone had to go to the bathroom that many times.

Maybe it was Sahara's fault. When she'd returned from Cairo last year, she decided not to tell Vicky about any of the weird magical stuff that had happened. It wasn't that she didn't trust Vicky. It was that she wanted to keep her safe. And though Naima still reported on their weekly phone calls that El Ghoula had not resurfaced, Sahara couldn't chance endangering her friend by involving her in her family's secret. But she did wonder if Vicky could sense she was hiding something, and that's why she was spending so much time looking down lately.

"So how did robotics do?" Vicky asked as Mr. Avelino's oldest son walked over and slid two plates and cans of Fanta Orange soda in front of the girls. It had quickly become their go-to beverage after Sahara had told Vicky all about her cool cousin and his favorite drink—she hadn't hidden everything about last summer from her best friend.

Sahara inhaled the savory steam coming off her slice, then beamed. "Winner, winner . . ."

"Chicken dinner," Vicky cried. "You won?"

"Yup." Sahara fist-bumped her friend. Their usual celebration might have come late, but at least it had come.

"You won, and I missed it," Vicky said, her voice dropping.

Sahara waved her hand. "Pfft. No biggie. There'll be other Club Clashes."

"If you're upset, you can tell me. You're not lying, right?" Vicky asked.

Sahara shook her head. Maybe she'd been a little upset, but it didn't matter now.

Vicky raised her finger. "Pinkie promise."

"Promise." Sahara curled her pinkie around her friend's. She took a sip of her soda, trying to sink back the gnawing guilt climbing up her throat.

"So tell me. Did everyone love Omni's dance?" Vicky asked.

"They did." Sahara grinned, taking her first bite of pizza. The stretch of the cheese, the sweetness of the sauce, the crispiness of the crust—it was all . . . "A-maz-ing." Sahara sighed. Normally, she'd order another slice, but not today, when Amitu was busy cooking a special early dinner for her last day of school. Instead, she told Vicky all about how Omni's near fall had turned into an epic success.

"That's awesome. Maybe next year, you'll let me dress him in costume."

"Not a chance. There's no way Omni would've been able to do the "Y.M.C.A." arms with a leather jacket constricting his—"

"Radius of mobility." Vicky huffed. "Whatever that is."

Sahara brought her hands to her heart, feigning being upset. "Aren't you going to miss all my tech babble when you're at camp?"

Vicky's eyes dropped again. "I would miss it *if* I was still going."

Sahara did a double take. "*If* you were still going?

"I ... I changed my mind."

"Since when? You were so excited about it. What about the wedding?"

"There'll be other weddings. It's not a big deal."

Sahara couldn't believe what she was hearing. Vicky had talked her ear off about her two favorite counselors getting married at camp this summer.

"I've been going to Camp Stoneridge for the last five years. Believe me. I'm not missing out on much. I wanna do something different."

"Like what?"

Vicky sat up tall. Her eyes brightened and met Sahara's. "Like have my best friend show me around Cairo. Is the invitation to go still open?"

"Of course it's open." Sahara smiled, though she worried about Vicky's sudden change of heart. Maybe she was overreacting. Even though Sahara hadn't shared everything about her last summer in Egypt, she *had* gone on and on about her mom's awesome family, their cool shop, and seeing the Great Pyramids. Of course Vicky wanted to go. "Do you think your parents will say yes?"

"I haven't asked them yet, but you're not leaving for another few weeks. Just think"—Vicky flashed a mischievous grin—"the two of us together this summer getting into so much fun Egyptian trouble."

If she only knew how much Egyptian trouble Sahara had gotten into last year.

"What's better than *trouble*?" Vicky asked, quoting a line from one of their favorite TV shows.

"*Double* trouble," Sahara answered, chuckling nervously. It was one thing to talk about her friend joining her this summer but another for it actually to be happening. She'd have to make sure it was still okay with her dad and Amitu. And there was so much she had to plan for. *Unexpected magic, unexpected magic,* she repeated to herself, trying to quell her panic. There was still plenty of time to make a *Ten Things to Do With Your BFF in Cairo* list. Hopefully, it wouldn't include the return of a witch.

The Spectacular

965 CE

Princess Husnaya pulled the leaves apart, hoping to catch a glimpse of the spectacular. She sat high in a cork oak tree overlooking the Nasra palace in the Maghreb region of North Africa. Today, the caravan of pilgrims, which included her grandmother, was returning from Mecca. Every year, her father, the khalifa and supreme ruler of the empire, would commission his sage to put on a spectacle of magic to celebrate the arrival of the hajj and hajjas—the titles these men and women earned for completing their sacred pilgrimage. Husnaya's heart beat rapidly with anticipation like the wings of a fledgling about to take flight for the first time.

Meanwhile, her brother, Prince Hassan, struggled to stay awake in the next tree. "I don't understand"—Hassan yawned—"why you had us climb up here to watch the procession when we could've just watched from the tower."

"Because in about two seconds, Mama's going to realize we're not standing with the rest of the court to greet the pilgrims. And when she does, the first place she'll send Aziza to check is the tower. Everyone knows it will have the best view of the procession." Husnaya looked toward the palace steps. "Unless you'd prefer to be down there?"

Hassan grimaced like he'd drank sour milk. "And have to pretend to smile next to pompous Rashid while he stands beside Baba, claiming his spot as the next khalifa? No, thank you." He shook his head fervently.

"What show do you think Marwan will put on this year?" Husnaya asked, changing the subject from the sting of their brother Rashid being chosen to succeed their father over Hassan. There was no winning that argument, no matter how many times she'd had it with Hassan. Even though Rashid was two years older, Hassan believed that his having been born with the symbol of the hawa—a golden teardrop-shaped letter *hā* on his head representing the wind—trumped age. But his father had chosen to listen to his sage Marwan and go with the "elder and therefore wiser" son. Husnaya wasn't sure anyone was ready for that kind of power at thirteen *or* fifteen. As Hassan's twin, she was also born with the symbol of the wind, and never once had she whined about being passed over—not even considered—because she was a girl.

"Whatever Marwan has planned, I don't care to see it." Hassan turned his head. "Obviously, his judgment is lacking."

"Hawa twins!" someone shouted into the trees.

"Aziza." Husnaya groaned. The children's maid, who had started working at the palace ten years ago by helping her father in the kitchen, was the only one to ever refer to them by that name. "I swear that woman could find a needle in a sand dune."

"Hawa twins," Hassan groused. "Why does she insist on calling us that? We're not three anymore. In two days, the entire city will be celebrating our thirteenth birthday."

But Husnaya rather liked the nickname and the way Aziza's voice brimmed with endearment, even when she yelled it.

"I know you're up there, Husnaya. I can see the hem of your beautiful, now-dirty qamees and the soles of Hassan's muddy boots. Get down here before your mother sends the cavalry looking for you. And you know what happened last time."

"I can't do it. I won't spend another hour listening to Commander Osman bragging about his triumphant days on the battlefield and how he conquered the city of Fez." Hassan slid down to the next branch.

Husnaya followed him, defeated. The last time she and Hassan had shirked their royal greeting duties, he had to shadow the commander for two weeks, and she was forced to follow Sitt Jamila, one of the most prestigious and tradition-bound ladies of the court, who gave her an earful about proper table settings and the difference between brocade and damask. Husnaya still couldn't tell the two patterns of fabric apart.

"Look at you," Aziza scolded, dusting the stray leaves and branches off Husnaya's tunic. "Do you know how hard it is to scrub mud and grass out of silk?" She clicked her tongue disapprovingly, tucking some straggling strands of Husnaya's hair under her headscarf. "I know neither of you cares for your royal duties, but you mustn't take them for granted. Your father, like his father before him, has been ordained to lead our people. As you have as his kin." Aziza ushered the children toward the palace. She always reminded them how fortunate they were to be in their positions.

"We know, Aziza."

"You're right, Aziza."

"We're sorry, Aziza."

The twins took turns repeating their almost daily apology refrain as they made for the brick steps.

Husnaya could tell by how her mother, Dounya, steeled her chin, her eyes scrutinizing them from top to bottom, that she was not pleased. She was rarely pleased with anything Husnaya did, frequently chiding her for not spending more time learning how to be a dignified princess. Husnaya glanced back at Aziza, who nodded softly and gave her an encouraging smile. For all of the maid's incessant fussing, there was a tenderness in her warm eyes Husnaya didn't find anywhere else.

Standing up taller, Husnaya slid to Dounya's side on the second step while Hassan joined their father and brothers on the first. The emerald on the pommel of the khalifa's sword shimmered in the sunlight. Since it had been gifted to him by his commander upon the fall of Fez, Husnaya's father carried the steel blade with him everywhere he went. Hassan joked that he even slept with it. And he was determined that the sword, like the khalifate, should pass to him, not Rashid, in the unfortunate event of their father's death.

As the palace musicians blew their mizwads announcing the arrival of the pilgrims, Zain, Husnaya's ten-year-old brother, turned around and stuck his tongue out at her. He loved when the twins got reprimanded because it deflected attention from his thumb-sucking habit. Though he'd managed to keep it in check most times, it still reared its infantile and disgraceful head—Mama's words, not Husnaya's—when he was tired or upset. Despite Zain's penchant for getting her in trouble, Husnaya had a soft spot for her little brother. He was the only one who didn't nag her about being more princess-like. Just last night, she'd pretended to enchant the carpet in Zain's room so they could fly to China.

Husnaya remembered the wild excitement in his eyes as she now stood watching the cavalry trot through the towering wooden gates and under the pointed arch leading to the palace first, with Commander Osman at the helm. Her gaze flickered down to the right, where the soldiers' wives and children assembled under the arched portico. As happy an occasion as today was, glassy eyes accompanied their smiles. For, in a few days, the men would be heading east toward Egypt to seize the capital from its ruler. For months, Marwan had been advising their father that the conquest of Egypt was critical to cementing the khalifa's power among rivals, even if the cost was the lives of his men—the court's fathers, sons, and husbands.

After the last steeds crossed the gate, Marwan exited the palace doors, sporting a new silk cloak for the occasion. He bowed before the khalifa and his family when he reached the bottom of the steps. Husnaya could feel Hassan's eyes rolling. Marwan nodded toward the commander, who gave a signal to his men. In seconds, the cavalry parted, revealing a sea of pilgrims. Led by Husnaya's grandmother, they marched around the expansive rectangular pool and trickling fountains situated before the stairs.

"Welcome to our new hajjs and hajjas," Marwan declared, holding out his hands like he was holding up the sky.

Husnaya heard the wind first, but judging by the way Hassan raised his head, he had too. They always heard the hawa or any movement against it, from the likes of horses or carriages, before anyone else. Aziza had told them it was because they were children of the wind, born on the night of one of the worst windstorms of the century. "It's a gift," she'd said, which made Husnaya smile. But Hassan griped over what a curse it was in the middle of the night when even the slightest whisper of the wind awakened him.

Husnaya stood on her toes to get a better view of the sage's magic. Hundreds of paper birds ascended from the palace roof into the sky, scattering over the procession. She marveled as Marwan flourished his hands through the air directing the flock, their fluttering reflections shimmering in the waters of the pool.

The crowd broke out into thundering applause. Hassan gave a low snort meant to evade his parents, but Husnaya had still heard it under the clapping. Marwan was by no means her favorite person. She didn't like his presumptuous air or how he counseled her father with self-serving advice. But she would give anything to possess that kind of power—that kind of magic!

She could hear Aziza in her head. Anytime Husnaya brought up how much she'd rather learn magic than how to be a proper and boring lady, Aziza would warn, "The strongest of men have fallen victim to magic's illusion of power."

"Thankfully, Allah has not made me a man," Husnaya would quip back.

Speaking of Aziza, she must've stepped away from the other servants. Husnaya scanned the crowd until she found her hiding behind one of the palace's columns. It wasn't the best place to view Marwan's magic. Nonetheless, the maid craned her neck, fixing her eyes on the paper birds in the sky. She mouthed words Husnaya couldn't decipher from where she was standing. With her arms at her side, Aziza circled her leather-cuffed wrists. She never took off the wide brown bracelets, which had once belonged to her deceased mother.

"What's Aziza do—" Husnaya started to whisper to Mama but stopped at her jidda's arrival in front of the khalifa. Husnaya had only ever seen her father bow to two people— his wife and his mother.

"Welcome home, Hajja Zubayda." The khalifa flashed the smile he reserved for his family. In front of everyone else, he had to be fierce and serious. "How was your pilgrimage?"

"Glorious." His mother sighed. "But it's good to be home."

"It is delightful to have you back, Zubayda." Marwan bowed before her.

"It's *Hajja* Zubayda now," Husnaya's jidda corrected. "Miss me?" It was no secret in the court that the khalifa's mother and his sage did not always see eye to eye.

"Tab'an," he conceded, turning his gaze toward the soldiers on horseback. "Does the cavalry not look ready to triumphantly march on Egyptian soil?"

"About that." Zubayda leaned toward her son. "I am happy to inform you of the gracious hospitality and safe passage Egypt's ruler showed me, showed all your people, while we passed through Egypt. It doesn't seem right to invade his lands when he has bestowed such a courtesy."

"Hajja, surely you're not suggesting we delay our mission east." Marwan let out a nervous laugh.

"That is exactly what I am suggesting." She twisted away from him and toward the khalifa. "I am sure you will do the honorable thing, my son."

"But . . . Khalifa." The sage stepped toward his leader. "You aren't considering waiting?"

"Now there, Marwan," the khalifa appeased. "I'm sure the soldiers would appreciate a few more months with their families." He looked to his men. "How would you like more time at home?" he yelled over to them. The calvary cheered their approval. Joy filled Husnaya as the soldiers' wives and children hugged each other, grateful for the delay. She beamed at her grandmother, who had made that possible. Marwan may have amazed the court with his sorcery, but it was the khalifa's mother who won them over with her spectacular influence.

"It's settled." Husnaya's grandmother clapped her hands, then turned to her grandchildren and held her arms out, inviting them to her.

"Jidda!" Husnaya cried, running over before her siblings and nestling into her grandmother's majestic embrace. Maybe it wouldn't be so bad to learn to be a royal lady if she could also stop war in its tracks.

Heck Yeah

Occasionally, what starts as a chance affair becomes a beloved tradition. Last June might have been the first time Sahara's dad had come home early for her final day of school, but it would not be the last.

Sahara entered the apartment a little past three.

"So that's it? One year of junior high complete," her father called.

She smiled, following his voice to the dining table where he was unloading the wallet from his suit jacket. "I thought you weren't supposed to be back until four. You beat me home."

He gazed at his watch. "By three minutes, to be exact. I couldn't wait to hear all about"—his voice turned gravelly—"Club Clash Wars." He sounded like the voice-over for an action movie trailer.

Sahara laughed. "If you're talking about the Club Clash competition, you should know something." She slid her backpack off and then raced over to him. "We won!"

"Oh! Well done." He pulled her into his arms. Sahara sank into the warmth of their shared pride.

Within seconds, Amitu called them into the kitchen for their now-annual end-of-year early dinner extravaganza. The wara ainab was a staple. Though today, they'd have Amitu's signature grape leaves *plus* lamb stew for the first day of Eid el Adha.

Whenever the holiday rolled around, Sahara's father would tell her the story behind the holy festival. "One night, the prophet Ibrahim, peace be upon him, dreamed that God commanded him to sacrifice his son Ismail to prove his devotion. But just as the ever-faithful Sayidna Ibrahim was about to go through with the act"—her dad's voice would always rise with excitement at this part—"Allah sent his angel Jibreel with a ram to sacrifice instead. That is why we celebrate Eid el Adha." Supposedly, in Egypt, people ate lamb around the clock during the festival. Hence today's menu addition.

Sahara's mouth watered at the platter of steaming grape leaves and bowl of savory stew as she hugged her aunt, who was seated at the kitchen table.

"Not only did Sahara's team win the school contest . . ." Her father turned to his sister. "Ahem."

The excited gasp he'd anticipated came a second later, followed by an equally enthusiastic congratulations. "Mabrook!" Amitu cried, squeezing Sahara's hand. "Of course you won. You all worked so hard."

"Thank you." Sahara beamed and pulled her chair out. She stopped midway, her gaze flitting to her dad. "Wait. You said 'not only did Sahara's team win' like there was more news."

"There is." He cocked his head toward his sister.

Amitu, who had been celebrating Sahara's victory seconds ago, was now staring into space with a bewildered smile. What was going on?

"Just because we're continuing our end-of-year early dinner doesn't mean everything has to be the same," Sahara told them. "Trust me, last year's 'Khalu Omar's getting married' news was enough."

"I just got off the phone with the Cairo Museum of Islamic Art." A giggle escaped Amitu's lips. "They offered me a summer internship." The surprise in her voice shifted to a squeal. "I can't believe it!"

Phew. No surprise weddings this time. "That's awesome!" Sahara said, finally sitting down. As an art history major at Queens College, an internship at a historical museum was a dream come true for her aunt, let alone one in the country where she was from. "So does that mean you don't have to take classes this summer and can come with us to Egypt?"

Amitu nodded. "The internship will fulfill my Islamic Art course requirement." She hesitated, biting her lip. "But unfortunately, it can't wait two weeks. It begins on Monday."

"I know you hadn't planned on leaving this early, Susu," Sahara's dad said. "But if you want to go with—"

"Heck yeah!" Sahara slapped the table, making her dad and

aunt jump. She wouldn't have much time to pack *again*, but it was worth it to see her family earlier. Sahara suddenly remembered that her grandmother was in the middle of a pilgrimage to Mecca, which Amitu had explained as a spiritual journey every Muslim yearns to make in their lifetime.

Sahara folded her square napkin into a triangle. "If we leave so soon, won't Sittu still be away when we get there?"

"Only for a few days." Amitu scooped some stew onto Sahara's plate. "But you'll get *plenty* of time with her when she gets home."

Amitu's emphasis on *plenty* made Sahara ask, "How long are we going to be there for?"

"Six weeks," Amitu answered.

Sahara's eyes darted to her father. There was no way he could take all that time off. "What about work?"

"It's too late to change my vacation days, but I will join you in mid-July as planned."

The tightness seizing her throat made Sahara hold off on taking her first bite. She had never been away from her father except for the occasional sleepover at Vicky's. But at least she'd be back in Shobra. Back with her mom's family.

And closer to the chamber.

Just as she thought this, the hamsa pulsed. The amulet had done that often when she thought of Cairo and even more as her trip approached.

"Promise me you'll be careful," her dad said softly.

Sahara knew he was thinking about a certain witch. She

crossed her heart. "Don't worry. No one has seen or heard of Fayrouz since last summer. And we can't let her keep us away from our family."

"No, your mother wouldn't want that." He raised his glass of soda. "To all of today's wonderful news and another unforgettable summer."

Sahara clinked her glass, realization hitting her. These new plans weren't just about her. She smacked her head. "Vicky!"

SAHARA COULDN'T BELIEVE Mr. and Mrs. Miller had agreed to let Vicky join them on such short notice. Though lately, Mrs. Miller said yes more, and Mr. Miller bought Vicky and her brothers gifts they didn't need. He'd just gotten Vicky a portable music player, when she already had the latest one. Usually, Vicky had to earn things like that by doing endless chores. She was always taking out the trash or walking the family's dog, but not anymore. Oh well. Who was Sahara to look a gift horse in the mouth?

With so much excitement coursing through her, it had been almost impossible to fall asleep. She would be spending the summer with her two favorite people—Naima and Vicky! When Sahara finally drifted off, it was to a familiar dream. One she'd repeatedly had this past year.

She was in the chamber, where her ancestor Morgana had hidden the magical treasures that Sahara's family would continue to protect for centuries. Only Sahara didn't see herself.

It was like she was watching a movie, and the star of the show was her mother, Amani. She was standing in the middle of the quiet, dark chamber, holding up a small lantern. Its faint beam barely illuminated the surrounding rocky walls. Dressed in a pale yellow nightgown, she appeared older than the young Amani with braids Sahara had seen in Sittu's Room of Photos but younger than in her wedding day picture. She tiptoed to the curio, shooting one quick look up at the entrance before twisting the handle. Sahara could feel her mom's heart drum and her hand tremble.

"Amani?" A deep female voice came from behind, echoing around the chamber. Her mother jumped, waking Sahara up.

She sucked in air as her eyes opened. A blue glow blanketed her moonlit bedroom. It was coming from the amulet's sapphire tucked under her shirt. She pressed the hamsa to her chest, its warmth quieting her nerves.

Mom. This wasn't the first time Sahara had dreamed of her mother in the chamber. But it was the first time she felt like her mom knew she shouldn't be there. And she wasn't sure if the person who had called her mother's name knew that too.

4

Returning Home

Earlier this year, when Sahara had found out that Sittu was
making a pilgrimage to Mecca, she asked Amitu why it
was so important. "Just as all waves return to the sea," her
aunt answered softly, "Muslims near and far return to God's
home." Sahara quite liked that explanation at the time, and
she couldn't help but think of those words as she landed in
Egypt again. She may not have been on a spiritual journey
like her grandmother, but she was on a journey, nonetheless.
One in which she'd left one home behind only to find she'd
returned to another.

"I don't think I've ever seen this many people," Vicky
marveled as they followed Amitu into the arrivals terminal.

Sahara smiled. "It's a lot, but you'll get used to—"

A piercing whistle cut through the hubbub of the crowd.
Sahara spun around excitedly to find her cousin Naima pushing through the masses, leaving an aisle open that her mom,
dad, and brother, Fanta, strolled through. A rushing stream

of affection for the people headed toward her—*her* people—coursed through Sahara.

Home.

Naima ran toward her. She threw her arms around Sahara, nearly knocking her over.

"I missed you so much!" the girls cried simultaneously.

"Jinx." Naima winked, then slid over toward Vicky.

"Naima?" Vicky asked.

Naima answered with an enormous hug that surprised Vicky. "I guess I was right." She laughed. Only Sahara could detect the hint of nervousness in her voice.

Meanwhile, Khaltu Layla descended on Sahara and Amitu, passing each of them to the next family member for hugs and kisses. As full as Sahara's heart was, her belly twisted with missing. She wished her dad and Sittu could be here too.

Fanta, a head taller than last year and sporting his signature bandana, sidled to her side. "Are you ready for Summer in Cairo Part II?"

"Only if you're in that movie too." Sahara giggled, hugging him.

"Tab'an, I'm the star."

Same old Fanta, Sahara thought as Vicky stepped toward her cousin. "And you must be—"

"Fanta . . . Fanta Saeed," he answered, saying his name like James Bond.

He kissed Vicky's hand. *Gross.* Sahara was surprised Vicky, whose cheeks flushed, didn't pull it away. Instead, she said, "Your karate bandana is really cool," making Fanta stand taller.

"Come help with the luggage, Mr. Cool." Naima snickered, grabbing one of the suitcases and heaving it at him.

Same old Naima. Sahara's eyes darted between her family members. She was thrilled they all had come, but there was no way everyone would fit in Uncle Gamal's Fiat.

Amitu must have been thinking the same thing. "The girls and I can take a taxi back to Shobra," she said.

Khaltu waved a dismissive hand. "The Fiat gave out last month. Allah has blessed us with a new car. One we can *all* fit in." She bent down and kissed Sahara's head, her floral perfume warming Sahara's nose.

Uncle Gamal spun the cart and nodded toward the exit. "To the Saeedmobile."

THE FAMILY'S SKY-BLUE Volkswagen van might have been new, but Uncle Gamal's driving was as stomach-flip-flopping as ever. Vicky's nails dug into Sahara's hand as they swiveled and swerved through the city, which radiated with golden light from the streetlamps, car beams, building windows, and boats on the Nile. Other than the navy sky, there was no sign that it was actually nighttime. Cairo was bursting at the seams with a vitality usually reserved for busy weekday afternoons in other places.

When the van briefly stopped at an intersection, Sahara smiled out the window at a young man crooning loudly over the blare of the intermittent car horns to a smiling woman holding a toddler and waving to him from across the street. *Only in Cairo,* Sahara thought as the Saeedmobile made its way onto the 6th of October Bridge.

It wasn't until the van slowed down for traffic that Vicky let go of her hand. Sahara cringed at the sight of nail prints on the back of her palm, stretching her fingers to release the tension of her friend's twenty-two-minute death grip.

"Sorry," Vicky whispered, her face pale. "I thought I was gonna die."

"Die, no. Throw up, maybe. But hopefully not." Sahara chuckled to herself, remembering how freaked out she'd been last summer when she'd first gotten into Uncle Gamal's car.

Naima must have heard Vicky. She leaned over her seat to grab a bottle of water from the trunk and passed it to her. "No one has died yet," she teased.

The timing of Naima's joke couldn't have been worse. Within seconds, el Borg came into view. It had been almost a year since Sahara had faced off with El Ghoula at the top of the Cairo Tower, reclaiming her amulet and the family's magical lamp. But seeing it again made her muscles clench tighter than Vicky's killer grasp.

"No one has seen her. I promise," Naima said softly to Sahara.

Sahara nodded, but her heart pounded in her ears. She

wanted so badly to believe her cousin. Even though there was no proof that the witch would return, something deep inside Sahara said otherwise. And after last year, Sahara had learned not to ignore that innermost voice, even when she didn't understand it right away. Eventually, it always guided her toward the truth. It had known all along that there was something wrong with her uncle's fiancée, Magda, and that the necklace her mother had saved for her before she'd died was more than just a beautiful hamsa.

Vicky poked Sahara's shoulder. "You okay? Now *you* look like you're about to throw up."

Think fast. "Yeah. I must be a little carsick too."

"Here, your turn." Vicky held out her hand to Sahara.

Sahara took it, swallowing back the sour taste of lying in her mouth. She hated not being able to tell Vicky the truth, even if it was to keep her safe. They'd never kept secrets from each other before.

As the van finally picked up speed and Sahara could no longer see the tower, her breathing—and guilt—began to settle. Unfortunately, Vicky wasn't as lucky.

"Breathe." Sahara squeezed her friend's knee. "It gets better," she reassured her, though truthfully, Uncle Gamal's driving would never get better. Vicky would eventually get used to it like she had. "Think of all the cool things we're gonna do here," Sahara reminded her.

Vicky mustered a smile. "You're right. We—well, *you* made some awesome plans for us."

Since they hadn't had much time to prepare, Sahara used the fourteen-hour plane ride to jot down, in the margins of the airline's magazine, all the places they would visit. She couldn't wait to return to the Pyramids with Vicky, but she was really pumped to go to the famous Khan el Khalili market. There hadn't been enough time to last summer.

Much to his father's dismay, Fanta leaned over into the front seat and pressed play on the radio's tape deck. He looked back at Vicky, an eager smile on his face. "Do you like INXS?"

Vicky perked up momentarily. "I . . ." She hesitated for a second. "I love them."

Sahara rolled her eyes. Why was her friend acting so weird around Fanta? Besides, Vicky *liked* the band INXS, not *loved*.

The rest of the car ride Fanta and his father sparred over the music. Every few minutes, Uncle Gamal would say something snarky about the song playing and eject Fanta's mixtape, then Fanta would groan and pop it back in. Luckily, it wasn't long before the family's building came into view.

Sahara peeked at her watch as they pulled up in front of it. Nine thirteen p.m.—two minutes earlier than she'd arrived last year. When she looked up, her uncle Omar and his wife, Noora, stepped out of the shop, hand in hand. Ali's, the convenience store located on the lower level of the building, had been in the family for as long as the chamber.

As Khaltu Layla slid the rear door open, Sahara bounced in her seat. She couldn't wait to greet Khalu Omar and Noora. But before they reached the van, Kitmeer bounded up the shop's steps and cut in front of them. He sniffed Sahara's legs as she hopped out.

"Kitmeer!" Sahara crouched and rubbed his head. After a second, his tail wagged so fast it was a blur. "I missed you too."

Vicky backed away. Compared to her schnauzer, Maisy, Kitmeer was a beast. "I've heard a lot about you, Kitmeer," she said from a safe distance. Her face was still white from the ride.

"You need more than water. Some gum may help," Naima suggested, leading Vicky into the shop.

Kitmeer followed, giving Omar and Noora room to finally greet Sahara. They embraced her tightly together.

"My Sahara." Khalu Omar smiled brightly. Sahara basked in the light of his love. "Cairo hasn't been the same without you." Her uncle always knew the right thing to say.

"We're so happy you're back." Noora winked. "Hopefully, we can get off to a better start this summer."

"Of course, *darling*." Sahara giggled at the infamous words. It had been awful when Fayrouz's spell had turned Noora into vile Magda, but at least they'd gotten a good catchphrase out of it.

Behind Khalu and Noora, Sahara spotted a curly-haired man, who appeared to be about her dad's age, and a girl dressed as if she'd stepped out of an equestrian magazine, riding helmet and all, approaching from across the street. And a few paces behind them was none other than Umm Zalabya. Sahara would always be grateful to the seer for her enchanted jasmine garlands and the way they'd protected her family last year, but she wasn't sure she fully trusted Umm Zalabya. It was hard to when the woman always spoke in cryptic riddles. But Sahara could at least give her a chance this summer. Especially since she was trying to lean into the mysterious and magical, even when they were hard to explain.

"What's Umm Zalabya doing here?" Sahara asked as Naima exited the shop with Vicky—she'd finally regained the color in her face. "Umm Zalabya's the woman who grows yasmeen on her roof," she whispered to Vicky. Sahara had told her about Umm Zalabya, minus all the divination and enchanted ful parts.

"She's here to welcome you." Naima smiled coyly. "I would've told you, but I wanted it to be a surprise."

"Good job, I think? I'm definitely surprised." Sahara stopped before she said anything negative about Umm Zalabya. *Lean into the mysterious,* she reminded herself.

Vicky pointed to the man and girl who'd now stopped several feet before the shop and were in the middle of a heated discussion. At least it looked that way from the hard look the girl was giving him. "Are those two with Umm Zalabya?"

"That's her son, Zalabya—" Naima started.

"Wait a minute. He has the same name as his mom?" Vicky interjected.

"No. Umm Zalabya is kind of like a title. It means 'Mother of Zalabya.' I don't know what her real name is. Do you?" Sahara asked her cousin.

Naima shrugged. "Everyone always just calls her that. But I do know that the girl next to him is his daughter, Yara."

"Ooh, I love her costume," Vicky gushed.

"It's not a costume." Naima giggled. "Yara rides horses. She's always competing in those big-shot races."

"No wonder she's dressed like that," Sahara said. "But isn't she dying, wearing that heavy helmet in the middle of summer?"

"Mama said she always has it on." Naima looked around to make sure no one else was listening. "Mama also said that Zalabya's been staying with his mother because he and his rich wife itallaqu. That's why Yara's here for the summer instead of on some fancy European vacation."

"*Itallaqu* means divorced," Sahara clarified after seeing the confusion on Vicky's face.

"I didn't know people got divorced here too," Vicky said.

"It's not very common," Naima explained, "but it does happen, and when it does, *everyone* talks about it."

"That's awful." Vicky's voice turned sad. "For their daughter, I mean. We should go say hi. Looks like she's done talking to her dad." Vicky turned on her heel.

Sahara gripped her friend's arm. "You're just gonna go over and say hi to a complete stranger?" Vicky was friendly, but not *that* friendly.

"She's not a stranger. She's Umm Za-la-bya's granddaughter." The seer's name didn't exactly roll off Vicky's tongue. She winked, then hurried toward Yara.

Sahara huffed and started to follow, coming to a halt as Umm Zalabya slunk in front of her. "The desert rose has at last returned," the seer said slowly and deliberately. Her silver widow's peak jutted out of her loosely tied headscarf.

Sahara quickly bowed. It may have come across as respectful when, truthfully, she was trying to get out of the whole hug-and-kisses ordeal.

Luckily, Umm Zalabya's attention shifted toward Amitu, who had just finished saying hello to Omar and Noora. "And I see you've brought your amitu Malak with you this time."

"It's nice to see you again, Umm Zalabya." Amitu kissed the woman's cheeks.

Umm Zalabya smiled her toothless grin and then waved to her son. "Ta'ala. Come meet the desert rose and welcome Malak back."

"Desert rose." Fanta snickered, rolling one of their suitcases toward the building's entrance. "I bet you missed being called that."

Sahara gave him a curt look that warned he would pay for that joke later. Meanwhile, Zalabya came to a stop in front of her aunt. *Not missing any teeth,* Sahara thought as he smiled at Amitu. "I'm looking forward to showing you around the museum," he said in an oddly robotic voice.

"You work at the museum too?" Sahara asked, eyeing his goatee. He may have been the first person she'd met with one.

"Ustaz Zalabya is the *director* of the museum," Amitu corrected. "He offered me the internship, remember?"

But Sahara didn't remember because Amitu had never told her. She definitely wouldn't have forgotten that the museum's director was Umm Zalabya's *son*.

"Last time I saw you, we were kids graduating from high school." Amitu smiled back at him. "You've done well for yourself."

In New York, Amitu was just her aunt. But in Egypt, like Sahara's mom and dad, Amitu had a history rooted in its people and places. And Sahara would have to share her with them.

The sound of Vicky's laughter caught Sahara off guard. In that moment, Sahara realized she hadn't heard her friend laugh this carefree in a long time. She turned to see what had made Vicky crack up. But it had been a who, not a what. Apparently, Umm Zalabya's granddaughter was a riot.

"Are we going to bring our guests upstairs or keep them out here all night?" Uncle Gamal bellowed.

Khaltu Layla slapped his arm playfully. "You and Omar get them settled, and I'll help Noora close up the shop."

One by one, they cleared out of the street, including Vicky, who was busy talking to Yara. Too busy to notice Sahara lurch back as she passed the shop.

The amulet. It was pulling her backward. Toward the shop. And the chamber.

Sahara pressed the pendant against her chest. It quieted at her touch. *Phew.* Despite her relief, she couldn't shake the feeling that there was a reason the hamsa had drawn her in that direction. She wasn't sure exactly what that was yet, but she had a strong hunch there was something it wanted her to see or do in the chamber.

"Everything all right?" Noora asked from the shop's steps.

Sahara gave a faint smile. "I'm probably just a little dizzy from the plane and the drive." But she knew it wasn't that. Curse her newfound intuition!

Make a Wish

The Saeedmobile may have fit everyone, but their four-seat dining table would not. Dinner would have to be at Sittu's, especially after Amitu had insisted Zalabya and his family stay to thank him for the internship and celebrate the third night of Eid el Adha. "You don't want to miss Layla's fatteh," she'd said. Amitu had also talked up Khaltu's famous fatteh on the plane, but Sahara wasn't sure how pita bread, rice, yogurt, and lamb would taste together. She was about to find out.

Once Noora and Khaltu had arrived upstairs, everyone headed for Sittu's table. Sahara slid into the chair next to her best friend, signaling for Naima to join them, but Yara beat her to the empty spot to the left of Vicky.

Khaltu had been right about Yara always wearing her velvet riding helmet. She didn't even take it off at the table. Sahara's father frequently wore a fedora when they went out to dinner, but he always took it off before he sat down to eat.

As Sahara got ready to take her first bite of fatteh, she spotted Khaltu Layla eyeing her. Hopefully, she would like it and not have to say it was good just to be polite. But it was better than good. "Delicious," Sahara told Khaltu.

"Nobody knows why these ingredients work together"— Uncle Gamal pointed to his plate—"but they do." He laughed heartily, scooping up a large spoonful.

A year ago, Uncle Gamal's boisterous laugh had made Sahara jump, but now it was another familiar note in the sweet symphony of home that brought a smile to her face. She tried to focus on that and not on how Umm Zalabya's granddaughter kept turning to talk to Vicky every five seconds. It was *her* job, not Yara's, to explain to Vicky what they were eating and translate it from Arabic to English. *Shake it off*, she told herself. Yara was probably just trying to make Vicky feel welcome. Regardless, Sahara was more than happy to say goodbye to Umm Zalabya and her crew once the evening ended.

Meanwhile, Naima was working on rejiggering the sleeping arrangements. The plan had been for Amitu and the girls to stay at Sittu's, but Naima begged her mother and father to let Sahara and Vicky sleep downstairs with her. Unbeknownst to Fanta—and much to his present ticked-offness—his sister had already dragged his mattress into her bedroom. Now she wanted to borrow one from Sittu's.

Sahara loved the idea of camping out in Naima's room with

her two favorite people all summer. "We can help carry the mattress down," she threw out.

Khaltu Layla turned to Amitu. "As long as it's all right with you, Malak?"

"I don't see why not," Amitu answered. "They'll be right downstairs."

Wahoo! The girls exchanged excited glances.

"Where am I supposed to go?" Fanta griped. "Even the dog has a place to sleep!" Kitmeer's heroism at el Borg had landed him an upgrade from the street to Naima's cozy room.

"There's plenty of space at our place. If you stay with us, think of all the fun games of chess I can beat you in," Khalu Omar teased. Sahara seemed to remember Naima mentioning something about their uncle and Fanta's chess rivalry on one of their calls.

"Ha ha," Fanta sneered. "And have to move my stuff across Shobra? Forget it. I'll just sleep in there." He nodded toward the room with the balcony.

After some swift mattress maneuvering, the girls and Kitmeer headed to their tight but cozy abode at Chez Naima.

"Your family's super nice," Vicky told the girls as she plopped down onto one of the mattresses on the floor. "Especially Yara."

"She's not family," Sahara corrected, lying down on her elbows on the other.

"Right. But she's really nice too."

"Sure," Sahara conceded through gritted teeth as Naima hopped down beside them.

"The rabbit's foot!" Vicky squealed at the lime-green fur in Naima's hand.

Sahara squinted. She'd forgotten how bright it was. "I told you Naima would keep it safe."

"Tab'an." Naima opened her palm. "Let's hold it together and make a wish like I did last year when Sahara gave it to me."

As she placed her hand on top of Naima's, Sahara remembered how they'd wished for a way to stop Magda when they thought she was the actual El Ghoula.

"No cheating," Vicky said as she added her hand. "It's gotta be the first thing you think of, or it doesn't count."

"Totally. On three." Sahara closed her eyes.

"Wahid, itnin, talata," Naima counted.

Sahara wasn't surprised by the first thing that popped into her head. All year, she had thought about the vision she'd had last summer of her pregnant mother talking to her unborn self and reminding her of how strong she was. It had given Sahara the courage to use the amulet to lock the lamp and stop Fayrouz from unleashing the jinni inside. She'd had dreams of her mom since then, but nothing that felt that *real*. Sahara squeezed her eyes shut tighter, rubbed the soft tufts of fur in her cousin's palm, and made her wish.

Even after Naima had turned off the lights and Vicky fell asleep listening to the *Les Misérables* soundtrack—she was obsessed with the Broadway musical, especially that "On My Own" song—all Sahara could think about was seeing her mother again. At first, the hamsa just pulsed. Then, as she thought more about her vision, the amulet glowed through her shirt. She flung her hand over it to keep it from waking the girls. But when it began to shake, her cousin's eyes blinked open.

"Ya Allah. It's happening," Naima murmured, her tired gaze quickly giving way to glimmering excitement.

Sahara held her finger to her lips and pointed to the door. Naima threw her hands up to her mouth. Sahara could only imagine the restraint it took for her cousin not to yell out something wild about the enchanted amulet. As the girls tiptoed into the fancy-furniture living room, Kitmeer followed, but Naima sent him right back to bed.

"You told me it moved a few times," her cousin whispered, putting her ear to her parents' door, then giving Sahara a thumbs-up. "But you didn't say anything about it shaking and turning everything blue."

"That's because it hasn't done any of *this*"—Sahara pointed to her chest—"since last summer." The vibrating suddenly subsided, only to be replaced by a tugging. Sahara held on to the wooden arm of a chair to keep from being swept outside. "It's pulling me toward the door," Sahara cried, trying to keep her voice down.

Naima gasped. "Its magic is waking up!"

"Shh!" Sahara hissed at Naima's way-too-loud declaration. The last thing they needed was for anyone else to wake up. Especially not Vicky, who'd have no idea what was going on. Sahara wasn't sure how long she'd be able to hang on with the hamsa's pull intensifying.

Naima grabbed her other hand. "Where does it want you to go?"

But Sahara didn't have to answer. And the flash of light in her cousin's eyes told her she knew too.

"Back to the chamber," Naima muttered to herself. She sucked in so much air Sahara was afraid she'd explode. Finally, her cousin let out a breath and whispered, "We have to follow it. I'm going to let go and get Mama's keys, okay?"

Sahara nodded. Back in Queens, she'd often imagined what it would feel like to return to Morgana's chamber. An idea that always filled her with alternating waves of "Let's go!" and "Oh no!" Not only was it her family's duty to protect the magical treasures, but it was up to her—thanks to the pendant around her neck—to ensure the jinni lamp stayed locked. Thrilling or scary, the responsibility of all that was a lot.

Seriously! Sahara railed in her head at the amulet as she fought to keep her hands from slipping off the armchair. It wasn't that she didn't want to go back to the chamber. She just wasn't ready to go tonight. Her first night. Before she'd had a chance to rest after a long trip. Before she'd had a chance to talk to Naima and figure out why her necklace was acting up again. What it wanted her to see so bad . . .

The hamsa jerked forward, seeming to mock her backslide into the realm of reason. Sahara blew out a hefty breath and released her grip. Detouring once more from the measured and methodical to the messy and magical.

6

Click, Boom

I t had been a waste of time retrieving Khaltu Layla's keys. The closer the girls got to the chamber, the more powerful the amulet's draw became. Naima could scarcely hold on to Sahara as she stumbled out of the building. It was a good thing the street was empty—there was no way Sahara could've explained why she looked like a puppet being pulled by invisible strings. And even better that both the locked gate at the shop's entrance and the door to the old refrigerator succumbed to the hamsa's power, opening a moment before she'd have crashed into them.

Sahara's knees ached from how fast she had to crawl to keep it from dragging her through the tunnel. Climbing down the rope ladder proved to be even more precarious. Her fingers burned as she struggled to keep hold of the rope's rough fibers, the necklace's pull threatening to hurl her down into the chamber. When she finally reached the bottom, she dropped to her knees. If the carpet beneath her hadn't been one thousand years old and never vacuumed, she would've kissed it.

Naima trailed behind with the matches. But there was no need to illuminate the lanterns lining the chamber's walls. The amulet's sapphire provided plenty of light, blazing brighter and brighter as it pulled Sahara forward, hurling her straight toward the curio. She shut her eyes, bracing for impact.

"Sahara!" Naima screamed from behind.

But the collision never came. Instead, the amulet got very still. Sahara opened one eye, then the next. She was inches away from the cabinet.

Naima raced to her side, out of breath. Sahara couldn't speak if she'd wanted to. Not that there was time. Something stirred in the cabinet, activating a second wind in the hamsa. Its force blew the doors open. The girls ducked, just barely escaping getting clocked by them.

Sahara rose, coming face-to-face with the enchanted contents—the vial of healing water, the ivory spyglass, and the brass lamp. All now glowing blue. The amulet might've relaxed again, but it would be a while before Sahara's pulse leveled. Despite the unsettling way she'd gotten here tonight, excitement overtook panic. She was back in the chamber. Back where her family's legacy had begun, surrounded by the portraits of the women who had come before her to protect it.

"Are you okay?" Naima cried.

"I . . . think . . . so." Sahara panted, then looked down at her amulet and mouthed, just in case it could hear her, *It's stopped.*

She scanned the curio, thanking God that before she'd left last summer, she'd had the foresight to Velcro the tiny vial and the spyglass tube to the inside of the shelf. Otherwise, the magical glass that had revealed where El Ghoula had taken the lamp last year, and the water, which had wakened everyone who'd attended the wedding from El Ghoula's sharbat sleeping curse, would've rolled out and smashed to the floor. And it wasn't like Sahara's family could go to the mall and replace them. Though somewhere out there was a golden apple with healing magic too. But it had never made it to the chamber.

She turned to Naima. "Did you ever find out what happened to that apple?"

Naima shook her head, her eyes wide like saucers. She pointed a trembling finger at the cabinet. Sahara spun around.

"It's . . . flying," Naima stammered. The jinni lamp floated out of the curio, then made a beeline for Sahara. "At you!"

Sahara tried to jump back, but it was no use. The necklace flew out of the collar of her shirt and toward the lamp. Its chain dug into her neck as the amulet wedged itself into the hamsa-shaped notch on the lamp's lid, then rotated half a turn with a soft click. A thunderous boom followed as the top flipped open, releasing a whirlwind of darkness.

"The jinni," Naima yelled before Sahara was thrust into the spinning vortex of the lamp, just like last year. She kept her eyes shut until the twisting stopped, which happened quickly—thankfully, because she was moments away from puking. She swallowed, trying to drive back the nausea.

The lamp now dangled in her right hand, and the amulet rested against her chest. They must've come apart during the twirling. She lifted her eyes, recognizing the bookshelf holding her dad's engineering books, which stood in the living room of her Queens apartment. And across from it . . . *Mom.* Just like last time, she was pregnant and sitting on the couch.

As Amani tenderly caressed her stomach, adoration enveloped Sahara like a warm blanket. Her wish had come true. Was the lamp showing her this again *because* of that wish?

Sahara followed her mother's soft eyes to the ivory jewelry box sitting beside her. The very one Amitu had given Sahara last year that held the hamsa. She must've missed this detail last time.

"Sahara," her mother whispered to her stomach.

Hearing her mother utter her name again filled Sahara's eyes with hot tears and her chest with an aching longing. Before she could stop the word from coming out, *Mom* fell from her lips. Amani turned in her direction.

Sahara panicked, and the lamp shook. The twisting immediately returned, sucking and spinning her farther and farther away until she bounced onto the chamber's carpet.

Naima's mouth hung open as she ran over and offered Sahara a hand.

"I . . ." Sahara's voice shook as she held on to Naima and struggled to get back on her feet. "I had that vision of my . . . my mom again."

Naima said nothing but her eyes were wide and wild.

Something was wrong. "What happened? Why do you look so spooked?" Sahara blurted.

Naima remained speechless. Sahara couldn't wait for a response. She had to lock the lamp now. *How?* She'd never actually done it on purpose. But somehow her hands knew what to do. She lifted the lamp and pressed the amulet to it. The lid slammed shut. *Phew.* Sahara shoved it back into the curio and secured the doors, then slipped the hamsa, which had calmed down again, under her shirt before it caused any more trouble.

It was then that Naima finally spoke. "I'm not sure that was a vision. You"—she swallowed hard—"you disappeared into the lamp."

"Naima! Sahara!" A voice came from the top of the ladder. It was Fanta.

"How did you know we were here?" his sister yelled back.

He didn't answer her question, but what he did say rang through the chamber.

"Umm Zalabya's been attacked."

The Best Gift

965 CE

The hawa twins' thirteenth birthday fell on the twentieth day of the month of Muharram this year. The night before, the Hall of Lions bustled with all the court's opulent pleasures—music, dance, and, of course, food. Husnaya did her best to present herself as a proper princess, but by the end of the night, her cheeks hurt from smiling and thanking guests for coming to their celebration. Still, it felt good to have Mama look approvingly her way instead of eyeing her like a toad covered in warts.

After dinner, the khalifa raised his glass in honor of his children. With a proud lilt in his voice, he announced, "Tomorrow, you begin your journeys as adult prince and princess." This morning, Husnaya had been a girl, but in a matter of hours, she would be an adult. She didn't feel any different than she had last night, lying in her bed and cradling the bone doll Aziza had bought her when she was eight.

"Hassan will begin his training in the science of divination and sorcery with my sage, Marwan," the khalifa continued, "while Husnaya will train in the art of personal conduct and royal duties with Sitt Jamila."

Husnaya forced another smile onto her face though her stomach churned with frustration and disappointment. It felt like Hassan was being offered a juicy pomegranate while she was left with the bitter, inedible peel.

The festivities continued deep into the night. Husnaya could still hear the dancing from her bedroom. She tried to fall asleep, but her mind replayed her father's speech. What she would give to be in Hassan's shoes, even though he was too busy moping about Rashid getting to sit closest to the khalifa on *his* day. "*Our* day," she'd had to correct him repeatedly.

If only Aziza were here. She'd probably insist on reminding Husnaya of the importance and advantage of her royal position, but afterward, she'd tuck her tightly into bed and kiss her forehead. That always made the world seem more tolerable. It was odd that the maid had not checked on her yet. She had every night for as long as Husnaya could remember. Did this wretched birthday mean the end of that too? Or worse, what if something bad had happened to Aziza?

Husnaya couldn't sleep without knowing Aziza was all right. Even though she wasn't supposed to leave her room at this late hour, she threw the sheets off and peeked her head out the doorway. Finding the hallway empty, Husnaya hurried toward the steps. But just as she descended the first stair, a door creaked open. She spun around, bracing for the possibility of coming face-to-face with her mother.

Phew. It was only Zain. "What are you doing out of bed?" she railed.

"What are *you* doing out of bed?" he repeated, giving a conniving grin.

"Pretend you never saw me, and I won't tell Mama how long it's been since I've seen you . . ." Husnaya brought her thumb to her lips. It was just a threat. She'd never actually tell on him, especially since, lately, their mother had a new doctor coming every week to find an underlying physical cause for his unyielding habit. Husnaya hated how they examined her brother like a sick patient when all he needed was more time to grow up.

"Only if you also promise to enchant my rug again so we can fly to the Great Pyramids this time."

"Certainly, my prince." Husnaya winked as Zain turned on his heel and ran back into his room.

She didn't waste another moment, racing down the steps on tiptoe toward the female servants' quarters. But the sound of a man's voice brought her to a halt. Not just any man's voice—Marwan's.

"You will do as I say." His voice seethed with venom. "Sit in on the lessons, claiming the boy needs help to stay focused. If I get so much as a whiff of betrayal, I will personally see to it your father returns to debtor's prison."

"Yes . . . Hadir, Marwan."

Aziza. Husnaya's stomach turned at the shaking in her maid's voice. Curse that treacherous Marwan and the way he flaunted his power. If she hadn't been sneaking out of her room, she would have run in there and blasted him for speaking so harshly to Aziza. Instead, she tiptoed down another two steps to see if she could hear why Marwan was demanding a maid join his lessons with Hassan.

"Then it's settled. Keep to our deal. It would be a shame for the court to no longer have your father's delicious tagine."

"Of course. But—"

"But what?" Marwan's voice tightened.

"Prince Hassan may be easily distracted, but he is not foolish. Won't he notice where . . . where the magic is coming from?"

"Then do your best to distract him," Marwan hissed. "And I will do my part to feign the sorcery he's witnessing is coming from me."

Ya Allah. Husnaya covered her mouth, stifling a gasp.

"If I can convince the court I fashioned the flight of a flock of paper birds, I can surely convince one absent-minded boy I am reading his fortune."

Husnaya clenched her fists. Marwan was a fraud. He had no powers. It was Aziza. It had been her all along.

At the sound of footsteps, Husnaya scurried up the stairs and back to her room. She didn't need to unbox any of her presents to know that nothing could best the gift she'd just been given. Of course, she hated that Marwan was blackmailing her dear maid. But Aziza, her Aziza, was the palace sorceress, not Marwan, putting magic within Husnaya's reach.

AFTER EVERYTHING SHE'D overheard, Husnaya had barely been able to sleep more than a few hours. She tossed and turned, reeling over Marwan's treachery. But despite her exhaustion, she hopped out of bed the next morning, brimming with excitement over the discovery she'd made last night.

Unfortunately, Aziza did not share her enthusiasm. In all the years she'd helped Husnaya get dressed for the day, she'd never looked this glum. Husnaya's heart ached for the maid and the position Marwan had put her in. For years, he'd been pawning off her magic as his own, and Aziza had been forced to stay silent to protect her father. The last thing Husnaya wanted to do was risk the cook's freedom, but she couldn't bear the thought of Hassan wasting time learning rubbish.

"Come out with it," Aziza said, pulling the comb through Husnaya's hair. "You always protest when I get the surly knots out of your hair. But you've barely flinched this morning. What's got your mind so busy?"

"The same thing that's troubling *you* this morning." Husnaya spoke to Aziza's reflection in the dressing mirror. "I swear to Allah I didn't mean to eavesdrop last night. I was only looking for you because you hadn't come to tuck me in or even say good night."

"You snuck out of your room?" Aziza narrowed her eyes at Husnaya. "You know your mother doesn't like you roaming around the palace that late, especially with so many visitors around."

"It's fine. No one saw me. But I heard Marwan threatening you. Why didn't you tell me what he's been doing all these years? Why didn't you tell me about your magic?"

Aziza froze, face as white as the scarf covering her hair. A knock at the door brought her back to the present and she pleaded to Husnaya, "No one can know. Promise me."

The maid hurried to the chamber's entrance and bowed deeply as Dounya entered the room, the hem of her embroidered robe sliding along the marble floor.

Husnaya leaped up. "Mama, I wasn't expecting you this early."

Dounya remained silent, her eyes slowly traveling down the collar of her daughter's silk qamees to the sash around her waist, then to the pants peeking out under her tunic, and finally to her leather shoes. It was Husnaya's footwear that made her mother gasp.

Dounya spun toward Aziza and spoke curtly. "Before my daughter leaves this room, see to it that she takes off the shoes she has muddied climbing trees with her brother and replaces them with one of the new pairs she was gifted for her birthday. We don't want to scare Sitt Jamila off."

"Of course, Mistress Dounya." Aziza bowed again.

Husnaya's mother headed out, pausing momentarily to shoot one final frown in her daughter's direction. "You heard your father yesterday. You are an adult princess now. You can't show up to your royal training looking like you've been skipping around the garden all morning."

"And what's wrong with that?"

Mama winced as if Husnaya had said a curse word. "What's wrong with it is that it's not how we do things here. There is enough threat and chaos coming from your father's enemies. We do not need it from our own daughter and her rebellious notions," she chided, then left, shutting the door with a bang.

Husnaya slumped down onto the stool in front of her dressing mirror. "I swear she only comes in here to criticize me." She huffed. "I'd prefer to skip in the garden all day than practice how to hold a finjan properly. To heck with teacups!"

Aziza rushed to the wardrobe and pulled out a new pair of shoes. "Your mother is just looking out for you," she said as she bent down and slid the old ones off Husnaya's feet. "As princess, you are expected to present yourself in the most dignified way."

"Then I don't want to be one," Husnaya scoffed. She shook the gold bangle dangling from her wrist, eyeing the cuffs around Aziza's. "I fancy leather more than gold." A smile crept across her face. "And I'd much rather be a sorceress."

Aziza quickly raised a finger to her mouth. "Shh. Whatever you think you heard last night, scrub it from your mind," she urged.

"How?" Husnaya whispered. "I can't just forget that you've been behind all the extraordinary magic I've seen—that this palace has seen. I know you want to keep your father safe.

I want that too. But you must tell Mama. We can't let that wretched Marwan get away with years of deceit."

Aziza's eyes darkened in the mirror. "Men like him have always gotten away with using others to advance themselves. Why should it be any different now?" Aziza's shoulders fell. "Which is why you must promise to say nothing for my sake and my father's," she pressed.

"I promise," Husnaya grumbled.

Aziza bowed her head and then hurried out of the room, leaving Husnaya staring at her hopeless reflection.

8

What Jinni?

Sahara's amulet might have finally chilled out, but that didn't stop her from speeding out of the tunnel as fast as she'd sped in. She had to find out what had happened to Umm Zalabya. Fanta didn't add much other than that Zalabya had called ten minutes ago with news of the attack on his mother. Sahara exited the refrigerator, expecting to see Khaltu Layla's face. And boy was it there—her reproach smoldering in the lantern's light.

"How could you be so careless?" Khaltu scolded, trying to keep her voice down. "After everything that happened last year, you should know better than to come down here alone in the middle of the night. It's not safe." She carefully shut the refrigerator door and locked it, shooting a nervous glance outside.

It was then that Sahara saw who was waiting in front of the van—Uncle Gamal, Amitu, and Vicky. *Crap!* While Uncle Gamal and Amitu disapprovingly shook their heads, at least they had an inkling of why the girls were down here. But Vicky had no clue.

Naima threw out a bunch of excuses, none of which her mother was having. "We'll talk about what you were doing here later. But we must get to Umm Zalabya's, now!" Khaltu cried, pushing them up the steps.

All Sahara could think of was how confused Vicky must be. And she was right to worry.

"What's going on?" her best friend asked as Fanta locked the shop. Vicky's voice quivered with fear and a hint of anger. "What were you doing in there so late?"

Sahara didn't know how to answer. "I'm sorry." It was the only thing she could think of. Besides, she didn't have time to say anything else. Amitu ushered them into the van, flashing a disappointed look at Sahara.

The Saeedmobile raced across town to Umm Zalabya's. Vicky grabbed the sides of the seat in front of her during the first of many sharp turns but did not reach for Sahara's hand. Sahara's eyes fell to the floor. Vicky and everyone in the family, except Naima, were upset with her. She wanted to tell them that it wasn't her fault. She hadn't *chosen* to go to the chamber. But she couldn't find the words to explain the hamsa's antics tonight, so she said nothing.

"Was it necessary to wake everyone up and bring them?" Naima asked, daring to speak after her mother had chewed them out.

"It was when Zalabya's call had already woken them, and you and your cousin were missing," Khaltu answered curtly as they pulled up to the seer's building.

Despite his bad leg, Uncle Gamal led the charge to the rooftop garden. Zalabya and his daughter paced around the seer, whose eyes remained fixed on the crescent moon as she sat rubbing her head in a wicker rocking chair with Almaz in her lap. The cat raised her head to peer at their visitors, then nestled against her owner's hip with a purr. A light breeze blew, dispersing the sweet smell of jasmine throughout the garden.

Yara stopped in her tracks and brought her hands to her hips. "I knew something like this would happen. Mama warned me your mother's life wasn't safe," she railed at her father, her resentful gaze darting between him and her grandmother. "I knew I shouldn't have come here. I should have gone away with Mama."

"Then why didn't you?" Naima seethed under her breath.

Sahara wasn't Umm Zalabya's number one fan. Still, she didn't appreciate how Yara, who'd traded in her riding attire and helmet for a long nightgown and bonnet, talked about her grandmother like she wasn't even there.

Khaltu Layla rushed over to Umm Zalabya. "Are you hurt?" No answer. She knelt in front of the older woman. "Umm Zalabya!"

Khaltu's panic roused the seer. "It's all right, Layla . . . I'm all right." Umm Zalabya's usually booming voice sounded weak. But even in its tired state, there was no mistaking its message.

"Fayrouz is back."

Everyone in Sahara's family gasped at the seer's revelation. Sahara's breathing might have quickened, but she didn't share their shock. Deep inside, she'd always known Fayrouz would be back. She had been the last to see the witch before she fled el Borg. The last to see the desperate hunger in her eyes as she tried to unlock the lamp. A hunger that could wait a year but not forever to return for the lamp she insisted belonged to her family.

Uncle Gamal leaned on the ledge, surveying the street below. "Izay?" he asked, shaking his head. "How has she stayed under the radar for this long? Morsy's had half of Cairo searching for her."

Khaltu Layla walked over and rubbed his back. "You mustn't blame yourself."

"Listen to your wife," Umm Zalabya told him. "El Ghoula's been hiding in the shadows, ones nobody, even your ex-military friend and his partners, would dare go near."

"Is this El Ghoula responsible for the attack on Mama?" Zalabya asked.

Khaltu looked toward him. "We owe you the truth. Your mother's life was compromised tonight, and it was because of our family's—" she began.

"Mama," Naima cried, stopping her mother from spilling the family's ancient secret.

"Layla." Umm Zalabya stared hard at Khaltu. "There is no need to rehash the past. No one is at fault but Fayrouz."

"Tab'an." Khaltu nodded, rethinking her near indiscretion.

Sahara had suspected Umm Zalabya knew about the chamber, but she was sure of it now by the way she'd looked at Khaltu Layla, imploring her not to say anything she'd regret later. And thank God she had. If anyone was going to explain to Vicky what was going on, it should be Sahara.

"What's an *el goo-lah*?" Vicky whispered to Sahara, struggling to pronounce the last word. "And did you know about her?"

Sahara was relieved her friend was talking to her but hesitated before answering, knowing Vicky would stop as soon as she heard her response. "It's . . . it's a witch. And I . . . I did know," Sahara stammered.

Vicky shook her head, her face cycling through fear, confusion, shock, and finally settling on betrayal.

"I promise I'll explain everything later," Sahara threw in, but nothing she could say would erase the look on her best friend's face.

"Don't do me any favors." Vicky huffed and walked away, settling in next to Yara. Sahara couldn't blame her friend for being confused and scared. She was thousands of miles from home, and a dangerous witch had just attacked. Anyone would be upset. But why was Vicky this upset with *her*?

"You've been so careful." Naima spoke to Umm Zalabya.

"None of your divination revealed that Fayrouz was coming back."

"None till today." The seer's gaze shifted to Sahara. "When our desert rose returned, there was a subtle shift in the wind. So subtle I was convinced El Ghoula must still be far away." Her hand returned to her head. "But trust me when I say there was nothing subtle about her emergence tonight. I was busy picking the yasmeen that had bloomed, when something smacked me in the back, sending me crashing to the ground. I looked up and found Fayrouz glowering above me, sand and wind blasting out of her palm."

Sahara shivered, remembering how the witch's menacing power had knocked out both Noora and Fanta on the tower last year.

"I heard a commotion on the roof. By the time I came up here, Mama was lying on the ground unconscious," Zalabya added, barely batting an eye. Sahara didn't know what to make of him. His words were those of a son concerned about his mother, but his demeanor was not.

Almaz hopped off the seer's lap and circled Zalabya as Uncle Gamal moved to console him. "Your mother is strong. She will make a quick recovery, insha Allah."

"God willing," Amitu repeated. "It's a good thing you were here to find her."

"*Pfft.*" Yara narrowed her eyes at Amitu. "How could you say that? He . . . *we* could've been hurt."

"I just meant—" Amitu started.

"This is why I won't learn her magic," Yara told her father, pointing her finger at Umm Zalabya. "It's the reason you and Mama aren't together anymore. I won't let it be the reason something else awful happens to us."

"Mind yourself, my granddaughter," Umm Zalabya warned, struggling to stand. Fanta ran over to give her a hand. She nodded her gratitude, then turned back to Yara. "You are not wrong. Magic is not without its costs, but it is not to blame for the demise of your parents' marriage. Love and the unfortunate loss of it are beyond even *its* control."

Umm Zalabya was right about that. Despite all the ways Fayrouz's transformation had backfired on Noora last year, it hadn't stopped Khalu Omar from loving her. If Yara's parents weren't together anymore, something other than magic was to blame. Speaking of magic, Sahara couldn't imagine how Vicky was taking all this talk about it. She glanced over at her best friend. If Vicky was surprised, she wasn't showing it. Her face remained steely.

Yara brushed tears from her eyes. "I'm going back inside," she huffed, running for the door. A gust of wind trailed, slamming it behind her.

"See to your daughter," Umm Zalabya directed her son, whose unfazed expression hadn't faltered even during the battle royale between his mom and daughter.

"Are you sure he's not a robot?" Sahara whispered to Naima

as Zalabya marched after his daughter. There had to be wires, not veins, running through his body.

Meanwhile, Vicky turned to Amitu. "Would it be okay if I go inside with them? I'm cold." She wrapped her arms around her shoulders, which were exposed by her pajama tank.

"Of course. I'll come to get you before we leave," Amitu replied. "We'll just be a few more minutes."

Fanta raced to grab the door for Vicky. She gave him a faint smile before disappearing inside. Sahara thought about going after her friend, but with Vicky, Yara, and Zalabya gone, her family and Umm Zalabya could finally talk freely about what had happened.

As soon as he shut the door, Fanta straightened his bandana and asked, "Why is El Ghoula back *now*? Did she say what she wanted?"

"What she's always wanted," Umm Zalabya answered. "And what those who came before her, beginning with the wretched sorcerer, have always wanted—to reclaim the lamp. But Fayrouz has more at stake than they did. That is why she went mad when I wouldn't give up the lamp's location."

Sahara didn't understand the last part. "What do you mean 'more at stake'?"

"Her identity hinges on the lamp. She was raised to believe *she* was the prophesied one." Umm Zalabya's eyes darted to where the necklace hung under Sahara's shirt. "The one meant to join the hamsa and the lamp and unleash a great power.

What she plans on doing with that power is something only she knows. I have not been able to see it in the wind."

"That's why she mentioned the prophecy at el Borg," Sahara muttered.

Umm Zalabya nodded. "Not only did your ability to wield the amulet thwart her plans, but it also contradicted her truth."

"But Sahara is the one with the power to lock and unlock the lamp." Naima smiled at her cousin. "And Fayrouz knows that. So why bother coming back?"

Umm Zalabya chuckled to herself. "Because she knows it in here"—she pointed to her head, then her heart—"*not* in here. And her need to preserve her version of the truth is unrelenting. Perhaps more so than her quest for the lamp. She's been lying in wait for the opportunity to prove that her whole life hasn't been a lie. And this time, she's not going to risk failing. Right before her wind knocked me unconscious, El Ghoula delivered a warning. This would not be the last or the worst I'd be seeing of her. She will return for the lamp and the amulet at the end of the month."

"And what will happen if we don't give it to her?" Amitu put a protective arm around Sahara.

"It won't come to that," Uncle Gamal insisted. "Morsy and I will find her before then. I won't sleep until we do." Sahara had never seen her uncle so determined.

"What's so special about the end of the month anyway?" Fanta asked. "Why is the witch waiting until then?"

"The last day of the month is marked by the absence of the

moon. The qamar's noor balances the threat of darkness," Umm Zalabya explained. "And without the moon's light, that balance is thrown off. Throughout time, evil sorcerers have cast their most wretched spells then."

"So Fayrouz thinks she has a better chance of unlocking the lamp when the moon isn't there to stop her," Naima thought aloud.

If Umm Zalabya could enchant ful and read the future from some dots in the dirt, like Sahara had seen her do last summer, who knew what else she could do? As unsure as Sahara was of the seer, she had to admit it—they needed her strange powers. "Is there anything *you* can do to stop her?" Sahara asked.

"I'm afraid not. The witch's attack has compromised my magical abilities." Umm Zalabya flinched as she sat back down. She looked to Naima and Sahara. "Until my powers return, the enchantments I once cast to keep El Ghoula from using her magic to locate the chamber have likely been weakened. You must stay away from the lamp at all costs."

Sahara cast a nervous glance at Naima.

"Good luck getting them to do that." Fanta snickered.

"You must," the seer pressed. "Fayrouz can sense when the amulet"—she gestured toward the necklace—"is near it."

Sahara bit her lip. Had El Ghoula returned tonight because of her? Because she'd gone back into the chamber?

Khaltu Layla's gaze seared into the girls. "Do you hear that? The last thing we need is for Fayrouz to find the chamber. As far as we know, she has no knowledge of it or any of the treasures hidden there with the jinni lamp."

What jinni? Sahara wanted to yell. But she couldn't without revealing she'd just unlocked the lamp and only seen her mom, not a powerful jinni. Khaltu had been livid at the girls for going into the chamber. She'd have a fit if she found out Sahara's hamsa had opened the lamp. Besides, Sahara wasn't sure what power it possessed, other than showing her a pregnant Amani.

Ugh. How could she protect something she didn't understand? And since *she* had the key to the lamp around her neck, *she* needed to discover the truth about it. There were four days left to figure out what exactly this lamp did before Fayrouz returned.

ON THE VAN ride back, Vicky stared out the window, refusing to look Sahara's way. As they climbed the steps to the Saeeds' apartment, Sahara stared at the back of Vicky's head, wishing she'd turn around and yell at her like she did at her brothers when she was mad at them. Anything was better than this silent treatment.

"I'm sorry I didn't tell you about El Ghoula," Sahara said to Vicky, shutting the door to Naima's room.

"There had better not be any more sneaking out." Khaltu Layla's voice pierced through the door. Poor Naima was on the other side, taking one for the team. But Sahara wasn't sure it was any better on this one.

Vicky turned to face Sahara, her cheeks crimson. "At least I know the truth now. If Umm Zalabya hadn't been attacked, I don't think you would've ever told me that a nasty witch who can shoot sand out of her hand was on the loose!"

"I wasn't sure how . . . I was scared if I told you . . ." Sahara paused, searching for the right words, any words that would make Vicky less mad.

"Scared of what? Of the witch coming back?" Vicky snorted, then plunked down on the mattress and lay down. "Some good your secret did." She twisted onto her side as Naima entered. "I'm tired, and I want to go to sleep. Please turn off the lights."

Naima mouthed, "What happened?" to her cousin, but Sahara just shook her head. Involving Naima would only push Vicky further over the edge. Sahara quickly settled into bed and whispered, "Good night." Though, what a ridiculous thing to say tonight. Aside from seeing her mother again, it had *not* been a good night.

The family's legacy was important, but for years they'd protected the lamp without knowing what it did or how. Sahara had done the same this year. And in the end, that might've cost her Vicky's friendship.

Pyramid Pad

Olololololoee. The sound of a woman's trilling outside the window woke Sahara up. She couldn't imagine what good news someone was celebrating so early. She opened her eyes and raised her watch—12:03 p.m. It *wasn't* early. The only other time Sahara had woken up this late was last summer. The only other time bizarre things had happened—like witches attacking and carpets flying—was last summer.

How was Sahara supposed to explain any of this to Vicky? She had to say something, though. She flipped to her other side, only to find Vicky's bed empty. Well, technically not empty—Kitmeer lay on top, his legs stretched across it. Vicky was probably just in the bathroom.

Sahara scratched under the dog's chin. "Do you know what the magic lamp the scary witch wants to steal does?" she cooed as Naima entered.

"He probably does. Animals see things we don't. They're not busy worrying about what they said or didn't say yesterday or what might happen next week."

"Technically, we're animals too," Sahara pointed out. "But I know what you mean. We should all be more like Kitmeer. What do you see with those sweet brown eyes?" Sahara asked the dog.

Naima deepened her voice, pretending to answer for Kitmeer. "Your friend Vicky loves you very much."

Sahara giggled as her cousin continued her adorable dog impersonation.

"But she's also hurt," Naima continued. "That's why she left with Mama . . . I mean, Naima's mama, to check on Umm Zalabya."

Sahara's shoulders slumped with disappointment, putting an end to her laughter. "Shoot. I wanted to talk to her this morning . . . try to explain things to her." But now Vicky was at Umm Zalabya's, probably cracking up at something clever Yara, her Cairo BFF, had said.

Naima sensed her upset. And in her normal voice said, "They didn't want to wake you. I'm sure they won't be gone too long."

Sahara shook off her dismay. "You're probably right. We can talk when she gets back. Until then, you and I have critical and necessary research to conduct. We've got to figure out what the lamp's power is. I definitely didn't see a jinni last night, unless it was an invisible one." She ran to her backpack and pulled out her mother's journal.

Naima's eyes widened with affection like she was reuniting with a long-lost friend. Sahara turned to the "The Fisherman and the Jinni" story and started reciting the opening aloud.

"Inty bi tiqri!" Naima marveled.

Sahara looked up and grinned. "I thought about telling you I'd learned to read Arabic, but I wanted to see the look on your face. And it was so worth it." She laughed, pointing at her cousin's fallen jaw. "I made Amitu teach me this year." There was no way Sahara could have a piece of her mother and not be able to decipher it.

Sahara traced one of the lines on the page with her finger. "It talks about a brass lamp with an afreet imprisoned inside." Amitu had told her *afreet* meant evil monster. "And then there's Ala el-Din's wish-granting genie." Sahara flipped through the journal. "But there's nothing about a lamp that you—" She hesitated, unable to repeat the unbelievable.

"Disappear into," Naima finished.

Sahara didn't think her cousin was lying, but she still had to ask. "Are you sure that's what happened? To me, it just felt like I was spinning superfast."

"Yes," Naima huffed. "And with the end of the month six days away, there's no time for your doubt. Believe me. You got sucked into the lamp, and then both you and the lamp, *poof*, were gone."

"I believe you," Sahara insisted. "I guess if the carpet can shrink and fly through the chamber's tunnel, I can disappear into the lamp." She twisted her scrunchie around her hair. "But there are only three days, not six, until the end of the month."

Her cousin pointed to the sun streaming through the

open shutters. "Three days according to the sun, *not* the qamar's phases. Remember how Umm Zalabya said the moon wouldn't be visible at the end of the month?"

Sahara nodded, recalling that and how Amitu had once explained that the Islamic calendar was a lunar one. That's why certain holidays like the Eids and Ramadan didn't always fall on the same day. "Right. There are thirty-three fewer days in a lunar year than the three hundred sixty-five solar. So the end of the month, according to each, is different." Sahara breathed out a sigh of relief. "Kudos to the lunar calendar. That gives us more time to—"

Naima jumped up, then ran to the treasure chest and back, hiding something behind her. "I almost forgot! If we're going to find out what the lamp does, we need a new nuta. Since we used up your planet pad last summer, I bought you a . . . *tun tun tuuun* . . ." After a dramatic pause, Naima whipped out a notebook. "A pyramid pad!"

Sahara beamed as she traced an illustration of the Giza pyramids on the cover. "I love it! And you're right. We're gonna need it." They'd filled her other pad brainstorming ways to stop El Ghoula and working out that the prophecy, *the two that must not join become one*, was about her hamsa and the lamp.

Sahara flipped to the first page as Naima handed her a pencil. *Possible Lamp Powers,* she wrote, underlining it twice.

"Maybe it's a portal into another world?" Naima suggested. Sahara added the idea, then quickly scribbled underneath,

A portal into memories. "Both times, I saw the same memory of my mom talking to me before I was born."

"Mama says babies can remember things from when they were inside their mothers."

Sahara wasn't so sure about that, even though she had read something similar in biology class. "I was thinking more like a portal into my mom's memories, not mine."

"Ooh, yes!" Naima's eyes danced. "There are so many amazing powers the lamp *could* have. Do you think El Ghoula knows what it does?"

"I'm not sure. I wish we knew what she wanted to use it for. 'Cause what she plans to do with the lamp might lead us to how it works. At least we've got six days to figure that out before Fayrouz crawls out of whatever hole she's hiding in. "

"We might not need that long. Get dressed and meet me at the shop." Naima hurried toward the door, Kitmeer bounding after her. "It's Noora's shift, and if anyone can help us get inside Fayrouz's head, it's the woman she nearly destroyed last year."

Into the Unknown

Outside the building, Uncle Gamal was deep in conversation with a tall and brawny man. So deep that he didn't notice the girls walk by on their way to the shop. But the other man had, his eyes darting to the girls and back to Uncle Gamal. Between his khaki uniform and discreet-but-intent countenance, Sahara had a feeling this was Uncle Gamal's army friend.

"Is that Morsy?" she asked.

Naima nodded. "Aywa. Before Mama left, she said that Morsy and Baba were up all night planning a strategy to find Fayrouz. You're not the only one who likes plans." She winked at Sahara. "But until they find El Ghoula, Morsy and some more of Baba's old army officers will be keeping a close watch here and at Umm Zalabya's."

Sahara glanced back at Uncle Gamal, appreciating how much he looked out for their family. His eyes were dark with worry as he talked to Morsy. Come to think of it—he was the one doing all the talking. His friend just listened, nodding every few seconds.

"Does Morsy speak?" Sahara asked, stopping in front of the shop. "I thought your dad said his friend knows everything that happens in Shobra."

"He knows everything because he *doesn't* talk a lot. But he listens carefully. Baba says people are either put off or comforted by his silence—either way, they end up telling him way more than they should." Her cousin laughed, stepping inside the shop, where Noora was replenishing the chips rack. Naima looked around. "Good, no customers."

Noora raised her eyebrows. "How is that good?"

"I mean, bad for business but good for us, because we need to talk to you *alone*." Naima whispered the last word. "I'm sure Mama has already told you and Khalu Omar what happened last night."

"I haven't been able to stop thinking about Umm Zalabya." Noora wrung her hands. "I'll check on her when the shop closes for lunch."

Naima leaned in, resting her elbows on the newspapers stacked on the counter. "Noora, I know your memory of the time you were Magda is hazy, but is there anything you can remember Fayrouz saying about the lamp or what she planned to do with it?"

Noora rubbed her forehead and grimaced.

Sahara felt terrible making her remember when it caused

her such pain. "I'm sorry to upset you, but we want to understand as much as we can to stop Fayrouz."

"And I want to help. It's just..." Noora hesitated as Kitmeer jumped up and sniffed the scar on her wrist from his bite when she'd been Magda. He whimpered.

"No matter how many times I tell him I've forgiven him, he still cries." Noora patted his head, then turned back to the girls. "I've been on edge since hearing about El Ghoula's return, jumping every time someone comes in." Her voice trembled. "I won't let her hurt anyone I love again."

Naima took hold of her hand. "That's why we need you to remember."

Noora inhaled deeply. Her gaze grew distant. "There was this one time... Fayrouz was threatening to tell everyone I... Magda... was really Noora if she didn't get the lamp by the end of the night. Something slipped out of her mouth about someone she had to bring back."

"Did she say anything about who that person was?" Sahara asked. For all she knew, El Ghoula was trying to resurrect some cursed witch or monster.

Noora squeezed her eyes shut, trying hard to remember. After a few seconds, she opened them and threw her hands up in frustration. "I wish I could iftikir more," she groaned. "But that's all I can recall."

With Noora's memory being so spotty, there was only one thing left to do. And it wasn't more brainstorming—as much as Sahara loved doing that—in Naima's room. It was time for some field research. Last night, Sahara had agreed to stay out of the chamber to keep Fayrouz from locating it, but she wasn't sure that was the right thing to do anymore. If the lamp had shown her Amani when she'd thought about her mom, would it show her its power if she asked to see that? She pressed the hamsa to her chest and stared intently at the old refrigerator. "I've gotta get back into the chamber."

"What do you mean *I*? *We* need to," Naima told her.

"No. I can't let you get in trouble again." Sahara slid the hamsa out of her shirt. "It's because of this that I have to go. I have to know what power it unlocks so I can protect it."

"You may be the one with the amulet around your neck, but we're a team. I won't let you go alone."

It meant a lot to Sahara that her cousin was willing to risk Khaltu's wrath for her. But until she figured out how to control the berserk magnetism between her necklace and the lamp, she'd have to brave it alone. She couldn't chance both of them getting sucked into the lamp.

"Neither of you is going," Noora said with a hard "don't mess with me" expression on her face.

But Sahara didn't back down from her uncle's wife. She rolled her shoulders back and put on her bravest voice. "I have to. I don't want Fayrouz to hurt anyone else either. But I can't do that unless I understand *how* the lamp works and *why* she thinks she can use it to bring someone back."

"What's to understand? Isn't there a jinni inside that can grant her whatever wish she wants?" Noora spat out.

"There isn't——" Naima started.

"Much time," Sahara broke in. This wasn't the moment to explain how Sahara had disappeared into the lamp. It would only scare Noora more and make her double down on not letting Sahara go. "I need to get in there now," Sahara pressed.

Naima hurried behind the counter and stood in front of the fridge. "Not without me."

"Or me." Fanta entered the shop, sliding his headphones down and around his neck. "You think after last year, I didn't know what the two of you would be up to today? I knew you wouldn't be able to just let Baba and Morsy do their job."

"We are letting them do it. But we're doing ours," Naima snapped back.

There was no time to argue. "Fine," Sahara groaned. "You both can come. Just stay away from the lamp." She peeked at her watch—12:55 p.m. "We'd better hurry. When I was getting dressed, your mom called. She's staying with Umm Zalabya through lunch to make sure she eats something. She and Vicky will be back right after."

Naima turned to Noora. "Can you buy us some time, *please*?"

Noora pressed her lips together. "Allah forgive me. If I don't say yes, you'll just sneak in here in the middle of the night." She glanced at the shelf holding the small clocks for sale. "The shop closes at one for lunch. I'll lock up a few minutes early.

But you must be back before three. If your mother comes looking for you, I'll think of some errand to say I've sent you on." She grabbed her purse from underneath the counter.

"What would we do without you?" Naima kissed Noora's cheek.

"Get into more trouble," Noora huffed.

As Noora turned off the lights and lowered the gate, the Zuhr adhan echoed from the mosque across the street. Hearing the call to prayer, Sahara closed her eyes and thought of her mom, hoping they were doing the right thing while Naima entered the code A-M-A-N-I into the combination lock. The minute it opened, the amulet yanked Sahara forward as it had done last night, thrusting her past her cousins and into the refrigerator.

JUST LIKE LAST summer, when the kids had entered the chamber prior to heading to el Borg to stop the witch, Kitmeer insisted on joining them. He raced into the refrigerator before Naima or Fanta could stop him. But unlike the first time, there was no way he was going to jump to get inside his family's secret cavern of treasures. Having once made the mighty leap herself, Sahara couldn't imagine doing it again. And thankfully, neither one of them had to.

After dragging Sahara down the rope ladder and toward the curio, the hamsa's pull let up momentarily, giving her just enough time to witness Kitmeer's magical miracle. As the dog reached the edge of the tunnel, he ignored Naima's reassurances about the jump not being that high. Instead, he honed in on the rug several feet below him and let out an echoing *ow-ooooooooooh*. The enchanted carpet immediately responded by floating up to its canine summoner. Kitmeer hopped aboard, allowing the rug to gently carry him down to the chamber.

"You're brilliant, Kitmeer!" Naima praised, hurrying down the ladder.

Fanta, who trailed his sister, had missed Kitmeer's incredible feat. "Why's he brilliant, and what do you mean Sahara vanished inside—" He stopped mid-sentence, gasping as the curio doors flew open and the lamp floated toward the glowing pendant, which stretched to meet it.

Click. Boom!

This time, Sahara didn't think about her mom but about the lamp. "Teach me how you work," she whispered.

Within seconds, the spinning started, pulling her away from the chamber. Then, out of nowhere, came a tug, then another, and another. She glanced back to find Fanta hanging on to one leg of her pants and Naima the other while Kitmeer dug his teeth into the hem.

"I told you to stay baaack!" Sahara yelled. The twisting ramped up, making her dizzy. She hugged her arms tightly, tucked her head between them, and braced herself for whatever came next as they all got sucked into the lamp. And into the unknown.

One More Condition

Husnaya trudged down the stairs in her new shoes to the banquet hall where Sitt Jamila was waiting to begin their first lesson: How to Host a Dinner at the Court. At least that's what Mama had Aziza tell her a few minutes ago. How hard could that be? Cook would prepare delicious platters of food, and guests would eat it. All *she* had to do was pretend to smile, donning layers of uncomfortable clothing.

As Husnaya passed Marwan's study, she snuck a peek at his so-called sorcery lessons with her brother through the partially open door. Hassan's shoulders were slumped, his bottom lip quivering the way it had when they were nine and he'd fallen off his horse and twisted his ankle.

"Until that worthless maid of yours arrives to keep you in line, you must pay attention, boy!" Marwan growled.

Husnaya gritted her teeth at the awful way this brute talked to her brother and referred to Aziza. What a mistake it had been for Mama to send the maid on a last-minute errand to the tailor's shop, leaving Hassan to fend for himself at his first lesson.

Marwan poked Hassan in the center of his chest. "Your frivolousness is the very reason I told your father you were not fit to be the next khalifa."

Husnaya had seen enough. Promise or no promise to Aziza, she couldn't let Marwan humiliate her brother.

She threw the door all the way open. "And you're not fit to be the heel of his boot!"

Hassan's jaw dropped, his eyes glimmering with a combination of gratitude and fear.

Marwan's face turned red. "How dare you—"

Even though Husnaya could hear her pulse throb in her ears, she still stood on her toes and glared into his eyes. "I *dare* because I know your secret."

'What secret?" Hassan asked as Marwan peered out the door, then quickly shut it.

For the next few minutes, Husnaya happily answered her brother's question. When she was done, she turned to Marwan. "I won't tell my father about your deceit and will allow you to continue this charade if, and only if, you leave Aziza and her father alone. For good."

The cornered sage—if he could even still be called that— mumbled some words under his breath, then reluctantly nodded.

This was going better than expected. "Actually, I have one more condition," Husnaya added.

"I've already agreed to one," Marwan grumbled.

"I don't think you're in a position to be limiting terms."

Husnaya flashed a grin at Hassan, then repeated, "One more condition—you let Aziza secretly train my brother and me in *actual* sorcery."

"But it would not be appropriate for a princess to learn such things. It is the domain of men," Marwan insisted, looking to Hassan for support but getting none.

Husnaya put her ear against the door. "I think I hear Baba's footsteps."

"Fine," Marwan seethed.

Husnaya winked at her brother and turned on her heel. "I'll leave you to the domain of men." She could feel Hassan smiling at the back of her head.

PART TWO
Secrets and Lies

12

Where Are We?

The lamp's twirling and whirling lasted way longer than before, leaving Sahara wondering how much more it would go on for and if it would ever stop. But could whatever was happening even be measured in *time*? They were spinning so swiftly she thought they'd broken the sound barrier—or some other kind of barrier. And when they'd finally come through, they crash-landed, knocking the air out of them. "Oof!" they groaned in tandem.

With her eyes still closed, Sahara ran her hand—the one not clinging to the lamp—over the rocky ground, then quickly recoiled it. The earth was hot—scorching. Her eyes flung open. Above her, a fiery sun blazed high in the sky.

Fanta was the first to speak, his voice shaking. "What just happened?" He looked around. "And where are we?"

"Not in the chamber," Naima said, giddy with excitement. "This is incredible!"

"It's some kind of valley . . . or canyon." Sahara raised

herself onto her elbows, which wasn't easy given that her cousins and Kitmeer were still hanging on to her, and scanned the steep, craggy cliffs towering in the distance. With the exception of a few tenacious plants, the surrounding land was barren. Whatever the lamp was showing them was definitely not Shobra or Queens. And now she had to worry about how she would get herself and her stubborn cousins back to the chamber.

"I told you to stay away from the lamp. Why didn't you?" she railed. They quickly let go of her pants.

Naima turned to Sahara. "What were we supposed . . ." She dropped her gaze as the ground underneath them shook.

Sahara's eyes darted to the lamp, worrying it might pull them back into its twisting madness. But it was oddly calm. Seconds later, the whinny of a horse echoed through the canyon, coupled with an escalating pounding. *Hoofbeats.* And judging by their intensity, fast ones.

"Horses!" Naima pointed at the galloping animals in the distance.

But an icy shiver ran down Sahara's spine. Unless these were wild horses, they were carrying riders. Sahara searched for cover, but with the exception of the jagged cliffs, which they'd never reach in time, there was no place to hide. She slipped her necklace under her shirt and concealed the lamp behind her back.

As the three tall black horses approached, the figures of their riders grew more lucid by the second. Scarves were wrapped around their heads, and they donned beige-colored galabeyas like the tunics Amitu wore.

Kitmeer bared his teeth at their unexpected company, which was quickly closing in on the children and showing no sign of slowing down. The last thing Sahara wanted to do was attract attention, but she waved her hands wildly in case they didn't see them.

"Stop!" Naima shouted to the riders, who still charged ahead.

Sahara's heart pounded as loud as the hooves beating toward them. The horses and their passengers were going to crash right into them. "Run," she yelled to her cousins and Kitmeer.

They leaped out of the way just as the horses reared up, coming to an abrupt, booming stop where the children had been a second ago.

"You could've killed us," Naima cried at the surly men who hovered above them.

From up close, all three Bedouin riders appeared to be of a similar age—their faces lined with their fair share of life but not enough to be at the end of it.

One of the men jumped down and sauntered over. "You should have seen your faces," he cackled, exposing a mouthful of rotting teeth. His companions snickered behind him. He leaned in closer to the kids, his foul breath stinking up the hot air between them. "Are you lost?" he asked in a dialect of Arabic Sahara hadn't heard before but managed to make out.

"Separated from your caravan? Fallen out of your carriage?" He stared at them, then turned and smiled at his friends, stretching the dry, leathery skin of his face.

Sahara quickly slid the lamp under the back of her shirt while his attention was momentarily on the other riders. Though when the man began circling her and her cousins, scrutinizing their clothes, she wasn't sure her last-ditch covert effort would make much of a difference.

"Have you come from a masquerade ball?" he scoffed, making his cronies crack up. His gaze settled on Sahara's short-sleeve shirt. "Tut, tut, tut. Showing your arms. Has no one taught you modesty, girl?" Sahara felt the simultaneous urge to hide behind the cliffs *and* punch him in the face.

"Leave her alone. She's not from here," Naima blared as Kitmeer growled.

Sahara appreciated her cousin's defense, but Naima wasn't from here—wherever that was—either.

"Then where is she from? Waq el Waq?" The man sneered. Sahara rolled her eyes, recognizing the name of the fictional island—known for strange creatures like talking crocodiles and winged vipers—from her mother's journal.

"No, America." Fanta puffed out his chest.

"America!" The two companions, clearly the lead man's underlings, repeated, pretending to be impressed.

"You dare lie to me?" The rotten-toothed leader heaved Fanta to the ground.

Kitmeer jumped in front of Fanta, barking and snapping.

"Bil raha," the leader said, cautiously signaling the dog to take it easy. "A quick word with your owners, and we'll be off. You see, we run the lands of Wadi el Qelt. And if you want to pass, you must pay the appropriate tariff."

"We don't have money. And if we did, we wouldn't give it to you anyway." Naima helped her brother to his feet.

The leader bared his gross teeth at Naima. "Hold your tongue before I cut it out of your mouth," he warned, furling his fingers around the handle of a dagger secured to his belt.

Sahara threw a cautionary glance at Naima, begging her to back down. Luckily, her cousin kept any further gutsy comebacks to herself.

"You expect me to believe you are out here alone *and* empty-handed," the leader continued to rant. His eyes shifted to Sahara's concealed hand. She froze.

"I have money," Fanta yelled, reaching into his pocket and taking out a few crumpled Egyptian pounds.

The leader grabbed the bills out of his hands. "Paper!" he yelled. "You think I'm daft enough to mistake paper for money? He ripped it up and then grabbed Fanta by the collar of his tracksuit jacket. His eyes flickered to the headphones around his neck. "What do we have here?" He yanked them off and nodded toward his minions. Immediately, they dismounted their horses and walked over to their leader for a closer look. They eyed the headphones suspiciously.

"There might be some silver here we can trade, boss," one of the cronies said.

"What else are you holding out from us?" The foul-breathed rider came back to Sahara.

"Nothing." She bit her lip, her brain crying, *Please don't find the lamp, please don't find the lamp.*

"We have more," Naima blurted. "Don't you, my brother?" She jerked her head toward his pocket, where his music player resided.

Fanta shot a look of contempt at his sister. He'd already lost his headphones. At least those could be easily replaced. The music player could not. But what choice did they have? They hadn't come this far to protect the lamp only to lose it now. Sahara's heart sank as Fanta reached into his pocket and surrendered his precious device.

The leader raised his eyebrows, weighing it in his hand to judge its worth.

"You need to press this button first," Fanta explained.

As a tinny sound of music came out of the player's small speaker, the man's face darkened.

"What witchcraft is this?" He threw it to the ground and stomped on it with his foot, breaking it into pieces.

"No!" Fanta cried.

"I don't know where you children have come from or if the devil sent you, but I don't have time for more games." He approached Sahara. "I can see you're hiding something behind your back. Now turn it over, or I will slay you all."

The hairs on the back of Sahara's neck stood at attention as he tore the blade out of his belt. She couldn't let him hurt her cousins, even if it meant giving up the lamp. Sahara reached behind, until—

A flicker of shimmering wings.

Then, a fierce wind, howling and pushing against Sahara, her cousins, and the riders. From inside the gale, a silver horse emerged, carrying two women, one with long hair whipping behind her, and the other with a scarf wrapped around her head.

The men's faces turned ashen. "The wind has brought them to punish us," one of the men screamed. "Jinniyas," another cried, then all three ran toward their steeds.

The scarved Bedouin woman jumped off her horse, raising her palm and releasing a burst of wind that launched the men toward the remote cliffs. "Good luck getting home, you brutes." She glowered at them from afar as they struggled to their feet, then turned and whispered something to the scoundrels' horses that sent them galloping in the opposite direction of their wretched owners.

"Well done." The long-haired woman touched her friend's shoulder.

Next to their heads, a tiny fairy hovered. She squealed in delight, her golden wings whirring.

The Bedouin woman stepped forward, making Sahara jump back. She'd only seen this kind of wind-bursting magic come out of one other person's hand: Fayrouz's.

The woman with the long hair approached the children too. Something about the way she glided as she moved toward them, her midnight hair and flowy gown rippling with each step, gave Sahara a major case of déjà vu. *Where have I seen you before?* she thought as the woman spoke. "Do not fear us, dear children."

"Why shouldn't we?" Fanta asked defensively while Naima gaped at them like they were rare comets, absent from the night sky for centuries, whizzing past—blink, and she might miss them.

"Because you asked the lamp to lead you here," the Bedouin answered.

"And to us," the fairy chirped.

"To you?" Sahara shook her head. "I did not. I asked the lamp to show us its power."

"And it has." The long-haired woman reached for Sahara's empty hand, sending a wave of warmth through her. The amulet quivered in response. "Welcome, Sahara, Ahmed, Naima, and Kitmeer the Brave."

"Ya Allah," Naima sighed, and fell back. Luckily, Fanta was close enough to catch her.

The Bedouin eyed the silver chain around Sahara's neck, then bowed her head. "We have been waiting for you."

13

The Magical Trio

Sahara had seen people faint in the movies, like when a monster with three heads popped out of the closet, but never in real life. At least not until now. She fanned Naima's face, trying to get her to wake up, but it wasn't working. The woman with the long hair and iridescent billowy gown bent beside her cousin, setting her lithe fingers on Naima's forehead.

Within seconds, Naima stirred, a wide smile spreading across her face.

"Are you all right?" Fanta asked his sister, his eyes fixed on the woman whose touch had woken her.

"Tab'an. Better than all right." Naima giggled, propping herself up on her elbows as Kitmeer licked her face.

"Pfft. How can you laugh? Ten seconds ago, you were passed out!" her brother griped.

"Look who we're with," she told him, then spun her head toward Sahara. "They're from the tales in your mother's journal.

The mermaid queen, the jinn fairy, and the princess-turned–greatest sorceress of all time are here! Standing in front of us!"

Sahara stared at the trio, trying to make sense of what she saw before her with what she remembered from the stories. Even though she'd accepted, even come to love, that Morgana was real, doubt still crept into Sahara's mind. She wanted so badly to embrace the mysterious as wholeheartedly as Naima, but what were the chances that these women were who her cousin claimed them to be?

The long-haired woman leaned in closer to Sahara. "It's a lot to take in, my dear," she said, seemingly reading Sahara's mind. "How about we start by introducing ourselves? As you've already deduced, I'm Julnar of the Sea." The mermaid queen smiled—Sahara had only ever seen teeth that pearly white in toothpaste commercials—then turned to the fairy.

The jinniya pointed a tiny thumb at herself. "Call me Peri, short for Peri Banu." She winked.

Then the Bedouin woman stepped forward with her towering horse. She ran her sun-kissed fingers through the animal's silver mane as she stated, "This is Almaz."

Sahara would have to remember to ask Naima if that was a common Arabic name for animal companions, since that was also what Umm Zalabya called her cat. But for now, she couldn't take her eyes off of Almaz's owner.

The woman brought her hands—adorned with leather cuffs—together at her head, bowed, and proclaimed, "I am Sitt Husnaya."

Despite Sahara's misgivings about the trio, there was no denying that everything about them, especially the supposed Sitt Husnaya, screamed: *Incredible!*

Peri waved her hand over her ruby dress, fluttering her wings excitedly. "How do we look compared to what you pictured? Better, right?"

"Uh, sure." Sahara tightened her scrunchie. "But where are we?"

"The lamp has brought you to Wadi el Qelt," Husnaya answered plainly. "It connects the cities of Jericho and Jerusalem." She pointed ahead. "That way is Jericho." Then behind. "That way is Jerusalem."

"The lamp flew us *here*?" Fanta asked, helping his sister to her feet. "All the way across the Sinai Peninsula?"

"You could say that." Peri giggled.

"Speaking of here"—Julnar cleared her throat—"it may be best to find somewhere more private to talk. I'm certain you have many more questions, but perhaps this close to where those awful thieves descended upon you isn't the best place to answer them. Who knows who else is lurking around?"

"Down by the stream it is." Sitt Husnaya clapped her hands together. "I'm sure the animals would appreciate a drink." She helped Julnar onto Almaz, then hopped up behind her onto the silver-studded saddle. Peri perched herself on the mermaid queen's shoulder as Husnaya slyly glanced back at the children. "I would suggest following Almaz's wind. There is no finer way to travel."

As the horse began to trot, she kicked up a light breeze that blew cool, refreshing air onto Sahara and her cousins' faces.

Naima closed her eyes and sighed, letting the wind gently sweep her feet off the ground. Kitmeer hurried after her as she glided down the rocky trail, quickly getting whisked away himself.

"Wait," Fanta called to his sister and her dog.

"For what?" she yelled back. Naima would've followed the trio to the ends of the earth.

"She always just goes. Never thinks first," Fanta scoffed. "How do we know it's not a trap?" he asked Sahara, his voice quivering.

"We don't," she answered. Sahara stared at the remote cliffs, still trying to wrap her head around where they were. "I'm not sure about these women either," she said as a dark shadow raced above, disappearing before she could make out what it was. Her stomach clenched with fear. "But they are all on the good side in their stories. Plus, if the lamp brought us here, we'd better find out why."

She grabbed Fanta's hand, and together they let the wind carry them off.

MINUTES LATER, THE arid ground of the desert gave way to the green and lush earth leading to the water. As reticent as Sahara had been about following the trio, she couldn't complain about their ride. Almaz's wind was smooth, comfortably drifting them down toward the stream.

When they reached the reeds and wildflowers on the bank, the wind slowly lowered Sahara and her cousins beside the trio. Peri dove off of Julnar's shoulder. Her wings whizzed across the water's surface, spraying a fine mist.

Julnar leaned into the spray. "Ah. Much better."

"How are they here? Now?" Fanta whispered to Naima, eyeing the trio suspiciously. "Those stories you read are always about people that lived a thousand years ago."

Fanta had a point. As jinn, Peri and Julnar could be eternal, but *not* Husnaya. She was human. Sahara narrowed her eyes at the bronze-skinned sorceress. "If you really are Sitt Husnaya, you can't still be alive. Are you a ghost?"

Peri pinched her friend's arm. "She's very much alive. See for yourself." She flew a few inches back, suggesting Sahara do the same.

After the wind magic Sahara had seen come out of Husnaya's hand, there was no way she was pinching her. She'd take Peri's word for it. There had to be some other explanation. "Did you use your powers to become eternal?" Sahara asked the sorceress.

Husnaya fervently shook her head. "Magic should never be used for such a transformation."

Julnar's deep blue eyes pierced into hers. "You're as intelligent as they come, my dear. But all these questions distract you from what you know to be true."

A veil of uncertainty lifted from Sahara's heart. If Husnaya was alive but not eternal, that could only mean one thing. She turned to Naima, whose eyes glimmered in awe at the impossible, confirming what Sahara understood within.

"Not only did the lamp take us to Wadi el Qelt," Sahara murmured, "but it took us back in *time*."

"Ding, ding, ding." Peri's voice rang with affirmation. "Welcome to 985!"

14

985?

Sahara's legs wobbled. She sat down on a boulder before she, too, fainted, and then she stared at the sky, clearer and more vivid than the bluest sky back home. Everything was brighter. It was like all her life she'd been looking at the world through a streaky glass window that had suddenly been wiped clean.

"This is the best day! I've always wanted to travel to the past." Naima beamed at the trio.

"No, no, no. It can't be," Fanta muttered, his face losing color with each word.

"The lamp's power is time travel." Sahara spoke slowly and deliberately as if saying it this way would make it easier to understand. "And it brought us here. To 985."

"You wanted it to show you how it works, and it has," Husnaya told her. "It might not be what you expected, but it has led you to the answers you seek. They are here—over three hundred miles from Cairo and one thousand years back in time."

Sahara quickly did the math in her head. *One thousand and three years, to be exact.*

"But what about the lamp's jinni?" Fanta's voice was weak as he pointed at the trio. "Is one of you the jinni?"

Naima glanced from the mermaid queen and fairy to Sahara. "They *are* jinn."

"But neither is *the* jinni," Sahara retorted. "The one that's supposed to be locked in the lamp—the one that should never be unleashed, so its power doesn't destroy the world." The momentary peace Sahara had experienced floating down here gave way to indignation. She hated being duped. Sharp anger clawed its way up her throat. "And this," she growled, raising the lamp into the air, "is not that kind of lamp." She leaped up and faced the trio. "Why call it a jinni lamp at all? To fool us?"

"Of course not, my dear," Julnar asserted. "Along with evil sorcery, the blood of jinn was used to create the lamp. It *is* a jinni lamp, just not the kind you assumed it was."

"*You* let us assume that. For the last one thousand and three years, our family has *assumed* that," Sahara blasted. "Did Morgana at least know what the lamp did when she ran off with it?"

Peri shook her head, making the tiny gold-and-ruby earrings dangling from her ears jingle.

Sahara's cheeks burned. "So she risked her life, and everyone's that came after, without knowing what she was protecting?"

"The fewer who know the truth of the lamp's powers, the safer everyone will be. The lamp was created to alter that which should not be altered," Husnaya pressed.

"That excuse might've worked for over a millennium, but not anymore," Sahara argued. "There's an evil witch running around with your kinda magic"—Sahara looked at Husnaya's hand—"and she'll stop at nothing to get the lamp."

Fanta, who appeared to have regained his composure, raised his bandana away from his eyes and turned toward Husnaya. "How do we know you're here to help us if you can do that too?" He thrust out his palm, pretending to shoot wind out of it. "What if you're just as bad as El Ghoula?"

Husnaya lifted her hand. A breeze rippled out, gently rustling Fanta's hair. "The magic of the wind is neither good nor bad. It is the channeler who makes it such."

"Curse that witch!" Peri filled her cheeks with air, puffing it out angrily. "First, she attacks Morgana, and now she's after you."

"Fayrouz attacked Morgana? Izay?" Naima asked in disbelief.

Kitmeer stopped drinking from the stream long enough to snarl at the mention of the witch's name.

"She hasn't had the lamp since el Borg," Naima continued. "And even there, Sahara locked it right away. How?"

"Time doesn't move in a straight line. Think of it more like an infinite wheel spinning around and around." Julnar waved her hand in a smooth and hypnotic circular motion. "At some point, El Ghoula travels through the lamp, and when she does, she attacks Morgana and steals the healing apple."

Fanta smacked his bandana. "So that's why the apple was missing from the chamber. It never made it."

"Exactly." Peri whirred her wings. "But I was able to replace it with the vial from the lion's spring before Morgana left for Cairo. Alhamdulillah."

"Thank God" was right. If not for the jinniya's generosity, half of Shobra, their family included, would still be under Fayrouz's sharbat curse. Gratitude thawed the chilly distrust in Sahara's heart.

"We were on Morgana's side, my dears, and we are on yours," Julnar said softly.

Sahara's clenched muscles relaxed at the earnestness in the mermaid queen's voice.

"But what would El Ghoula want with the apple anyway?" Fanta screwed up his face. "Who could she possibly want to heal?"

"Noora!" Naima cried.

"She doesn't want to save Noora. She nearly killed her last year," her brother scoffed.

"No. Noora remembered something strange back from when she was Magda. Something about Fayrouz needing to use the lamp to save someone. But she couldn't remember who." Naima turned to the trio. "Do you know who it could be?"

Husnaya and Peri nervously glanced at Julnar, whose long fingers curled into tight fists. "Jauhara," she seethed.

Judging by the reaction of the mermaid queen—who up until now had been the epitome of calm and benevolence—this Jauhara was a total nightmare.

"Jauhara?" Naima whispered to Sahara. "Which story is she from?"

Sahara shrugged. She thought she recognized the name from her mother's journal but couldn't recall more than that.

Julnar's luminous face dimmed. "A vile jinniya with access to a ring that can unlock the hidden lamps that have, for centuries, confined the wickedest of jinn and prevented them from carrying out the most treacherous deeds. Which is why she's being kept in a bewitched sleep. But the healing apple can wake her."

"This is worse than we imagined." Husnaya wrung her cuffed hands. "If the witch succeeds in waking Jauhara and freeing the trapped jinn, she will have an army of darkness at her disposal."

Peri's wings shivered. "Dark enough to destroy all of us and anything else in their paths."

15

Why Me?

Fanta threw karate chops at the air. "First, my music player is smashed to pieces by a group of . . ." He hesitated, not knowing what to call them.

"Wretched bandits," Peri inserted.

"Wretched bandits!" Fanta repeated louder. "And now El Ghoula wants to release a bunch of wicked jinn that could kill us all!"

This day was getting more convoluted by the second. Sahara stared at a large brown bird—an eagle or hawk perhaps—perched high atop the canyons. She mentally flipped through what they'd learned so far: The lamp was some sort of magical time machine that Fayrouz intended to use to travel to the past, steal the golden apple, and bring back a dangerous jinniya. All so she could unleash even more danger on the world.

Despite this newfound knowledge, one question remained to be answered. "*Why* does Fayrouz want to unleash all these terrible jinn?" Sahara asked.

Naima placed her hands on her hips. "Because she's an evil witch and wants to let out more evil until it destroys the good. That's why."

"There's gotta be more to it," Sahara huffed. "What would she gain by doing that?"

"What she has lost," Husnaya answered. "When the moon and Saturn aligned last time you saw El Ghoula, the two that must not join *did* become one. Though not at her hands." The sorceress's gaze shifted from the lamp to the necklace. "At *yours*. This failure has only further fueled her inherited hunger. What started as a quest for one power"—Husnaya gestured toward the lamp—"has grown into an obsession for *infinite* power. And she will do anything not to fail *again*, which is why she is hellbent on unlocking the lamp at what she perceives to be the most favorable time." Husnaya sounded a lot like Umm Zalabya. "When its vile sorcery will be at its most powerful."

"The end of the month," Naima muttered. "When the moon is invisible."

Husnaya nodded.

"*And* the anniversary of the lamp's creation." Peri made her voice as deep and dark as possible for her tiny throat. "Magic is strongest on the anniversary of its birth."

Husnaya cocked an eyebrow at the fairy. "You know when the lamp was created?"

Peri wings whirred. "It's common knowledge in the jinn world, isn't it?"

Husnaya turned to Julnar. The mermaid queen shrugged.

Sahara was still thinking about the prophecy from her mother's journal. "The two that must not join become one. Who told you about that?" she asked Husnaya.

Peri swooped down by Sahara. "Sitt Husnaya was the one to see it in the wind."

Fanta's face mirrored the confusion Sahara felt. Meanwhile, Naima's eyes twinkled their fascinated acceptance. "I told you she was the greatest sorceress of all time."

The edges of Husnaya's mouth curled into a semi-smile.

"Show them," Peri squeaked.

Husnaya lifted her palm above the stream. With a tap of her finger, hundreds of droplets of water floated up into the sky. The sun shone through, filling them with tiny rainbows. When the sorceress waved her hand, they followed her movement, just as the dots in the dirt had done with Umm Zalabya. She arranged them into a prismatic image. A face. But not just any face—Morgana's.

"The hamsa around your neck is ingrained with the collective power of the four elements, though it wasn't always such," Husnaya told Sahara. "But from the start, Morgana cherished it with an earthly humanity that made it possible for us to join our wind, water, and fire energies with hers to create an amulet capable of locking the lamp."

"Capable of locking the lamp?" Fanta's brows rose to his bandana. "You mean it wasn't always locked? Anybody could open it?"

Julnar put her hands on his shoulders. By the way they

dropped and his eyes softened, Sahara could tell he'd experienced the wave of warmth that came with the mermaid's touch. Unfortunately, *her* head was still spinning. Everything she believed about the origin of the amulet was wrong. The hamsa twitched against Sahara's chest. "So you're saying my necklace belonged to Morgana? How could that be? My mother got it from a fortune teller when she was sixteen."

Husnaya flourished her hands through the air once more, organizing the remaining drops into another face.

"Sahara!" Naima squealed almost as high as Peri.

"It was always meant to pass from Morgana to you. And through someone you loved just as much as she loved the person who gifted it to her."

"But why me?" Sahara asked. Morgana slayed an evil sorcerer and took the lamp on the run before his family returned for it, starting a legacy to protect magic that has lasted for generations. But what had Sahara done? Of all of Morgana's descendants, why had the amulet chosen her?

"That is a question she, too, contemplated." Julnar smiled, pointing to Morgana's face.

"Seriously?" Sahara found that hard to believe.

"It seems to be the burden of the prophesied one to ask why, needing an explanation for the reason the winds of fate have blown in her direction," Husnaya stated. "Meanwhile, those who are not worthy have no trouble accepting the title." Her dark brown eyes peered into Sahara's. "Are you not the one who stopped Fayrouz from possessing the lamp?"

Peri soared to Sahara's image in the sky. "That's definitely you."

Julnar stroked Sahara's hair. "Was it not your courage to embrace your mother's love, despite the pain surrounding it, that allowed you to wield the amulet's power?"

Sahara's lip quivered at the mention of her mom. She remembered the boundless affection and certainty in her mother's voice as she spoke to her stomach. *My daughter, you are as vast and powerful as the great desert. And so is my love for you.* Sahara didn't want to let her mom down. She wanted so badly to live up to her expectations, to *all* the expectations that came with the prophecy.

"It's just so hard." Sahara bit her lip. "What if I make more mistakes? I've already messed up things with my best friend," she said, even though she was thinking about more than how upset Vicky was. She'd only been in Cairo one day and had already unlocked the lamp twice.

"You *will* make more mistakes," Husnaya said matter-of-factly, which was no comfort to Sahara. Could the sorceress somehow see that she wouldn't be able to control the pull of her amulet again in the future? But then Husnaya spoke softer than Sahara thought she was capable of. "It's not your mistakes that will define you. It's what you do after that will."

The bird sitting on the cliff extended its grand wings and dove down, flying past Sahara's rainbow image in the sky.

As the sun inched closer to the horizon, Peri announced, "It is nearly time for the Asr prayer—"

"Oh my God!" It couldn't be late in the afternoon already. Sahara's eyes darted to her watch and then to her cousins. "It's 4:02! We promised Noora we'd be back by three."

"Do not fret, my dear. You won't be late," Julnar reassured her.

"Huh? We *already* are." Sahara didn't want to be rude, but the eternal jinniya's concept of time was clearly off.

Husnaya must've picked up on Sahara's confusion. "Time speeds up when you travel through the lamp," she explained. "For every hour you have been away from home, three have passed here. When you return, you'll find that you haven't been gone long. That being said, you'd best be on your way. The longer the lamp is unlocked, the more its power will call to the witch. As soon as you're back home, you must lock it and avoid using it. At all times," the seer pressed.

Easier said than done. Sahara hadn't exactly had much of a choice last night. But how was she supposed to admit that she, "the prophesied one," couldn't control her amulet? Not to mention that the wish she'd made on the rabbit's foot may have set off a series of events culminating in the attack on Umm Zalabya. Before she could chide herself further, her cheeks burned with a painful realization. *I shouldn't try to see my mother again?*

Julnar stared softly into her eyes, kindly nodding in response to her silent question.

Sahara let out a resigned sigh. As much as she yearned to visit her mom, staying far away from the lamp might be best until she figured out how to keep her necklace from going off the wall.

The mermaid queen lifted Sahara's face to the water vision in the sky. "Without Morgana, there would be no amulet. And without you, its power to keep the lamp at bay would be lost. I know the burden is heavy, but the hamsa chose you for a reason. *You* are the wielder of the amulet."

Sahara looked down, praying she could live up to this duty.

"Don't worry about Vicky. She will forgive you." Naima wrapped her arm around her cousin.

Julnar sighed and turned to Peri and Husnaya. "The bond between two human hearts—magic can't hold a candle to it," she told them as Sahara nestled into Naima's embrace.

Sahara wanted so badly to admit she was worried about more than just fixing things with Vicky, but she wouldn't put that on her cousin when there was nothing Naima, or anyone for that matter, could do. This responsibility was hers, so she'd have to figure out how to handle it. Instead, she turned to Husnaya and asked, "Is there anything we can do to stop El Ghoula before she comes—"

"She's not coming back," Fanta blurted. "Baba and Morsy are going to find her."

Sahara didn't mention that Fayrouz had eluded Uncle Gamal and his army friend all year because she could see in her cousin's wide eyes how badly he needed to believe that the witch would be caught. "You're right. They'll find her first," she told him.

"In the end, things always work out as they are meant to—as Allah has intended, my dears," Julnar added. Though Sahara wasn't sure that meant the mermaid queen agreed Fayrouz would be caught.

Naima bent her fingers into a heart and aimed it at the trio. "I will miss you when we return to our time—" she started, then gasped. "Ya Allah! Since Peri and Julnar are eternal jinn, they're still alive in our time." She beamed at the two jinniyas, but her face fell when her gaze shifted to the sorceress.

Husnaya wasn't alive in the present—a reality that not only made Sahara sad too but also worried. "You said we shouldn't use the lamp anymore, but what if we need your help?"

"You will always have it." Husnaya bowed her head. "Look to the moon, and we will come."

"But you won't be . . ." Sahara struggled to get the word out.

"Alive." Husnaya shook her head. "Not in this form, but another."

Sahara wasn't sure why she did it. Maybe it was because she had lost someone early in life. Someone she desperately yearned to touch. But before she knew it, she'd thrown her arms around the sorceress. And Sahara wasn't alone. Her cousins did the same.

Husnaya smiled fully this time as she squeezed the children back. Up close, she smelled of cinnamon and cloves. For a few seconds, they curled up into her sweet, warm embrace.

Fanta was the first to pull away. He cleared his throat and said, "We'd better get back."

"It is time," the sorceress proclaimed as Sahara slid the necklace out of her shirt.

Peri flew closer, admiring the amulet. It was nearly the same size as her fairy body. "Spectacular as ever." Peri grinned. She spiraled her hands, producing sparks of light. From them emerged a tiny red candle, which she held out to Sahara. "A gift. In case you ever find yourself in the dark." She winked.

"Thank you," Sahara said, slipping it into her pocket. She couldn't imagine how such a little candle could scarcely produce more than a flicker, but she didn't want to insult the jinniya.

In seconds, the hamsa and lamp pulled toward each other. Sahara quickly reached for her cousins' arms, and Naima took hold of Kitmeer's collar, which was way better than him hanging off Sahara's pants with his teeth.

"Back to our time," Sahara whispered as the familiar twisting started. Before disappearing into the lamp, Sahara exchanged one last look with Husnaya, a light twinkling in the great sorceress's eyes.

The In-Between

965 CE

A light twinkled in Husnaya's eyes. For today, she and Hassan would start their training with Aziza. It turned out Marwan's fraudulent magic hadn't been his only secret. Behind the tall wooden chests of books in his study, which Husnaya was now convinced he hadn't read, was a tunnel that led underground to the servants' quarters and below them to the dungeons. They had once served as a prison, but after becoming overrun with captives under Marwan's watch, he commissioned the construction of one outside the palace.

It was in this dark and grimy space, still reeking of human neglect, that Husnaya and Hassan reported for their first sorcery lesson. Husnaya worried that after breaking her promise to Aziza by confronting Marwan, she might be reluctant to train them. But ever since she'd told the maid about the deal she'd made with the conniving sage and how it would ensure her and her father's safety, Aziza walked with an exuberant bounce.

"The key to any good union is respect," Aziza began, suddenly assuming the didactic tone of the children's tutor. "The same is true for the union between sorcerer and sorcery, between the diviner and the divine."

"The only union I'm thinking about is mine with my bed." Hassan groaned. "Why must we get up before the rooster crows?"

Husnaya shot him a sharp look. "Because if Mama and Baba are to believe that Marwan is still teaching you, we must meet with Aziza when everyone is still asleep."

"All right." Hassan put his hands up in surrender, then turned to Aziza. "Go on, please." He yawned.

Aziza's face turned serious. "*You* were born children of the hawa. The wind is within you, but before you can wield its powers, you must make a pledge. Repeat after me: I swear to Allah and all that is good in his world." She turned toward the twins.

"I swear to Allah and all that is good in his world," they repeated.

"To never take for granted or misuse."

"To never take for granted or misuse."

"The divine power of the Almighty's wind."

"The divine power of the Almighty's wind."

Aziza brought her palms together in prayer and raised them to her forehead. With her eyes closed, she bowed.

Husnaya followed suit, then kicked Hassan in the foot so he would do the same.

Aziza took a deep breath that echoed through the dungeon and flickered the candles, then opened her eyes. "Good." She nodded, taking a step toward the twins. As she waved her hand before them, a soft breeze cooled their foreheads and rippled through their hair.

Hassan jumped back, fully awake now. "How did you do that?"

"My mother taught me, just as my grandmother taught her."

Husnaya pointed to Aziza's head. She'd never actually seen her hair under her scarf. "Does that mean you were born with the hawa symbol too?"

"Hundreds of years ago, my ancestors bore it," Aziza answered. "But unfortunately, the more they had to hide their magic in the darkness, the more the golden hā disappeared from their children and their children's children, until there was no symbol left."

"That's awful. Why hide their powers at all?"

"Not by choice but to survive. Men with magic are regarded as respected sorcerers while women with magic are condemned for being evil witches."

Husnaya's face dropped. Even though Hassan had to lie about the source of his newfound sorcery knowledge, he could still claim his magic. But Husnaya could not.

Aziza must have sensed her unease. "Let's not harp on what we can't control." She paused, waiting for agreement.

After a few seconds more of stewing in the unfairness of her circumstances, Husnaya finally nodded.

"To harness the wind here"—Aziza stretched out her hand—"one must connect with it here first." Her hand moved to her heart.

"But *how* do we do that?" Husnaya asked eagerly.

"By listening," Aziza said softly. "It might help to close your eyes and focus on what you feel instead of what you see."

Husnaya shut her eyes, but all she could hear was Hassan's groan. There was a time when her brother was just as excited about magic as she was, but ever since he'd been passed over to succeed his father, he didn't seem to care about anything but his hurt pride. She missed the days when Hassan woke her in the middle of the night to count shooting stars or sneak into the stables to watch the newborn foals sleep.

"I feel something," Hassan now yelled.

Husnaya opened her eyes, expecting to see him snickering for fooling her into looking. But his eyes remained closed and his palm stretched open wide, shaking. He waved his hand, and *whoosh*—a gust of wind blew through the room, knocking Husnaya off her feet. It was gone as quickly as it had come.

"Well done," Aziza said, but a look of fear flashed across her face as she helped Husnaya up.

Hassan raced over to his sister. "Are you all right?"

A large smile spread across Husnaya's face. "Hassan, you did it!"

Hassan's eyes darted to his hand. "I did." He stood up taller and beamed.

"My turn," Husnaya said, quickly shutting her eyes. In the

distance, she recognized the sound of the wind arriving from the east, where the sun had just risen. It swished through the leaves of the palace trees. "I can hear it," she whispered.

"Let it flow to you and—" Aziza started.

"Catch it!" Hassan blurted out, ruining Husnaya's concentration.

She inhaled, trying to refocus.

"Let it become part of you," Aziza instructed as Husnaya's first wind showed itself.

It rushed down her chest and to her hand, which trembled in response. Husnaya furled her fingers to make the quivering stop, inadvertently cutting off her connection to the hawa. It came out of her palm with a lackluster *fsst*.

Husnaya screwed up her face. Hassan had shaken the room, while she had barely blown a speck of dirt off the floor. "What did I do wrong?" she asked.

"Nothing," Aziza reassured her. "Everyone's first wind shows itself differently, and with it comes an important lesson. Bigger and stronger"—she looked at Hassan—"isn't always better. Your wild wind knocked your sister down." Her eyes shifted to Husnaya. "Whereas your restraint stifled your wind. We must find the place between wild and restrained. The in-between is where your power lies."

The in-between is where your power lies. The words accompanied Husnaya to breakfast, lessons with Sitt Jamila, piano practice, dinner, and into the night as Aziza braided her hair before bed.

"You did well today," Aziza told her.

"I could have done better." Husnaya recalled the way the wind had rolled through her body. "But I got scared."

"There's nothing wrong with fear. It can warn us when we've flown too close to the sun. Just don't let it keep you from flying." She kissed Husnaya's head. "Tomorrow, we try again."

17

My Boys

Noora let out a massive sigh of relief when the children and Kitmeer crawled out of the refrigerator into the dark shop. "Alhamdulillah, you're back."

"Of course we are. No need to worry," Fanta told her, then muttered, "It's not like we've been gone for a thousand years . . . Ow!"

Naima had pinched him.

Sahara peeked at her watch—2:02 p.m. Only an hour had passed. Husnaya had been right about time moving faster where they'd been. Sahara's chest twinged at the thought of not seeing the sorceress again.

"Why are you sitting here in the dark?" Naima asked as she locked the refrigerator.

"Because the shop doesn't open until three." Noora patted Kitmeer's head. "But I couldn't wait upstairs. I'd never forgive myself if something went wrong."

"Nothing went wrong. It couldn't have gone any better." Naima grinned. "How did everything go here?"

"Fine. No one suspects anything. But there was one small problem." Noora pressed her lips together, hesitating.

"Mama?" Naima asked.

"She and Vicky came by looking for you, but I told them I'd sent you to check in on the Nassers' apartment. Remember the one they bought two years ago on Kholoosy Street?"

"The one Baba says is making more money than they know what to do with?" Fanta snickered.

"That's the one," Noora said. "Their renters moved out last Monday. And we promised Madame Nasser before she headed to Alexandria for the summer that we'd make sure everything was in order for the new tenants."

"You're a genius!" Naima kissed Noora's cheek. "Mama's been nagging me to go there all week. You probably made her day."

Sahara could see why Naima trusted Noora. She was a loyal friend, not to mention a whiz at coming up with excuses to cover their time-traveling tracks.

Noora's eyes glowed in the dark. "Don't keep me waiting. Did you find out what the lamp does?"

"It was what we thought. It isn't an ordinary—" Naima stopped, feeling the burn of her brother's and Sahara's stares.

Discretion had never been Naima's strong suit. They hadn't even discussed if and who they would share their new knowledge with, and she was already blabbing about it.

"It isn't an ordinary what?" Noora asked.

"Let's just say we have never been surer that we have to keep Fayrouz from getting the lamp," Sahara answered as Fanta lifted the gate.

"I'm late for karate practice," he said, hurrying out of the shop.

Sahara followed. "And I'd better go upstairs to check on Vicky."

"You won't find her there," Noora said, making Sahara about-face. "It seems that Umm Zalabya and her grand-daughter got into another argument this afternoon. Yara came back here with Layla and Vicky. And when they couldn't find you, she suggested they head to the stables to visit her horse."

Sahara's shoulders slumped with disappointment. "How nice," she remarked. But it wasn't nice. It was crappy. Was she ever going to get to talk to Vicky?

"Vicky wanted to wait until you got back," Noora assured her. "But when Yara's driver showed up, they had to leave."

"Yara's driver." Naima snorted. "He's not *her* driver. He works for her mother. And with her away in Europe, he has the time to drive Mademoiselle Yara wherever she wants."

Who the driver worked for made no difference to Sahara. Vicky should've waited, period.

"They'll meet us for easha tonight," Noora threw in.

Great. Once again, Yara would be intruding on one of their family dinners. Amitu was so excited about eating at Khalid's

Café, her favorite restaurant in Cairo. She'd meet them there after she finished work at the museum. It was supposed to be a last-day-of-Eid celebration. But Sahara wasn't sure she felt like celebrating.

"Thank you again for covering us for today, Noora." Sahara lowered her head and turned toward the exit.

"I should go with Sahara." Naima started after her cousin.

"Not so fast, Naima Saeed." Noora grabbed Naima's arm. "I told your mother you were checking in on the Nassers' apartment. And I am not a liar."

The last thing Sahara heard as she left the shop was the jingle of keys and Naima's loud groan.

Sahara trudged up the steps, entering the Saeeds' apartment a few minutes later. "There you are." Khalu Omar smiled from the fancy sofa.

"You were looking for me?" Sahara raced to think of an alibi.

He shook his head. "Noora told me you were at the Nassers' apartment, but I wanted to be here when you returned. I heard about the attack on Umm Zalabya. Are you all right? I'm sure it was scary, after everything that happened last year."

Sahara puffed out her chest. "Nothing this girl can't handle." Nothing except the scary-strong magnetism between the hamsa and the lamp and a certain pesky witch.

"Good." He tapped her head. "But I've also come to see if you would like to join me while I deliver some Eid meals Noora made for the boys."

"What boys?" Sahara asked.

"*My* boys."

Even though Sahara could've used the time to devise a plan to keep her hamsa from going haywire again, she desperately needed a break. Today's adventure through the lamp had been a lot. And seeing as Vicky wasn't around, why not meet Khalu's boys—whoever they turned out to be? "I'd love to go."

"Follow me." He grinned.

COMPARED TO UNCLE Gamal's driving, Khalu Omar's was a dream. Not quite as pleasant as Almaz's wind, but a solid second. Sahara happily read all the shops' names as Khalu's sedan rolled smoothly past them. They were usually a blur from the back seat of the Saeedmobile.

"Bravo," Khalu Omar praised.

Sahara's cheeks tingled. "Thanks." She hadn't realized she'd been saying them *aloud*. She turned to Khalu. "You're kinda the reason I can read Arabic. After you gave me my mom's journal filled with Giddu's stories, I had to learn."

"Is that so? Well, then I'm glad I did." He smiled. "As I understand it, if not for those stories, most of Shobra, including me, would still be asleep."

He was right about that. The tale about Prince Ahmed had helped Sahara figure out that the vial of healing water in the curio could be used to wake everyone up. "That's true."

She stared out the window again. "I can't believe that was last year."

"It feels like yesterday," he said.

"I was gonna say it feels like forever ago."

Khalu Omar chuckled. "Oh, to be young again and enjoy how time drips slowly like honey."

Except if you happened to have just traveled through your family's enchanted lamp. Time definitely did not drip like honey then. *More like a gushing geyser,* Sahara thought as they pulled up in front of an odd-looking three-level building. It was small compared to the others on the street, but its bright teal-blue windows stood out in the sea of beige around it like the rainbow-colored marshmallows in a box of Lucky Charms.

There were several boys in the small courtyard behind the sunny yellow gate, playing soccer. They ran over to her uncle when he got out of the car. Sahara watched from the window as Khalu Omar stretched his arms around the children. Afterward, he handed them several shopping bags of food from the trunk, then opened the door for Sahara.

"Are those your boys?" she asked.

"Some of them," he answered, turning around and practically skipping toward the building's entry.

Inside, Sahara followed her uncle past several bedrooms filled with bunk beds, classrooms, and playrooms. The bright color scheme continued into the mint-green cafeteria. Just as Khalu Omar dropped the last bag onto one of the tables, a gaggle of boys, ranging in age from toddlers to teenagers, popped out of the kitchen, making Sahara jump.

"Eid Mubarak!" they shouted.

"You caught us. It certainly is a blessed Eid now." Khalu Omar laughed as they flocked around him. The boys bubbled with excitement as he greeted each of them individually.

Sahara had no idea where they were. *A school? A community center?* she wondered as a woman in a striped headscarf hurried over. She kissed both of Sahara's cheeks, then pointed to the plastic name tag on her blouse and said, "I'm Mervat Shaheen, the director of the orphanage."

Orphanage. That meant Khalu Omar's *boys* didn't have parents. Sahara had lost her mom, but she couldn't imagine what it would be like to grow up without her father or Amitu.

"Nawarteena, Anissa Sahara." Mervat beamed. "Your visit blesses us."

Sahara raised her brows. "You know who I am?"

"Tab'an. Ustaz Omar hasn't stopped talking about his niece from New York since he met you."

Sahara's heart ballooned in her chest, gently tickling her rib cage. She turned her gaze toward her uncle, who was absorbed in a game of hot hands with one of the younger boys and purposely losing.

"Does my khalu come here often?" Sahara asked.

"Once or twice a week. Without his generosity, this place

wouldn't be what it is," Mervat explained. "It used to be an orphanage, and now it's a home." She smiled.

Sahara smiled back and looked down. A young boy with dimples was pulling on her leg. "Did we surprise you when we yelled, 'Eid Mubarak'?" he asked, shouting it again.

"You did," Sahara answered. "Today has been full of surprises." *In more ways than one.*

The boy giggled. "I like surprises. Even the scary ones like in the Sindbad stories."

Sahara did a double take. "You can read already?"

He shook his head. "La'a, I'm five. But Ustaz Omar's wife reads them to us when she comes. I like her."

"Me too," Sahara agreed. If only this kid knew who Khalu Omar almost ended up with as a wife. She crouched down. "So tell me. What's your favorite part of Sindbad's voyages?"

"The one with the afreet with the red eyes and claws. Grrr." He growled and swiped at the air.

"Ooh, scary!" Sahara fake-trembled. "Thank God Sindbad was smart enough to build a boat and sail away from him."

"I'm not scared." The boy jutted out his chin. "Abla Noora told me a secret." He cupped his hands and whispered in Sahara's ear. "Afreets love stories."

"They do?" Sahara asked.

He nodded, his eyes flickering with excitement as if an afreet could jump out at any minute. "But it has to be a story about when they were good so they'll turn back to that."

"What if they were never good?"

"Abla Noora says everyone starts off good." He twirled the scrunchie around Sahara's wrist.

"I guess you're right. If I ever run into a scary afreet, I'll tell him a tale that will make him good again." If only this strategy worked for el ghoulas. "Your secret's safe with me." Sahara stood up and pretended to zip her lips.

The young boy did the same.

They spent another thirty more minutes at the orphanage, Khalu reminding Sahara of Santa as he handed each of the children a plate of food. Except, he didn't disappear up a chimney after but instead prepared a small serving—dinner with Vicky and the rest of the family was nearing—for himself and Sahara to enjoy along with them. And enjoy it, she did. Sahara let out an audible "Mmm" as Noora's roasted lamb melted in her mouth, making the boys laugh and her blush.

Before they left, one of the teenagers dawdled over to Sahara's uncle with a large present. "I . . . I made this with the paints you bought me," he stammered.

Khalu excitedly unwrapped it like a kid on his birthday, and everyone in the cafeteria froze at the painting of the orphanage's exterior. *Amazing!* Sahara didn't know much about art, but it was clear this boy had a knack for it. And not just because of how accurately he'd captured the building, down to the exact turquoise-blue shade of the windows. It was the way the sun rose behind the building, the upper rim surrounding it like a golden halo, that really got her. Sahara tingled with warmth—the kind she got from gooey, roasted marshmallows, cuddles with her dad, or the smell of Khaltu Layla's floral perfume, but all at once.

Khalu Omar looked the gifter straight in the eye and beamed. "I love it."

The boy stood up taller, practically growing a few inches. Sahara knew exactly how he felt. It was impossible not to bloom in Khalu Omar's light.

On the car ride home, Sahara turned to her uncle. "It's nice what you do with your boys. Amitu and my dad are always telling me how important it is to give back."

"They are right." Her uncle gave a firm nod. "Extending a hand to others is our duty as Muslims."

"I know it's the right thing and all. But why do you *really* help at the orphanage?" she asked. "Like, back home, I tutor this nine-year-old boy who lives next door in math. I get ten dollars a week for it. Even though it's nice to have pocket cash, that's not the real reason I do it. I like the feeling I get when he shows me he got a ninety on his last test."

Khalu Omar thought about her question for a moment, drumming the steering wheel with his fingers. "All their lives, those boys have been told they're unfortunate and *poor*. I don't like that word, especially when it is used to define a person. Your sittu always says that people's circumstances may be poor, but *they* aren't. Those boys are rich in other ways—why should money or food be the only measure of wealth?" He jerked his head toward the canvas painting in the back seat.

"The young man whose hands created that is a rich soul. As much as my time allows, I try to help all the boys see their valuable gifts. That's why, really. Does that make sense?"

"Complete sense," Sahara answered, laying her head on her uncle's shoulder as he gently steered them home.

18

Duct Tape

With thirty minutes to spare until it was time to leave for dinner, Sahara headed upstairs to strategize ways to keep her amulet and the lamp apart. As she reached the third floor, music blared through the Saeeds' front door. Sahara smiled and entered the apartment, not the least bit surprised to find Fanta shaking and shuffling around his room.

She slid inside and pointed to her watch. "Nobody told me it was dance o'clock."

Fanta laughed, lowering the music. "You should've heard Baba before he left for the shop." He flailed his arms, reenacting his father's annoyance. "'All of Shobra is going to think we are running a disco club here.'" Sahara cracked up. "But without my headphones and music player, what else am I supposed to do?" He huffed.

The memory of the nasty-breathed robber stomping on them made Sahara wince. "I'm so sorry. I know how much they meant to you."

"It's not your fault," Fanta groaned. "You didn't break them."

He removed some clothes from his dresser and tossed them onto the empty bedframe. "I just dropped by to pick up some hidoom for the next few days."

"Thanks for letting us borrow your mattress. I know it's a pain to have to sleep upstairs." She had majorly complicated her cousin's life. "I've only been here a day, and you've lost your music player *and* your bed. You must love having me back."

"Tab'an, I do." Sahara could tell from the earnest expression on Fanta's face that he meant it. "And sleeping at Sittu's isn't that bad. With your amitu at the museum, I get the place all to myself. But don't tell Naima I said so. Knowing her, she'll get it into Mama and Baba's heads that I should move there permanently so she can turn my room into a library."

Sahara wouldn't put that past his sister. "Cross my heart," she assured him. "Speaking of Naima, where is she anyway?" Sahara asked, pulling her hair back into a ponytail.

Fanta shrugged, then stared at her intently. "Probably still at the Nassers' apartment, which means we have time to talk." He leaned in closer. "Spill it. I can tell something's on your mind."

"How?"

"The tighter your ponytail, the more you've got going on in there." He pointed to her head.

He was right, but Sahara didn't know where to begin.

"Just say it," Fanta pressed. "I'm sure it's not as bad as you think."

"Okay, fine. I'm supposed to be"—she made air quotes

with her fingers—"*the wielder of the amulet*. But how can I be when I can't even control it? Whenever the hamsa's anywhere near the lamp, it goes ballistic."

Fanta's eyes darted to the chain around her neck.

"It's not acting up now," Sahara groaned. "That's the thing. I don't know when it will. Last night, Naima and I didn't sneak into the chamber on purpose." She tapped on her pendant. "*It dragged me down there.*"

Fanta shook his finger. "Don't use that excuse with Mama. She'll never go for it."

"It might sound ridiculous, but it's not an excuse."

"I believe you. I saw it in action this afternoon."

"Then you know. And you heard Umm Zalabya and the trio. Every time I unlock the lamp, El Ghoula senses it. I have to keep the amulet in check."

"I've got an idea!" Fanta yelled, then spun and rummaged through his dresser, emerging seconds later with a silver roll.

"Tape?" Sahara asked.

"Not just any tape," Fanta corrected. "*Duct* tape."

"I *know* what it is. My dad and I use it all the time to fix stuff at home."

Dad. Missing wriggled through Sahara. She pushed it down so she could focus. "How's duct tape gonna help me?"

Fanta ripped off a medium-sized piece and handed it to her. "Just try it," he said, pointing to her necklace.

"So you're suggesting I tape the hamsa to myself? I'm not sure that's a good idea."

"Not to yourself. That might hurt. But to your shirt." Fanta twirled the roll around his finger. "Baba says this is one of man's greatest creations. They use it in the army for lots of things because of how strong and sticky it is. And right now, you need strong and sticky."

Her cousin wasn't wrong about the durability of duct tape. "They don't call it magic tape for nothing," she said. Sahara had once heard from her robotics coach that it helped save the lives of the *Apollo 13* astronauts. When their spacecraft was damaged, they were forced to use the lunar module to return to Earth. There was just one problem. The carbon dioxide filters aboard the module wouldn't last long enough for them to make it back. And too much carbon dioxide was lethal for humans. But thanks to duct tape, and some other nifty materials, they created a gadget to scrub the air of CO_2 until they landed.

If it was good enough for NASA and the military, it was good enough for her. "It's worth a shot." Sahara grabbed the rest of the roll from Fanta. "I have a feeling I'm gonna need more than one piece. And just so you know, duct tape isn't one of *man's* greatest creations. A woman came up with the idea."

Fanta's jaw dropped. Sahara giggled at his shocked expression. She reached over and closed his mouth, then swiveled toward the doorway.

"I'll be right back," she shouted as she hurried to Naima's room. "And if this works, I'll use what I've saved in my piggy bank to buy you a new music player."

19

El Muizz

El Muizz li-Din Allah, El Muizz for short, is the oldest street in Cairo, named after the Fatimid khalifa who conquered it in the late tenth century," Amitu had explained to Sahara and Vicky on the plane. "It was one of your mother's favorite places. 'Think about how much history has taken place here, Malak,' she would say. 'What stories this street has to tell.'"

Sahara recalled her mother's words to her aunt as she followed Khaltu Layla, Uncle Gamal, and her cousins through Bab el-Futuh—one of the stone gates that remained from the walls that had once enclosed the Fatimid Palace and the original old city of Cairo. She pictured armed soldiers on the watch for intruders, standing tall at the top of its two round towers. After today's adventure into the past, she couldn't help but feel more connected to history, which had always seemed so distant. And she was surrounded by it on this cobblestone street flagged by ancient mosques, mansions, schools, and mausoleums with domes, arches, and towers.

She could see why her mother loved it here. What would she have thought if she knew her family was protecting a lamp that could travel back in time and allow her to meet the people who had lived, worked, prayed, and studied in these monuments? It didn't seem fair that her mom and so many others in their family had been kept in the dark. As much as Sahara wished they had known the artifact's true magic, she couldn't ignore the seriousness on Husnaya's face when she'd warned about how hard it was to resist the kind of power the lamp promised. Would her mother have been able to resist it? Hopefully, Sahara would. She pressed the hamsa to her chest, feeling the thick layer of duct tape she'd used to attach it to the inside of her shirt.

The lights of the apartment buildings, shops, cafés, and stands interspersed between El Muizz's historic architecture flickered on as the sun set. So did the flashes of the cameras held by the myriad of tourists attempting to capture the ancient landmarks.

Up ahead, the tables of Khalid's Café spilled onto the sidewalk. Aside from the one that Khalu Omar was waving them over to, every table in the restaurant was filled with customers. Amitu hadn't arrived yet, but Vicky was already seated with Omar and Noora. Maybe Yara had dropped her off and then left. *Yes!*

But as Sahara headed for the empty chair next to her friend, a knot of nerves formed in her stomach. Vicky had been pretty upset the last time they'd seen each other. Sahara took a deep breath, reminding herself that they'd been best friends since forever, then asked, "Anyone sitting here?"

Even though Vicky only shook her head, Sahara caught the flicker of a half smile. She'd take it. "How were the stables?" Sahara spat out, quickly sitting down.

"Fun. Yara's horse is gorgeous." Vicky was majorly smiling now. "Her name is Leila because she's dark as night. Isn't that so cool?"

After yesterday, Sahara was relieved to see her friend's spirits back up. But that didn't keep jealousy from slithering inside her. Why did Yara and her horse have to be responsible for her friend's good mood?

"It sounds really cool," Sahara said as the waiter dropped trays of pita bread and small plates of dip in front of them.

Vicky dipped a slice of pita into the baba ghanouj sparingly. "Ooh, that's good," she said, going back for more. "What's in it?"

"Eggplant and tahini. I like it too." Sahara smiled, noticing the thin string of silver and lapis-blue beads around Vicky's wrist. "I've never seen that bracelet before. Where'd you get it?"

"At the market today. You know, the one you told me about it with all the old shops. I forget its name." Vicky scratched her head.

"Khan el Khalili," Sahara answered, the knot in her belly retwisting. Vicky had no idea that a fortune teller had given Sahara's mom the jewelry box there, but she did know how much Sahara wanted to go. It was on the list of places to visit they'd made on the plane.

"Khan el Khalili," Vicky repeated, struggling to pronounce the *kh* sounds.

Sahara looked down. "But we were supposed to go. *Together.* Remember?"

"I know. It's just after we left the stables, Yara was still upset about the fight with her grandmother. She really wanted to go. And I thought it could cheer her up."

Of course, Miss Equestrian wanted to go to the greatest market in Cairo with *her* best friend!

"But I can't wait to go back." Vicky's shoulder playfully nudged Sahara's. "With *you.*"

Out of nowhere, Yara stuck her head between the girls. "Talking about anything good?"

Sahara jumped, nearly knocking over her water. *Crap!* Yara hadn't gone back home. "Where . . . where did you come from?"

"The bathroom." Yara flashed a devilish grin.

Umm Zalabya's granddaughter was like those annoying windup jack-in-the-box toys. The ones where a clown pops up with a weird and slightly scary smile on its face. At least *they* came with a musical warning.

"I was just showing Sahara the bracelet I got today," Vicky said. "I'm glad you convinced me to get it."

Yara touched Vicky's shoulder. "I could tell you wanted it."

Pfft. How could Yara tell anything about Vicky? She'd known her for a day. "It's really pretty," Sahara remarked.

"It is. Ma'lish, you couldn't make it." Yara tilted her helmeted head and batted her lashes, pretending to be sorry. "But we can go again."

"Definitely." Sahara feigned a smile. She wasn't going anywhere with that girl.

As the servers dropped more appetizers off, Khaltu Layla called to Yara. "There's an empty korsi here. Come sit before everything gets cold."

Thank you, Khaltu!

"I'll be right there, Tante Layla," Yara responded, then bent down and whispered to Vicky—still loud enough for Sahara to hear, "Thank you for being there for me today."

"Ditto," Vicky whispered back.

Sahara cringed at the buddy-buddy way they were acting. And she hated that anyone, especially Yara, needed to be there for Vicky today. *She* should've been there. She'd tried to be there last night, but Vicky had turned her away.

When Yara finally left for her seat, Sahara tapped Vicky's shoulder. "I know you didn't want to talk yesterday, but maybe we can when we get back to Naima's."

Before her friend could answer, Amitu hurried toward them. "I'm sorry I'm late," she huffed, breathless. "Got caught up at the museum. There are so many wonderful things to see!"

Despite the friction with Vicky, Sahara was happy for her aunt. "It sounds like you had a great first day."

"I did." Amitu yawned. "Though I'm still a bit tired from our travels, it was a great first day indeed. How would you both like to join me at the museum in the morning? Zalabya said I was welcome to show you around. Then after work, I can take you to see the Pyramids."

"Thumbs-up." Vicky beamed.

"Thumbs-up," Sahara said too. She might have missed out on Khan el Khalili today, but it would be awesome to return to Giza with her best friend. She'd told Vicky all about the nighttime Sound and Light show and how the Pyramids and Sphinx had lit up the desert.

Amitu kissed Sahara's head, then hurried to sit as the waiter filled their glasses with a red liquid.

Sahara's muscles clenched, remembering El Ghoula's cursed sleep sharbat. Her eyes darted to Naima.

Her cousin leaned across the table. "It's not sharbat, I promise," she assured Sahara. "Just karkaday. I think you call it hibiscus tea in English."

Sahara's tension eased. She let out a nervous giggle as Uncle Gamal clinked his glass with a fork to get the table's attention. "Ladies and gentlemen." He raised his glass the way he had as master of ceremonies at the fake wedding. "On this last night of Eid el Adha, let us drink to faith, loyalty, and family. And pray for our beloved Hajja Zainab's safe return from her pilgrimage." Unlike her experience with the sharbat, Sahara gladly took a sip of the karkaday, trying not to pucker her face at its tartness.

Dinner continued into the night with endless platters of savory spiced stews, rice-stuffed vegetables, and skewers of grilled tender meats. After Sahara took her last sweet lick of creamy rice pudding, they strolled down El Muizz Street to the van. Amitu pointed out a perpendicular road. "El Darb el Asfar. At one time, the Yellow Way was one of Cairo's richest and most prestigious streets. The government is talking about restoring some of its historic mansions and turning them into museums—"

HOOT! HOOT! HOOT! A symphony of owl calls pierced through the night. Sahara had never heard so many at once.

"El būm of El Darb el Asfar." Amitu chuckled. "Another thing the road is known for—owls!"

Sahara spun in the direction of the hooting, but all she could see was a massive dark structure looming over the street like a bad omen.

"Bayt Sultan," Amitu said. "The mansion was once the crown jewel of the road."

"Bayt Sss-oool-taaan." Fanta drew out its name like a ghost, sending a chill down Sahara's spine. His sister gave him a push. "What?" he railed at Naima. "Everyone knows it's haunted."

"He's right," Yara added. "My dad told me that for many years it was owned by a Turkish ambassador, who passed it down to his children, who then passed it down to theirs. Eventually, the family sold it to a wealthy businessman, Fareed Sultan, and returned to Turkey. He got married a few months later. The Sultans were so in love. But when the wife suddenly died, the husband couldn't live without her. He was so desperate, he used dark magic to bring her back. But it backfired, turning him into a vicious afreet instead. One that haunts the halls of the mansion at night."

"That's frightening." Vicky cowered.

"Don't worry. That afreet won't come near you as long as I'm around." Fanta flexed his bicep, making Vicky giggle and Naima retch.

Sahara gazed at the eerie house, noticing a broken wooden lattice hanging from the top window. *Thump.* Sahara wasn't sure if her heart or the hamsa—luckily, the tape held to her shirt—had drummed. Whatever it was, the house definitely gave her the creeps. She twisted away, nearly crashing into Yara.

"Do you like it?" she asked, shoving her wrist in Sahara's face and showing off a bracelet identical to the one Vicky wore. "Vicky bought me one too. You're lucky to have a friend like her. Don't lose her by keeping secrets," Yara warned before running ahead to join Vicky.

Sahara's eyes flitted from the eerie mansion to the sly way Yara slid her arm through Vicky's, unable to decide which she should be more afraid of.

20

Almaz

965 CE

As the days grew cooler and all the olives had been harvested from the groves on the southern edge of the palace grounds, Husnaya and her brother continued their training. Every lesson started with tuning in to the wind and Aziza frequently reminding them of its importance. "Not only will connecting with the hawa allow you to harness its power, but it will also allow you to call to others and hear their calls to you."

"So one day when Husnaya is married to some unfortunate soul, and I to the luckiest woman on earth, we can communicate through the wind," Hassan had once teased.

Even though Husnaya huffed at her brother's jab, she rather liked the idea of their winds keeping them united.

While Husnaya's ability to wield the wind without restraint progressed slowly, Hassan's only grew more uncontrollable. The wilder his power became, the more resistant he grew to Aziza's warnings to tamp it down.

"Why should I tame it? Did you hear how Baba praised my magic when my wind sped up the flow in the water clock so that the cymbals sounded twenty minutes early? I have the power to change time." Hassan puffed out his chest.

Husnaya had witnessed her father's admiration of Hassan's feat herself. She yearned to display her magic as freely as he could. Unfortunately, the price of that freedom would be the end of her lessons. Thus, she kept quiet and applauded her brother for his one-of-a-kind sorcery.

Aziza greeted them in the dungeon with a surprise this morning.

Husnaya's jaw dropped. "A magic carpet!" she said, her eyes fixed on the red-and-gold rug hovering by Aziza's shoulder. "Are we going to fly that?"

"Of course we are." Hassan approached the carpet.

Aziza's arm shot up in front of it. "Tut-tut! This one's mine. It's been in my family for generations. And when I die, it will find its way to its next rightful owner." Aziza stepped aside to reveal two rolled-up rugs. "You will enchant your own," she said, picking up a thick leather-bound book by her feet. "For centuries, this grimoire has passed through the hands of the women in my family. Inside are spells so powerful that the book itself is armed with a protective enchantment. *Never* touch the pages inside," she warned.

"What happens if you do?" Husnaya's voice quivered.

"The hemlock they've been soaked in will seep into your hands, ending your life in minutes."

"Calm down. She's obviously kidding," Hassan told his sister.

"I most certainly am not," Aziza insisted. "But you could give it a try if you doubt my seriousness."

Hassan shook his head, his confidence shrinking in the face of Aziza's challenge. "Then how are we supposed to read it?" he asked.

"You must use your wind." Aziza opened the book with a flourish of her hand. She flipped through it by sliding her finger back and forth in the air. "Here it is," she said, stopping at a page with the words *Elsijada elsiḥriya.*

"To turn these feet warmers into vessels that zip through the sky, we must spell them."

"Using what it says there?" Husnaya asked, looking down at the grimoire.

"Alone, they are merely words. But uttered at the right celestial time by a sorcerer in tune with the hawa, they are capable of much more."

Husnaya's whole body vibrated with excitement.

"Today, as the moon passes between the sun and the earth, you will use your wind to carry down the magic forged by the eclipse and transfer it to the carpets until they, too, are floating before us."

Aziza unrolled a rug in front of each of them. "As you are tuning in to the wind today, go deeper. Go farther into the cosmos, summoning the favorable power of the eclipse."

Husnaya shut her eyes and connected with the air, which came much more naturally now, pushing her mind past

Earth's sky to the stars, planets, and moons her tutor had taught her existed beyond it.

"Channel this fortune into your wind and bring it down into your hands," Aziza instructed.

Husnaya felt her right hand shake with an intensity greater than ever before.

"Direct the wind traveling through your hand to the sijada at your feet—picture it in your mind—and let your heart speak the words: *Teer, teer zay el asafeer.* Then tarta'ay." Aziza's snap echoed through the dungeon.

Husnaya repeated the incantation, commanding the carpet to fly like a bird, and then snapped. Within seconds, the fibers of the carpet brushed against her foot and traveled up her leg. "It tickles." She giggled as it made its way higher and higher, tousling her hair.

When she could no longer feel the rug, she opened her eyes. "It worked!" Husnaya smiled at the carpet floating a few feet above her.

"This is nonsense," Hassan griped, thrusting his hand at the carpet. An angry wind blew through the room, but the rug didn't budge.

Husnaya wiped the smile from her face, not wanting to make Hassan feel bad.

Meanwhile, Aziza shook her finger at him. "You are trying to get the fibers in the carpet to submit to you with force. They won't respond to the threat of your winds," she asserted. "The moon doesn't push away the sun. It sings it to sleep so that it might shine brighter tomorrow."

"So I should sing to my carpet." Hassan snickered.

Aziza narrowed her eyes at him. "No, you should respect it and all that went into creating it. Then and only then will it dare to fly."

Hassan's eyes flashed with fire. One Husnaya had never seen in them before. He turned his back and stomped toward the stairs.

Husnaya went to stop him, but Aziza took hold of her arm. "Leave him be." Aziza's voice was firm, making it clear this was not a suggestion but a command. She jerked her head toward Husnaya's carpet, her face softening. "You did well today. Celebrate *your* accomplishment." She squeezed Husnaya's hand, then followed Hassan up the steps.

THE ABRUPT END to this morning's lesson brought about by her brother's temper left Husnaya with an hour to spare before she was due at breakfast. Instead of retiring to her room, she headed out to the garden. She couldn't think of a better way to celebrate the flying success of her carpet spell than breathing in the lingering scent of the yasmeen, which had only bloomed hours before under the moonlight.

It felt strange not to check on Hassan when he was so upset. But perhaps Aziza was right. Maybe he needed time to clear his head. Husnaya took a seat on the iron bench in front of the round fountain in the yasmeen garden. This was one of her grandmother's favorite spots on the palace grounds. "All my troubles seem small compared to the beauty here," Jidda liked to say. Husnaya inhaled the sweet fragrance as an orange glow foreshadowed the sun's arrival. A soft wind blew through the flowers and toward Husnaya. It fluttered through her scarf, lightly loosening wisps of her hair, and tickled her cheeks with its warm whisper. Husnaya giggled. When the breeze shifted direction, she stood up and crept after it, yearning to stay close but not scare it away.

For a moment, she thought it might be Hassan's hawa calling to her. But his winds were never this calm. *Aziza?* Husnaya wondered, following the gentle hawa out of the garden and toward the olive groves far beyond the palace walls. As her home grew more and more distant, so did her worry. She'd never been this far on her own. Just as she considered turning back, a silver light flickered past, making the hairs on the back of her neck stand up.

A jinni? Husnaya had heard stories of the fire spirits that dwelled deep in the woods. This could be one. However, silver was an odd color for a fire jinni. The light flashed before her, then twisted around and around her body. Husnaya spun in place, growing dizzy trying to keep up with it—until the light finally came to a stop, exploding open with a blinding burst. She shielded her eyes, only daring to lower her hand several seconds later.

"Ya Allah. You're not a jinni." Husnaya's eyes widened with

wonder. Towering above her on lofty muscular legs was the most majestic horse Husnaya had ever seen. The expansive light immediately shrank into a ball behind the animal and zipped away.

"Was that your wind calling to me?" Husnaya asked the hisana, feeling oddly calm in her presence.

The horse lowered her head as if to answer *yes*. Husnaya traced her hand along the bridge of the animal's nose and asked, "Do you have a name?"

The hisana shook her head, her silky silver mane shimmering in the growing sunlight. "Then I shall call you Almaz, for your beauty rivals that of Mama's most precious diamonds."

The animal whinnied her approval.

And side by side, Husnaya and Almaz watched the sunrise—their first of many together.

21

Tea Time

A little after ten, Uncle Gamal backed the van into a spot between two tightly parked cars as everyone screamed, "It's too tight!" Much to his satisfaction, it wasn't. Sahara exhaled and flapped her lips, trying to rid herself of the hot jealousy twisting and turning in her stomach as she hopped out onto the sidewalk. Yara had said Vicky bought her the bracelet, but she could've been lying. For all Sahara knew, Yara had gotten it for herself and tried to pass it off as a gift.

When Sahara turned into the Saeeds' apartment, she felt a hand on her arm. She turned to find Amitu and Khaltu smiling at her.

"Shay bi laban before you go to bed?" Amitu asked, gesturing toward Sittu's apartment.

Sahara glanced back at Vicky. As much as she wanted to talk to her friend tonight, she could use some time cooling off first. Besides, Vicky wouldn't even notice she was gone. She and Naima were busy figuring out how to make room for

Yara. Her dad had told her she could sleep over if Uncle Gamal and Khaltu Layla said it was okay. Unfortunately, they'd said it was okay.

"Itfadali," Uncle Gamal welcomed Yara. "We are running a funduq for banat this summer." He roared with laughter, but Sahara didn't find his "inn for girls" joke funny. Not tonight.

As Amitu put the kettle on the stove and Khaltu pulled out the milk and sugar, Sahara wandered into the Room of Photos. This had been her first time in it since last summer. There were new additions to the family gallery—one of Sittu, dressed in a long white abaya and headscarf. Khaltu had mentioned taking photos of her before she left for her pilgrimage. "Libs il ihram," she'd called the clothes Sittu wore, symbolizing the state of holiness she would be entering on her hajj. Sahara stared into her grandmother's eyes. They'd always been warm and gentle, but there was a peace in them Sahara had never seen before. If only she could channel half of that calm.

Sahara slid down to a close-up of Noora and Omar's wedding. She traced the white blooms on the bride's crown, remembering how they'd replaced the silk, wannabe flowers that had been on Magda's head.

"Goomal." Amitu sighed. "Now that I've witnessed Umm Zalabya's beautiful yasmeen for myself, I can see why you said they were 'extraordinary.'"

They were—in more ways than one.

"But delicate too," Amitu added. "The most beautiful

things in life are. Including hearts and friendship. Don't you think?"

A lump formed in Sahara's throat. She turned to Amitu, her voice shaking. "I think mine is broken."

"Which one—your heart or your friendship?" Amitu asked, tucking Sahara's hair behind her ears.

"Both." Sahara sniffled as the kettle began to whistle.

Amitu led her to the table. "Lucky for you, there's nothing a cup of shay bi laban won't mend." She winked before disappearing into the kitchen.

The last time Sahara had sat at Sittu's table with a cup of tea with milk had been the night of Magda's laylat el henna, when Naima and her plan to out El Ghoula had gone south. Sahara wondered how many sorrowful hearts this table had seen, as her aunts took a seat on each side of her.

Khaltu set a steaming mug of tea in front of Sahara. "Drink first, then talk," she said, raising her cup to her lips. Sahara followed suit, the warm tea streaming down her throat and into her belly.

"I suspect this time with your friend in Egypt isn't going as you'd hoped."

Way to put it lightly, Khaltu. Between Vicky finding out about El Ghoula in the worst possible way and Yara's meddling every five seconds, *nothing* had gone as she'd hoped. "Definitely not," Sahara huffed, then took another sip. "This isn't how things were supposed to go. I wanted to show Vicky all the things I love about Cairo."

"But you still have over a month to do that," Amitu kindly pointed out.

"I know, but it won't be the way I imagined. *I* won't be the only one showing them to her."

"Naima?" Khaltu asked.

Sahara shook her head adamantly. "Yara," she grumbled.

"Ah." Khaltu nodded. "She *has* been hanging around here a lot lately."

"Exactly. Like an annoying fly I can't swat."

Her aunts giggled.

"It's not funny. What does Vicky see in her anyway?"

"I promise we're not laughing at you, Susu, but with you," Amitu assured her. "If anything, we're laughing at ourselves because we've both felt the sting of jealousy. And one day, you will laugh at it too."

"When we were little, Amani was very protective over her friendship with Malak," Khaltu explained. "Anytime I showed up around them, she would shoo me away with the same indignant look you have on your face now."

Hearing this made Sahara self-conscious. She wiped her face, trying to rid it of its scowl.

"I didn't know that," Amitu said softly to Layla.

"It was a long time ago." Khaltu waved a dismissive hand. "But I do remember Mama demanding that my sister be more welcoming, then Amani crying, 'I can't. If I let Layla in, she will steal Malak from me.'" Khaltu chuckled. "And Mama explained, 'Friendships, like flowers, can't bloom if they are held too tightly.'" Khaltu Layla hurried to her purse, returning with a small copper coin. "After, Mama placed five piasters in Amani's hand." Khaltu rolled her coin to Sahara.

Sahara slipped it off the table, quickly furling her fingers around it.

"'There are two ways we can approach life,' Mama told her." Khaltu pointed to Sahara's clenched hand. "'Hanging on'"—she rotated Sahara's palm and undid her fingers—"'or opening up.'"

Sahara stared at the side of the coin engraved with the Pyramids. Not only did it feel secure in her open palm, but her nails weren't digging into her hand. She relaxed her shoulders and smiled at her aunts. "Thank you," she said, returning the five piasters to Khaltu.

Khaltu slid it back. "Keep it, in case you need a reminder."

Just then, Uncle Gamal hurried through the door, his eyes wide with panic.

"Il lihassal?" Khaltu Layla ran over, inquiring what had happened.

"Morsy just stopped by. I'm afraid Mama won't be able to fly back home tomorrow. The city of Jeddah has been overtaken by winds, grounding all outgoing flights."

"For how long?" Amitu asked, her voice steeped with concern.

"Indefinitely," Uncle Gamal answered.

Disappointment wound itself around Sahara's heart and squeezed. She was so looking forward to Sittu's return.

"We can't just leave Mama there with no way to get home," Khaltu insisted.

"We won't. I will drive and get her. I leave for Jeddah in the van at dawn."

"Gamal!" his wife cried. "That will take days."

"Two, if I drive ten hours a day. And two is better than however long it could take for the matar in Jeddah to reopen. The airport officials say flights may be grounded for some time."

"And what about the search for Fayrouz?" Amitu asked.

"Morsy and his officers will continue it." He turned to Sahara. "I promise to return with your sittu, and soon, we will all celebrate El Ghoula's capture together. Wallahi," he swore.

Sahara mustered a smile for her uncle's sake. As he and Khaltu worked out logistics, she headed for the balcony.

Amitu followed. "Don't worry, Susu. Before planes, people made the trip to Mecca on horses and in carriages. Surely, the Saeedmobile can get there."

"Yeah, I guess." Sahara shrugged.

Amitu rubbed her back. "I know you've been charged with a lot at a young age, but you are not alone."

Then why do I feel alone? "I wish I could tell Vicky everything. But I'm trying to respect our family's legacy *and* keep her from getting mixed up in danger."

Amitu pointed across the street to the moon glowing above the mosque's minarets. "Generations of women who have looked at the same qamar with their own woes and wishes are holding you up."

Sahara stared at the crescent. The same one Sitt Husnaya had told her earlier today—one thousand and three years ago, actually—to look to if she needed help. Last summer, she would've scoffed at the idea. However, tonight it gave her some comfort. That didn't mean she wasn't searching her brain for a way to explain *how* the moon could summon the trio. But she didn't doubt that it would.

22

Daddy's Museum

"Time to wake up." Amitu peeked her head through the door. Even though it was only nine, Sahara was dressed and raring to go to the museum this morning and then the Pyramids at night. She'd practically done a happy dance when Yara left for Umm Zalabya's an hour ago.

There was no repeat performance of the amulet's antics last night—*thank you, magic tape*—Uncle Gamal was already on his way to get Sittu, and Sahara would have all morning to talk to Vicky without Yara's interference. Today was going better already. Too bad Naima couldn't join them at the museum. She was back at the Nassers' apartment, tidying up for their new tenants.

After a short taxi ride, Amitu and the girls arrived at the Museum of Islamic Art.

"Whoa! It looks like a palace," Vicky marveled.

"Tell me about it." Sahara couldn't take her eyes off the tall archway housing the entrance and the gagillion lattice windows. She was surprised not to see medieval guards flanking its lofty wooden doors.

The girls waited by the entrance as Amitu entered an office behind the ticket counter to pick up guest badges. Sahara seized the opportunity to talk to Vicky, joining her in front of a giant poster of the museum's artifacts.

She had no clue where to begin. "Those are just like Peri's," Sahara said, pointing to a pair of gold horseshoe-shaped earrings.

"Like whose?" Vicky scrunched her brows.

Sahara panicked. What was she thinking? Vicky had no idea who Peri was or that Sahara had met her yesterday in 985. "Like Amitu's," Sahara corrected herself.

"Oh. That reminds me." Vicky reached into her cross-body bag. "I meant to give you this last night, but we never had a second alone." She slipped out a bracelet resembling the one she'd brought from the khan for herself and, allegedly, Yara. "I know how much you love this shade of deep blue. The minute I saw it, I thought of you."

"You got me one too?" Of course Vicky had. They were best friends. Sahara should've trusted their friendship no matter what. Even if Vicky was being chummy with Yara.

As Vicky clasped the bracelet around her wrist, Sahara searched for the right words. Why was it so hard talking to her best friend lately? She fiddled with Khaltu's coin—tucked inside her shorts pocket—letting go of what she thought she should say. "Vicky."

"Sahara."

They'd spoken each other's names simultaneously, making them chuckle and releasing the tension between them.

"I'm sorry I didn't tell you about El Ghoula," Sahara blurted before she lost her nerve. "I thought I was doing the right thing."

Sunlight filtered through the stained glass square in the panel above the door, casting pink, blue, and red shapes on the tiled floor.

"I know." Vicky touched Sahara's hand. "I'm still hurt you didn't tell me about the witch, but now I get that it wasn't personal. This morning, your aunt Malak explained how she only found out about her last summer, and she's known your mom's family forever."

"That's true." Sahara snorted. Up until a year ago, she hadn't known Fayrouz existed either.

"*I'm* sorry I overreacted," Vicky continued. "It's just, lately, everyone's been keeping secrets from me. They say it's for my own good, only it's not. It definitely doesn't feel good."

If only Vicky knew how much Sahara wanted to tell her everything. But there was too much at stake.

"That's why I owe you the truth." Vicky hesitated like the time she'd accidentally broken the folding silk hand fan Amitu had purchased for Sahara from the gift shop at the Metropolitan Museum of Art. Just as she opened her mouth to speak, Amitu returned, and she wasn't alone.

"Look who I found in the back office with her father," Sahara's aunt said as if Yara's presence were a coincidence.

Ugh! Sahara squished her lips together to keep from screaming. This was *no* coincidence.

"Yara," Vicky cooed, making Sahara want to gag.

"Did you invite her?" Sahara spat out. Unsure who she had to thank for Yara's encore appearance, she widely aimed her question at her aunt and Vicky.

"Sahara," Amitu snapped at her loss of manners.

Vicky looked down, embarrassed.

"I don't need to be invited, because my father is the head of this museum." Yara's helmet bobbed from side to side as she spoke. "But if you'd rather I go—"

"No, of course not," Amitu interjected. She may have sympathized with Sahara's friendship woes, but she would not tolerate disrespect. She shot Sahara a stern "cut the attitude, *now*" look, then turned to Yara and smiled. "We're *all* so happy you're here."

"So happy," Sahara said through gritted teeth.

"Great. I have so much to show you. I know this museum like the back of my hand," Yara said. She skipped ahead of them.

Amitu followed, motioning sharply for Sahara to get moving.

"Ooh, an insider tour." Vicky clapped. "We always love those, right?"

"Right," Sahara muttered. She did love insider tours, just not ones led by a certain nosy equestrian.

"Finish our talk later?" Vicky asked, bounding off after Amitu and Yara before Sahara even answered.

"Sure," Sahara responded to herself, then trudged behind them. She hadn't realized she was clutching the five piasters in her pocket. *Open up,* she reminded herself, unfurling her fingers.

THE MUSEUM HOUSED thousands of incredible artifacts, including jewelry, textiles, manuscripts, furniture, and weapons. There was so much to see, but thanks to how well the collection was organized, it didn't feel overwhelming. In the right wing, exhibits were ordered chronologically by khalifates— the Islamic empire's dynasties—while in the left wing, they were arranged by categories like medicine and daily life.

Sahara was so fascinated by the science hall she'd completely missed the group leaving for another room. Amitu came looking for her.

"I had a feeling you'd still be here." Her aunt smiled, appearing to have gotten over Sahara's earlier misstep with Yara. *Phew.* "I knew the minute I saw this exhibit yesterday, Susu, that it would be your favorite part."

"How could it not be? Have you seen this?" Sahara pointed to a bronze disc with a ring at the top. "It's an astrolabe."

"I know," Amitu said. "I work here now."

"It can tell the position of the stars."

"I know," Amitu repeated, ushering Sahara into the weapons room, where the other girls were waiting.

Yara stood proudly in front of a glass display. Encased inside was a sword with a long and slightly curved steel blade. It had to be at least three feet in length. "Baba just procured this from a museum in Morocco."

Amitu walked over excitedly. "Yes, it belonged to a great Fatimid khalifa. His name is engraved on the hilt under the emerald. Strangely, it wasn't found here or back in Tunisia, where the khalifa would've lived, but in Baghdad, of all places. Nobody knows how it got there."

Yara leaned in. "Rumor has it, one of the khalifa's sons stole it and took it there," she told them discreetly, like she was gossiping in the school cafeteria.

As Sahara stared at the sparkling emerald, her hamsa quivered against her chest. She had no idea why. Maybe it was responding to being around objects as old as itself. Whatever it was, she was relieved the duct tape was keeping it secured to her chest.

"Everything okay?" Amitu asked. "Too much old stuff?"

Sahara nodded. Little did Amitu know how old the stuff around Sahara's neck was. So much history in such a small pendant. So much heaviness in one hamsa. For along with that history came the weight of duty. *Yeesh!* She might need another roll of tape.

They spent the last thirty minutes in the water and gardens

hall, Vicky still hanging on every one of Yara's boastful descriptions of the exhibits at "her father's museum," which Sahara was pretty sure belonged to the government, *not* Yara's dad. Sahara fingered the smooth beads of her new bracelet, eyeing Yara closely. Fayrouz might have been out to destroy the world, but Yara was out to destroy her friendship with Vicky. With the amulet presently under control and Morsy and his army tirelessly searching for El Ghoula, the second seemed more urgent.

Sahara didn't waste any time when their taxi rolled up in front of the museum while Yara was in the back office with her father. She grabbed Vicky and Amitu and raced inside it before Miss Busybody returned and finagled an invitation to the Pyramids tonight.

Except for Amitu's occasional small talk with the driver, the ride back home was fairly quiet. The girls sat silently in the back, the middle seat separating them like an ocean between two remote islands. Sahara leaned her head against the window, hoping they would be able to find their way back to each other.

23

Fiteer

Back in Queens, if Sahara had a bad day, she'd turn to a few go-to activities to feel better, like programming Omni or fixing something small—a loose toilet paper holder or a closet door off its track. Watching lines of code come together or feeling the tension of screws tightening and wheels sliding into place always cheered her up. Maybe she'd ask Khaltu Layla if there was anything that needed repair.

When they returned from the museum, Sahara's cousins were busy carrying crates of soda into the shop while Kitmeer basked in the shade of its awning.

"Don't stay in the sun too long," Amitu warned the girls as she headed upstairs.

Naima hopped up the shop steps, setting a bowl of water in front of her dog. She took one look at Sahara's sour face and asked, "The museum was that good?"

"It was awesome," Vicky answered. "I've never seen so many cool ancient things."

Awesome! Sahara scoffed in her head. "Yara was there and

showed us around her *father's* museum." She feigned excitement for Vicky's sake, but Naima narrowed her eyes in the "not buying it" sort of way.

"Ah, I see. Yara was there again." Naima twisted around and called inside to her brother. "Fanta, since we're done bringing in the azayiz of soda, why don't you unload them—"

"It's your shift," her brother griped, stomping outside. "I already worked an extra ten minutes when you were late coming back from the Nassers'."

"Vicky can help you," his sister tossed out. "You can tell her all about how you're training for your karate competition."

"Ooh." Vicky brought her hands to her chest in excited anticipation. "I'd love to hear about that."

Fanta's lips curled up. "After you." He gestured for Vicky to enter the shop.

"What did you do that for?" Sahara groaned. "I've gotta talk to Vic before we head to Giza tonight."

"You do. But not looking like that." Naima scrunched her face and pursed her lips. "Come with me."

"I do not 'look like that,'" Sahara railed as Naima pulled her into the maze of Shobra's people and shops.

After five long minutes of Sahara huffing about not knowing where they were going and Naima promising it wouldn't disappoint, the girls came to a stop in front of a small restaurant with a black awning that read AYOUB'S.

"We're here." Naima bounced up and down. "Have you ever had fiteer before?"

"No. But it had better be good."

"Just wait." Naima winked. She pushed open the door, making the bell at the top ring.

Behind the counter stood a large oven that reminded Sahara of the one at Avelino's pizzeria. Only instead of cheese, garlic, and basil, something sweet joined the scent of baked bread.

Two men in matching red aprons were busy at work—one kneading and stretching the dough, the other layering and folding it into a square.

"Itnin fiteer, Ammu Ayoub." Naima ordered two of whatever this fiteer was from the older gentleman and led Sahara to a table in the back.

Except for two men playing chess while they sipped on some very strong-smelling coffee, the restaurant was empty.

"This is the best time to come," Naima pointed out. "At night, you can't get a seat and have to wait hours for your fiteer. They make it fresh."

"It reminds me of this pizzeria back home," Sahara said. "Vicky and I were just there on the last day of school when she didn't feel like going to the park for the end-of-year celebration. Vicky hasn't been in the mood to do a lot of things lately. Well, until she got here and met Yara," Sahara grumbled. "I wish I knew why Vic's been acting so weird. At first, I thought keeping our family's secret from her was the reason, but maybe she'd just rather hang out with someone else."

"Like Mini Magda." Naima snickered.

Sahara hadn't thought of Yara as that before, but it was perfect. She was the same kind of snooty and self-involved as Magda had been. "Exactly," Sahara groaned.

"Have you and Vicky had a chance to talk at all yet?" Naima asked as Ammu Ayoub dropped two platters in front of them. If a croissant suddenly took the shape of pizza, it would look like fiteer.

"A little this morning." Sahara's mouth watered at the buttery scent of the flaky dough.

Naima tore off a slice, signaling for Sahara to do the same. She dug in as Naima sang, "Ready, steady"—bringing the fiteer to her lips—"go!"

The powdered sugar topping enveloped the pastry in a cloud of heavenly sweetness. Sahara's eyes rolled back. "Mmm. Why did I never have this last year?"

"It's more of a second-year thing," Naima teased. "First year, Bimbos. Second year, fiteer."

Sahara giggled.

"Feeling better?" Naima asked.

"Pfft. How could I not be? I'm eating yummy fiteer with one of my most favorite people in the world."

"Good." Naima grinned.

Sahara's voice turned serious again. "I know Vicky and I have to talk some more, but it's just so hard. Part of me wants to tell her everything."

"Even the time travel?" Naima whispered.

Sahara nodded and whispered back, "But then I remember how Husnaya said the fewer people that know about the lamp's real power, the better. And I feel the hamsa shake. This necklace"—Sahara pointed to her chest—"is the only thing standing in the way of Fayrouz unleashing a gang of evil jinn on the world. What good would it do to tell Vicky? It would only make her worry."

"The hamsa isn't the *only* thing standing in Fayrouz's way," Naima told her. "You are, and I'm right behind you. Let Vicky in. It doesn't have to be all or nothing. You don't have to tell her *everything*, but you can let her be there for you. She wants to be."

"How do you know that?" Sahara asked, wiping the powdered sugar off Naima's nose.

"Because she told me when you were having tea with Mama and your amitu last night. Vicky might like Yara, but she *loves* you."

Sahara squeezed Naima's hand. They spent the next few minutes silently devouring their fiteer.

"We'd better go before Fanta puts Vicky to sleep with his karate stories." Sahara laughed.

"Something tells me she's not bored." Naima smirked. "And if I'm going to have a sister-in-law, Vicky would make a fine one."

"Gross." Sahara made a heaving sound as she followed Naima toward the door. *Ring.* They stepped back into the street, cooler from the dwindled sunlight, the bell echoing behind them.

ON THEIR WAY back to the shop, Sahara spotted the central phone office across the street. She peeked at her watch, calculating the time in New York. Nine thirty. Her dad would be at work already. Luckily, his office number was one of the handful of phone numbers she'd memorized by heart.

"Would it be okay if we called—" She hesitated, not finding her cousin beside her.

"Over here," Naima yelled from outside the office. "Yalla. Let's go call your father."

"You are the bestest," Sahara told her as she crossed over.

"Is that the same as *best*?"

"Better than best." Sahara smiled and headed inside.

The central office was way more crowded than when she'd gone last summer to speak to Amitu. But that had also been earlier in the day.

After ten minutes of waiting in line, the phone rang at cubicle #8.

"Kareem Rashad speaking," her father answered formally.

"Surprise!" Sahara was so glad she'd caught him at his desk.

"Susu," her father cried, making her chin quiver. "Is everything all right?"

"Yeah, all good. Do you have a few minutes to talk?" she asked.

"For you, of course. How's everything going?"

"Great." Some things were going well, but definitely not everything. "I just called to see how New York is without me."

"Not the same. How's Cairo without me?"

"Not the same." She followed suit. It was the truth.

"Anything exciting happen since you arrived?" he asked.

Sahara wasn't sure if he'd spoken to her aunt and was testing her, so she deflected. "You should see how cool the museum that Amitu is interning at is."

"I *have* seen it, but it's probably changed a lot since then."

Sahara proceeded to tell him all about the astrolabe in the science hall.

"I can't wait to check it out together," he told her. "How's Vicky doing? Is she having fun?"

"Loads," Sahara responded. *Just not with me.* But that was about to change.

"I'm glad. She's had a hard year."

Sahara had no idea what her father was talking about. "What do you mean?"

"I just mean there have been a lot of changes. For both of you. The first year in junior high school isn't easy for anyone."

"I guess not," Sahara said, though she'd had a pretty good year.

"Lots of changes," her dad repeated as the clerk knocked on the glass, startling her. He held up one finger.

"I should go, Dad. My time's almost up."

"Okay. Say hello to Amitu and buseeli nafsik." *Kiss yourself for me* was one of those Arabic expressions that sounded odd in English. It was something her father and Amitu said to people far away or that they hadn't seen in a while and *couldn't* kiss.

"Kiss yourself for *me*," she told him before the line went dead.

As they left the office, Sahara thought about what her father had said about Vicky. She had this weird feeling. Like she'd missed something. Something she was supposed to know. Whatever it was, she was more determined than ever to set things right with her friend.

By the time they returned to the shop, Vicky was already gone. "See, she's not even here anymore," Sahara told Naima. Naima was totally wrong about Vicky and Fanta. Sahara rushed upstairs, but the Saeeds' apartment was empty.

Too winded to run back downstairs, she yelled down to her cousins from the balcony. "Vicky's not here. Are you sure she came up?"

"I watched her go into the building," Fanta shouted back, a goofy smirk on his face.

Sahara didn't want to think about him watching Vicky do anything, when out of the corner of her eye, she spotted her pyramid pad. It was open, lying facedown on the floor. *How?* She'd left it on her mattress this morning. Sahara picked it up and turned it over, immediately recognizing her best friend's curvy letters.

Sahara,

Sorry for using your cool new pad. It was the only paper I could find, and I had to write this down before I got too chicken. The reason I got so mad when I found out about the witch that hurt Yara's grandmother is cuz my family's been keeping a secret too. And I should've told you it before we left NY. So here goes nothing. My mom and dad are getting a divorce. Dad moved out in April, but Mom says things haven't been okay between them for a long time. That they "grew apart" cuz Dad kept things from her. I don't want that to ever happen to us, so I'm telling you now. I hope

Vicky's handwriting came to an abrupt stop. Underneath it were straight, pointy letters that had to belong to someone else:

MEET ME ON THE OLD SEER'S ROOFTOP AT DAWN ON THE LAST DAY OF THE MONTH. TO ENSURE YOUR COOPERATION, I'M KEEPING WHAT YOU WANT UNTIL I GET WHAT I WANT.

Sahara's mind spun into a dizzying black hole. But not because of the lamp. Because her world had flipped upside down.

Fayrouz had Vicky.

Seeing in the Sand

965 CE

The next few weeks at the Nasra palace were tense with the sudden disappearance of the khalifa's prized sword—half the army was out looking for its thief—and the continuous threats from rival empires to the east and west. Not to mention Marwan's incessant prodding to march into Egypt to assert the khalifate's power. But the khalifa held firm to his promise to Jidda. "If I go back on my vow to my own mother, I might as well never utter a truthful word again." Husnaya had beamed when she'd heard her father say this. Marwan may have been devoid of principles, but her father was not.

Despite Hassan's storm-out the day of the flying carpet lesson, both twins continued to report to their daily sorcery training. After her recent discovery outside the garden, Husnaya rose even earlier to spend an hour with her horse in the woods before heading to the dungeon. She wasn't sure why she'd kept Almaz a secret from Hassan and Aziza, especially since they were accomplices in her training scheme. Perhaps it was because being in her horse's presence filled her with a calm she didn't want to share. One of these days, she might actually muster the courage to ride Almaz.

"Now that we're all here"—Aziza shot Husnaya a cross look for being a few minutes late—"we can finally start our divination lesson."

"Sorry," Husnaya mouthed, taking a seat on a wooden crate next to her brother.

"Mama says that after she married Baba, Marwan divined she would deliver twins on a day when the palace saw the strongest desert winds." As the words departed Hassan's lips, a realization hit. "It wasn't Marwan." He aimed his finger at Aziza. "*You* predicted our birth."

Aziza smiled. "The hawa did. And now I will show you how."

Husnaya leaned forward, excited by today's lesson. How often had she heard Mama and Baba say things like, *If we only knew sooner, we would have done this instead*? And now she would know sooner so she could do the *instead* first. Too bad she couldn't share her skill with her parents.

"No material is better suited as a divination vessel than those of Allah's natural world." Aziza grabbed a handful of sand from the clay bowl at her feet. "As with all your training, your connection with the wind is paramount. Through it, you will coax the inherent wisdom in nature to predict a future outcome. But there is one important rule all seers must follow." Aziza's eyes flickered from Husnaya to Hassan, lingering on him. "You must never interfere with the evolution of that outcome. For it will create an imbalance. One that nature will seek to correct in catastrophic ways. Do you understand?"

Husnaya nodded her agreement, and out of the corner of her eye could see Hassan doing the same. Even he didn't dare contest the maid's stern warning.

"Now that we've gotten the serious part out of the way, it's time for some fun." A grin spread across Aziza's face right as she threw the sand up. Only it didn't fall to the ground. The dispersed tiny grains hovered in the air, and when Aziza lifted her palm, they combined into a series of random dots. She shut her eyes and moved them with flourishes of her hand. Soon, the dots formed a picture of a person with a shawl draped around her hair and a hamsa pendant dangling from her neck.

"It's a woman," Hassan blurted.

"Or a girl," Husnaya suggested.

Aziza opened her eyes. "The sand hasn't disclosed her age, but my winds have detected that she has not been born yet. Though eventually, she will play an important role in both of your lives."

"What will her name be?"

"When will we meet her?"

"Will she be a member of the court?

"Will this important role be good or bad?"

Endless queries flew out of the twins' mouths until Aziza finally shouted, "Khalas. Enough chatter. Divination through nature has always been clear but never as specific as man would like." Aziza waved, dispersing the sand. "Open your hands," she said, directing half of it to each of their palms.

Husnaya ran her fingers over the gritty grains. She couldn't remember the last time she'd felt the desert in her hands.

"Your turn." Aziza nodded toward the children. "You need not say your question aloud for the wind to hear it. Thinking it is enough."

Husnaya was too scared to ask about her future, so she wondered about Hassan's. Her first of many tries throwing the sand into the air, it instantly dropped to the floor. Each time, Aziza swept it up with her hawa, encouraging Husnaya to try again. It wasn't until the eleventh attempt that the grains hovered before her eyes. Husnaya smiled at the mess of floating sand. It was progress, at least.

"Don't forget your breath," Aziza reminded.

As Husnaya inhaled deeply, she felt an invisible tug on her hand. One that she allowed to direct her fingers and arrange the dots into an image. The two figures that appeared before her made her heart drop. She turned toward her brother, grateful to find his eyes closed. But Aziza had seen her vision. That look of fear Husnaya had spotted in Aziza's eyes the day of Hassan's first wind returned. Without hesitation, Aziza dispersed the sand and let it fall to the ground. If only she could permanently erase it from Husnaya's mind too.

Meanwhile, Hassan's dots formed the image of an oil lamp, like the ones evil jinn were imprisoned in.

"What did you ask it?" Husnaya inquired as her brother opened his eyes.

Hassan's stare blazed at the lamp. "What would make me powerful?" he answered proudly, noticing the pile of sand at her feet. "What happened?"

Husnaya's eyes flashed from Aziza to her brother. "Nothing. I suppose I need more practice."

"If you want, I can ask your question since it worked for me," he touted.

Husnaya's pride yearned to yell that hers had worked too. But before she could say anything, Aziza sputtered, "I'm . . . I'm afraid lessons will have to end early today. I just remembered I promised your mama I would hem her qamees before tonight's dinner." She whisked the children off, making Hassan's sand fall to the ground too.

"My lamp!" Hassan cried as Aziza rushed them up the stairs.

THROUGHOUT SITT JAMILA'S monologue on the merits of architectural patronage, Husnaya couldn't think about anything but what she'd seen in the future for her brother. A taller and brawnier version of Hassan was holding a baby. Tears spilled from his eyes as he looked down at the still infant. Husnaya had felt Hassan's endless grief and rage in her winds as the sands showed her this devastating vision. The darkness in his eyes had scared her. And it had scared Aziza too. She did not mince words when she came to ready Husnaya for bed.

"What you saw this morning in the sand, you must never share it with your brother."

"But I could warn him. And maybe then it wouldn't happen—"

"No," Aziza shouted. She drew in a deep breath. "I know you want to spare him pain." Aziza touched her shoulder, her voice softening. "But you must not interfere. Nothing good will come of it. As a seer, your job is to channel the winds of fate, not direct them, even when they blow toward the fire. For there is purpose in everything, whether we understand it or not. Never share it with Hassan," Aziza repeated.

"Never." Husnaya gave her word—one she would keep for all her days.

25

Look to the Moon

The dizziness slowly subsided, but not enough for Sahara to stand. Her enemy's threat played on a vicious loop in her head, every word plunging her deeper into the arctic waters of despair. Sahara's father had been worried about her safety when he should have been worried about everyone else's. Fayrouz wouldn't hurt her as long as she needed the lamp, but she wouldn't think twice about hurting the people closest to Sahara if it meant getting her wicked hands on it.

Sahara was still crouched on the balcony when Naima showed up with Kitmeer. "Did you find . . ." Her cousin stopped, spotting her on the ground. "Why are you on the 'ard? What happened?" she cried as Kitmeer frantically sniffed the terrace.

Sahara held out the pyramid pad in her trembling hand. Naima's eyes darted across the page, gasping when she reached the end. "Fayrouz!"

Kitmeer's tail stood at attention, his ears pinned back to his head, realizing, too, that El Ghoula had been here.

"But how did she get upstairs?" Naima asked.

The same way she got to Umm Zalabya's rooftop, Sahara wanted to say, but it was too hard to speak. She circled her finger in the air instead.

"Her cursed twister magic," Naima seethed, then looked to the mosque, whispering some words of prayer. After, she knelt beside Sahara and gently rubbed her arm.

The lump lodged in Sahara's throat released itself at her cousin's touch. And along with it came a deluge of tears. "What-am-I-going-to-do?" Sahara sobbed, struggling to get the words out. "My best friend, who flew miles and miles away from home to be with me, is missing. This is all my fault."

Naima's fingers caressed the back of Sahara's palm. "It's awful, but it's *not* your fault. Fayrouz attacked Umm Zalabya and kidnapped Vicky because she's evil. You can't blame your-self for her wickedness."

"But I should've been a better friend. Maybe then Vicky would've told me what was going on. And we would be in a better place—one El Ghoula couldn't dive in and swoop her up from." Sahara thwacked the ground with her foot.

"You know what you need?" Naima asked.

"What?"

"To get off the 'ard." Naima stood, then slowly helped Sahara up.

"Thanks." Sahara sniffled. "Now I've just gotta figure out how to tell Amitu and Dad . . ." She was so used to going to them with her problems, but this wasn't the kind they could fix. "There's nothing they can do," she said, dropping her head.

Naima lifted Sahara's chin. "I know someone who can."

"The last time you said that, we ended up on Umm Zalabya's rooftop."

"And it worked, didn't it? Without her yasmeen, El Ghoula's sharbat curse would've killed our parents and Sittu."

Her cousin did have a point. The eccentric seer might be exactly who they needed right now. "Fine," Sahara grumbled. "We can go and see . . ." She trailed off, following Naima's glimmering eyes to the sliver of the moon visible in the purple-and-orange evening sky.

"Remember what Husnaya told us," Naima said, her gaze fixed on the qamar.

"Look to the moon, and we will come," Sahara murmured. She didn't know *how* the trio would come. The only thing she knew for sure was that she needed their help to get her friend back.

Sahara crossed her fingers behind her back—*Please work. Please work*—as she concentrated on the crescent moon and pictured the enchanted women.

"Help," she sighed into the air.

At first, nothing happened, followed by more nothing for the next ten seconds. *Ugh.* She'd been foolish to put her faith in a silly moon signal. "This is ridiculous. We don't have time to wait for—"

"Isboori," Naima cut in, urging her to be patient. "They'll be here."

And then Sahara's ears picked up the sound of tinkling bells.

"Ya Allah!" Naima pointed her finger at a tiny glowing ball in the sky.

"It's working!" Excitement flooded Sahara like an unexpected summer storm.

The light whizzed closer and closer, stopping just short of their faces, where they could clearly see what their hearts had understood a moment ago. It wasn't a ball of light. It was a *fairy*.

"Peri! I knew you'd come," Naima shouted, rocking back and forth on her heels. She mouthed a stealthy "I told you so" to Sahara as Kitmeer barked at the airborne jinniya. Naima patted his head and assured him, "It's okay. She's a friend."

Sahara had never been happier to be wrong. She could've kissed the fairy. Instead, she waved eagerly. "Thank you for coming so fast," she said to Peri, who didn't look a day older than in 985.

"Missed me?" The fairy giggled.

"More than you know," Naima answered as a knock came from the apartment's front door. The girls shot each other nervous glances.

"Right on time," Peri squealed, zipping past them into the apartment.

"Wait," Sahara called out, racing after her. How would they explain the presence of the fairy to whoever was at the door?

But Peri didn't hesitate. She zipped around and around the doorknob, showering it with tiny sparks. Within seconds, the door flew open.

Sahara braced herself for the imminent shocked reaction of whoever was standing on the other side. She squeezed her eyes shut, not bearing to look.

"Ahlan, my dears."

Julnar. Sahara's eyes flew open.

"You're here too," Naima yelled as the mermaid queen gleamed a picture-perfect smile at them from the doorway. She wore a navy hooded cloak over her gown.

Sahara picked her jaw up from the floor. "I can't believe they're here," she muttered to her cousin.

"I can." Naima beamed.

"It certainly has been a while," Julnar said, lowering her hood and coasting into the apartment.

"But . . . but we just saw you yesterday," Naima said, confused.

"No, that was tenth-century us." Peri traced her figure with her hand. "This is *twentieth*-century us."

Something about seeing the jinniyas in the present in the middle of her cousin's apartment jogged Sahara's memory. She examined the mermaid queen, from her deep blue eyes and waist-length hair to the hem of her long, billowy gown. *Woo-woo Rapunzel!* "My elementary school's end-of-the-year fair—that's where I know you from. You were the fortune teller."

"Bingo! On the money! Bull's-eye! Hit the nail on the head . . ." Peri went on and on, blasting out every iteration of *You are right* she could think of. She'd picked up a lot over the last millennium.

"I didn't want to say anything until you figured it out," Julnar said softly to Sahara.

"But why? Why did you pretend to be a palm reader?"

"Because you needed reminding that what you know in your heart is as important as, if not more than, what you know in your head."

"Yeah, I'm still working on that one."

"We are all works in progress, my dear." Julnar rubbed Sahara's back.

"You've come a long way, baby," Peri squeaked above them.

Everyone laughed but Sahara.

"Don't get upset. We were just kidding," Naima said.

Sahara shook her head. "It's not that." She stared at her cousin, whose eyes now welled with the same realization that wrenched in Sahara's stomach. Husnaya *wasn't* coming.

Julnar reached for the girls' hands. "She's been gone for a long time for us but not for you. It's all right to miss her."

Even though technically Naima and Sahara had last seen Husnaya in the tenth century, it had only felt like yesterday to them. Shimmering, tiny tears fell from Peri's face.

Sahara looked down at her sneakers. She'd already cried

once today. But then a thought crawled into her head, nearly sending the tears spilling out. What if Julnar and Peri *couldn't* help her on their own?

"Fayrouz has taken my best friend." Sahara's voice trembled. She hurried to the balcony for the pad, then pointed to El Ghoula's words. "We..." The words caught in her throat. "We called you to help us get her back. Can you, if you're not... you're not still a trio?"

"Who said we were *not* still a trio?" Peri crossed her arms. She spun toward Julnar. "Modern-day logic is overrated," she huffed, then shot into the sky.

"Where are you going?" Naima yelled.

Peri turned around and winked. "To Umm Zalabya's, of course."

26

The 20th-Century Trio

Sahara scanned the street before they headed out of the building. "Fanta's outside the shop talking to one of Morsy's men," she whispered to Naima. *Crap.* With everything going on, Sahara had totally forgotten about the guards stationed here and in front of Umm Zalabya's building. Julnar's cloak might be discreet enough not to attract too much undue attention from pedestrians. But the same couldn't be said for the officer patrolling the shop. He was trained to catch anything or *anyone* out of the ordinary. Though he had missed Fayrouz descending on Vicky.

"*Psst. Psst.*" Sahara attempted to get Fanta's attention without the man noticing.

Her cousin turned his head, making quick eye contact with Sahara, before returning to his conversation with the officer.

"Did he hear you?" Naima asked.

"I think so, but he's talking to the guard again . . . Wait, he just stopped. He's coming."

As Fanta hurried over, Sahara ducked back into the building's entryway.

"Il li has—" Fanta started to ask what happened when he stepped inside. "Who's this?" he asked, scrutinizing the cloaked woman. His eyes locked with her ocean-blue ones. They nearly popped out of his head a second later. "Julnar!" Fanta staggered, making Sahara worry he might pass out. Fortunately, he regained his balance. He stared at the mermaid queen, his mouth open, but no words coming out.

"It's nice to see you too, Ahmed." Julnar smiled.

Fanta's eyes glossed over. "I must be dreaming." He pinched himself as his mother's voice rang from outside.

"Ahmed!"

Crap. Khaltu Layla was downstairs. Sahara froze.

"Mama's in the shop. You have to get out of here *now*," Fanta warned.

"That's what we're trying to do," his sister said under her breath.

"Ahmed!" his mother called even louder.

Fanta stuck his head outside. "I'll be right there, Mama," he yelled, then spun toward the girls. "*Phew.* She's still inside. Make a run for it"—he pointed a firm finger away from the shop—"*that* way. I'll try and keep the officer busy."

"We're headed to Umm Zalabya's," Sahara whispered. "Meet us there."

He nodded, walking back casually—like he hadn't just seen a thousand-year-old mermaid in the middle of Shobra.

As he chatted up the guard, Sahara and Naima grabbed Julnar's hands and bolted in the opposite direction.

The alternate route to Umm Zalabya's took precisely four minutes more than usual. Four minutes more of trying to play it cool with an eternal jinniya in tow. The streets were busy with shoppers picking up last-minute dinner items like lamb and chicken kebabs or pistachios to top their sweet baklawas with.

Sahara breathed out a sigh of relief as they rounded the corner to the seer's building. Until she spotted Morsy in front of it, that is. She couldn't fault him and his men for their commitment, but it was highly inconvenient when you were trying to sneak a mermaid queen onto an enchanted seer's rooftop.

Sahara shoved Naima and Julnar back. "What do we do now?" she asked as Fanta pulled up beside them, sucking in air. He must've sprinted to catch up.

"Why aren't you inside already?" he huffed.

Naima stood at attention, imitating the officer. "Morsy," she groaned.

"Right." Fanta slid his bandana, which must've ridden up while he was running, back down. "Leave it to me," he said, then sauntered over to his father's friend. He whispered something in Morsy's ear, which sent the man hurrying past the girls, not even flinching at the sight of Julnar.

"How'd you do that?" Sahara asked when they reached the door.

Fanta smiled. "I told him Mama had some leftover fatteh. Morsy never says no to fatteh, especially not Mama's."

"Genius!" Sahara clapped him on the back and dashed toward Umm Zalabya's.

PERI HOVERED OVER the yasmeen garden when Sahara swung the rooftop door open. The flowers didn't smell as fragrant tonight. Perhaps their vitality was connected to Umm Zalabya's. And with her powers on hiatus, so was their sweet floral perfume.

"I always knew you were a great seer." Naima bounced on her toes with such excitement Sahara was surprised she didn't take off. "But I had no idea you were friends with legends like Julnar and Peri."

Umm Zalabya's rocked in her chair, smirking. She didn't appear the least bit surprised by the jinn's arrival as Almaz purred and rubbed her head against Julnar's dress.

"Samya is a legend in her own right," the mermaid queen stated. "Not only is she a master at divination but a talented sorceress descended from the greatest sorceress to ever live."

Samya. That was the seer's first name. Sahara's eyes darted to Naima, who must've been thinking the same thing, because she was staring at Umm Zalabya and mouthing her name. Fanta, on the other hand, was not.

"Who's Samya?" he blurted.

The seer pointed to herself.

The greatest sorceress to ever live, Sahara repeated in her head. That couldn't possibly mean . . .

"Descended from the great Husnaya," Peri chirped.

Of course! The cryptic words, the dots in the dirt, the cat named Almaz—the evidence had been there all along. How could Sahara not have seen it? "So last year, all that 'desert rose we've been waiting ages for' stuff was true?" she asked.

"I may not be as old as my counterparts, but the ancient duty to help the Salem women protect the magical treasures lives deep in my bones," Umm Zalabya replied. "As does Sitt Husnaya's sorcery."

"Even this?" Fanta threw his palm out as they'd seen Husnaya do.

Umm Zalabya glanced at her hand, and her eyes darkened. "Not at the moment, I'm afraid." She rocked back and stared at the moon. "Now, which one of you summoned us tonight?"

"I did." Sahara stepped forward and knelt in front of the sorceress. "Because Fayrouz has . . ." She hesitated, her mouth going dry. She swallowed and started again. "Fayrouz has taken Vicky."

Umm Zalabya pressed her lips together tightly. "Yes, I know. Peri informed me of the unfortunate news when she arrived."

"Fayrouz has Vicky?!" Fanta's face fell. They'd been so busy trying to slink past everyone they hadn't gotten to fill him in.

"Han la'eeha, Ahmed," Naima insisted. "That's why we're here."

Fanta ran over to Sahara, who looked up at him and cried, "I . . . I need to get her back."

"Naima's right. We *will* find her," he reassured Sahara.

Sahara nodded, then turned back to Umm Zalabya. "Please help us," she pleaded. "I can't let El Ghoula hurt her."

"You did the right thing calling on us, my dear," Julnar said. "You don't have to brave this trouble by yourself."

"It's just that Fayrouz took Vicky because of *me*. So she could force *me* to give her the lamp. *I'm* the reason for this trouble. I should never have left Vicky alone knowing El Ghoula was still out there." An idea sprang into Sahara's head. Her gaze flitted to each face in the trio. "I know you said to stay away from the lamp, but what if I unlocked it quickly, went back in time, and stopped Vicky from going on the terrace?"

"Not only is it dangerous to open the lamp while Fayrouz is at large, but it wouldn't work, my dear." Julnar bent down beside Sahara. "The lamp's magic has certain limitations."

"What kind of limitations?" Sahara asked.

"When we joined with Morgana to create the amulet, not only did we create a key to lock it but a means to control its sorcery," Julnar explained. "Upon the hamsa's first union with the lamp came limits to govern its extensive power: The first, you cannot travel to a time between your birth and your death. The second, under no circumstances should you interfere with the beginning and ending of life. If you do, the consequences are most grave."

Sahara's heart sank like a heavy rock. Hard and fast. She

couldn't travel back to the past to save her friend. And she hadn't realized, until Julnar just cautioned against it, that a tiny seed had grown inside her when she'd learned what the lamp actually did. It had been filled with hopeful what-ifs. *What if I could keep my mom from dying? What if she was still alive?* But now that seed was crushed. She jammed the sorry thing back down, deep down, where it would never see the light of day.

"All is not lost, my dear." Julnar gently thumbed the chain around Sahara's neck. "The union of the four elements' energies created the Amulet of the Four—one element lifting up another." She slowly turned her head, peering at each person—or jinniya—on the rooftop. "Together, we will find your friend."

"Teamwork makes the dream work!" Peri zipped across the garden.

The Amulet of the Four. Sahara had never heard her hamsa called that, but she liked the sound of it.

"Wouldn't it be easier if we just looked in the spyglass to see where El Ghoula's taken Vicky?" Fanta asked.

Umm Zalabya shook her head. "I'm afraid that won't work either. Fayrouz may be wicked, but she's also smart. Smart enough to cover her tracks, especially after you stopped her at el Borg last year. I'm certain she's used a barrier spell to hide her location. And had my powers returned, I could counteract it." Her face hardened. "But not in this state."

Sahara wished more than anything for Umm Zalabya to

get her powers back. Mainly so she could help rescue Vicky. But also to erase the rigid lines of sorrow that had joined the soft wrinkles on the sorceress's forehead.

"And you?" Sahara looked to Peri and Julnar. "Can't you use any of your magic to find her?"

"Unfortunately, as noble jinn, we cannot use our magic to interfere with divine or human will," Julnar answered. "If we did, the cost would be severe. Our restraint is what separates us from jinn like Jauhara, who show no regard for consequences."

Sahara didn't like what she was hearing. "But what about last year?" she shot out. "You interfered then. You pretended to be a palm reader at the fair."

"Yes, but I was careful not to use my magic to alter your decisions," Julnar asserted. "I merely reminded you of a truth you'd forgotten."

"So it's God's will that my friend has been abducted by Fayrouz and hidden who knows where. Why?"

Umm Zalabya stood up with the help of the wooden cane by her side. She hobbled over to Sahara. "Many humans have spent years trying to make sense of Allah's will. All the time, I'm asked if I can change what I have foretold. The answer is always the same—I can, but I *won't*." She leaned in closer and stared straight at Sahara. Sahara had never noticed the hints of caramel in Umm Zalabya's eyes. "I know not what will come out of this, only *how* you will come out of it. How all of you will." She stepped back and shifted her gaze toward Naima and Fanta. "And that's closer to the truth of who you are."

Julnar wrapped her arm around Umm Zalabya and lamented, "I'm so sorry we weren't here sooner, Samya." Peri flew over. Sahara watched silently as the trio affectionately put their heads together. Seeing their bond made her miss Vicky even more.

"Now what?" Fanta asked.

"Now we get your friend back." Umm Zalabya pointed her cane at him. "I may not have my powers, but I can teach you the magic of the hawa so you can save your friend and fend off El Ghoula's dark sorcery in the process. Will you let me show you the ways of the wind?"

Naima's eyes glimmered yes.

Fanta shrugged. "If it helps us find Vicky." He turned to Sahara. "Morsy and his men will keep looking for her, but maybe we should."

"We should do anything to get Vicky back," Sahara agreed. Even learning Umm Zalabya's magic, which didn't seem as strange now, given its long and legitimate history. "I'm in," she declared.

"Me too," a quivering voice came from the doorway, where Yara stood.

"How long have you been over there?" Umm Zalabya asked her granddaughter.

"Long enough to know I should've let you train me. If I had, Vicky might still be here." Yara rushed toward her grand-mother, sneaking a glance at Peri and Julnar. "Can you forgive me, Nenna?"

Nenna. Sahara remembered Amitu telling her it was another way to address a grandmother in Egypt. She'd called her father's mother that.

Umm Zalabya kissed her head. "I already have."

Yara's gaze shifted to Sahara. "I know you don't like me very much, but I care about Vicky. Please let me help."

Sahara felt sucker-punched. Clearly, Vicky mattered way more to Yara than one-upping Sahara. "If it means finding Vicky, I'll take all the help I can get."

"Then it's settled." Peri clapped her tiny hands.

Fanta raised his. "Not so fast." He faced Umm Zalabya. "Does that mean you'll teach us how to shoot wind out of our hands?"

The sorceress chuckled. "There is much I can teach you, but I'm afraid that particular magic isn't something you learn but inherit."

"Do I have that magic?" Yara asked.

"We will have to wait and see," Umm Zalabya answered.

As the sunset adhan echoed across the rooftop, Julnar looked up at Peri. "Maghrib, already. We should be on our way."

"You're leaving?" Naima's voice slightly cracked.

"Only for now." Julnar faced the moon. "We'll stay close. If you need us, you know what to do. And we'll be here straightaway."

Peri pouted. "I'm enjoying the city life. Do we have to leave so soon?"

"We must before either of us is mistaken for an evil jinniya and trapped in a lamp for the rest of eternity."

"That doesn't happen anymore," Peri scoffed.

"I wouldn't be so sure." Julnar glanced cunningly at the fairy.

Peri's shoulders slumped. "Fine," she huffed.

"Where will you go?" Yara asked.

"My dear Peri will find a cozy tree to call home for now, and I'll return to the Nile." Julnar's eyes searched the garden. "This will do." She glided over to a clay water pitcher. "May I?" she asked Umm Zalabya. The sorceress nodded. Julnar placed one finger in the pitcher, and slowly, her body grew iridescent.

"She's disappearing!" Fanta yelled.

"I think she's returning to the river," Sahara said, unable to take her eyes off the mermaid.

"Our desert rose is right," Umm Zalabya told the children. "All water is connected. In seconds, she will be home."

When Julnar had fully faded, Peri swooped down toward the sorceress and bowed her head.

"See you next time, good friend." Umm Zalabya bowed back.

"Insha Allah." The fairy faced the children and showed off some more of her twentieth-century swanky jargon. "See you later, alligators." She winked, flapped her wings, then catapulted into the air. Soon she was a glimmering dot in the distance.

Sahara thought she'd seen it all last year—so many unreal

things she couldn't explain. But it had been just the beginning. She pressed the amulet to her chest and stared into the darkening sky, sending her best friend a message. One that she hoped one of those unreal things she couldn't explain would transport to Vicky.

I will find you.

PART THREE

The Hawa

27

Lesson One

Sahara had hated lying to Amitu last night. But she needed a good reason for bailing on the Pyramids, and she couldn't tell her aunt about Vicky yet. Not with Fayrouz still at large. If Amitu found out Vicky had been kidnapped, she'd flip. She'd feel responsible because Vicky was in her care and would insist on going out to look for her. That would only put her in danger. El Ghoula had taken Vicky to force Sahara's hand. To get her to give up the lamp and the amulet. Until Sahara figured out how to stop her, she couldn't let her hurt anyone else for leverage. So she came up with an excuse for delaying their visit to Giza that Amitu would buy.

"Vicky's not feeling so great." Sahara groaned and held her stomach. She contorted her face into a grimace that could only mean one thing.

Amitu's eyebrows shot up in alarm. "Don't tell me. Diarrhea!" Her voice shook with terror. She had reminded the girls at least once a day only to drink bottled water here so they *wouldn't* get diarrhea.

"It's bad." Sahara pressed her lips together. "But Vicky's super embarrassed, so you'd better let me handle it," she said, then sighed. "I hope she didn't drink the tap water, *especially* after all your helpful reminders." In retrospect, Sahara may have laid it on too thick. But luckily, Amitu was so busy digging through her suitcase for antidiarrheal medication she'd bought her lie. It wasn't the first and it wouldn't be the last lie Sahara and her cousins told this week.

Before training at Umm Zalabya's could begin today, the children had to ensure the adults didn't grow suspicious. They needed someone on the inside. Someone good at coming up with alibis. And after how well she'd done when they'd traveled to the past, that someone was Noora. But there was no way she would cover for them again unless she understood the gravity of the situation. So while Khaltu Layla was in town meeting with some local merchants and Amitu was at the museum, Sahara and her cousins headed down to the shop to see Noora.

"Any word from your father's men on El Ghoula?" Noora asked Fanta and Naima as they entered.

"They're still looking for her, but they don't know that . . ." Fanta hesitated, biting his lip.

"They don't know what?" Noora raised a skeptical brow.

Sahara didn't want to waste time when they could be learning ways to help Vicky. It was better just to rip the Band-Aid off. "That Fayrouz kidnapped Vicky," she blurted.

Noora gasped, leaning against the counter for support. "Who knows, then?"

"Just Umm Zalabya, and now, you." Naima edged closer and whispered, "We have to keep it that way."

"No, no, no." Noora shook her head fervently at the discretion Naima was implying. "No way."

Well, that hadn't gone well. It was time to beg. "Please," Sahara said. "I know we've asked you for a lot, and now we're asking for even more, but we can't tell anyone about Vicky yet. Morsy can keep looking for Fayrouz, but if we tell Amitu and Khaltu about Vicky, they'll freak out, and everyone will know. We can't risk that."

Noora didn't answer. She just continued to shake her head.

"You know better than anyone how dangerous El Ghoula is," Sahara added. "Last year, she put our family and half of Shobra to sleep with her awful sharbat so nobody would come after her when she tried to unlock the lamp. Who knows what she'll do now? We're only asking for a little bit more time. Fayrouz is supposed to return for the lamp and the amulet after four days. Give us three to get Vicky back. If we can't, *I'll* be the first to tell everyone. I promise."

Noora crossed her arms, but Sahara could tell by how her face had softened that they might have her. "If I'm going to lie to my husband and his family, I need to know everything."

Quickly, Sahara and her cousins took turns filling her

in, choosing to leave out the lamp's time-travel power and the magical trio. They stuck to Vicky's disappearance, El Ghoula's menacing note, Umm Zalabya's training, and Yara's offer to help.

"So, now that we've told you *everything*—" Naima winked at Sahara and Fanta. She was the worst liar.

Fanta half rolled his eyes, then quickly interjected, "Will you help us?" diverting Noora's attention from his sister and her pitiful attempt at playing it cool.

Noora looked away and murmured a bunch of words to herself. Sahara thought she heard her say, "At least Umm Zalabya's helping them." After a few more seconds of self-talk, Noora zeroed in on the children. "Talat tiyam." She huffed, agreeing to give them three more days to find Vicky. "And only because if it weren't for your stubborn resourcefulness, I might still be Magda."

"That would be *très* terrible, darling." Naima giggled.

Despite what they were asking of her, Noora laughed too. But it was a blink-and-you-miss-it kind of laugh. Within seconds, worry consumed her face again.

Sahara jerked her head toward the steps and mouthed, "Let's go," to her cousins before Khalu's wife changed her mind.

"*Don't* make me regret this," Noora warned as they raced out of the shop.

"You need to rest, Nenna," Yara insisted as Sahara and her cousins arrived on the roof. "You've been on your feet all morning."

"She's right, you know," Naima said, hugging Umm Zalabya.

"Enough rest." The sorceress huffed. "Over the last few days, I've had enough raha to last a lifetime." She touched Yara's hand softly. "I appreciate your concern, habibti, but I'm fine. No more worrying." She clanked her cane against the ground and gave a mischievous smile. "Now begins the fun. Lesson One: Tuning Into El Hawa."

Tuning into the wind—ha! Sahara winced at the sarcastic bite of her own doubt. Training was off to a stellar start. *This is for Vicky. This is for Vicky,* she repeated internally, pushing the distrust away and reminding herself that what Umm Zalabya was about to teach them had been passed down from the great Sitt Husnaya.

"All sorcery at its heart is a partnership. A dance between sorcerer and nature," Umm Zalabya professed. "And the key to this relationship is respect. To harness the power of the hawa, you must relinquish the urge to fill the silence with superfluous words. Only then will you be able to hear the wind's message. But we must begin with the basics. First, we tune into the air that keeps us alive—our breath." Umm Zalabya closed her eyes and took a slow, deep breath in. Then out. Then in again.

Were they supposed to be doing something while the

sorceress was practicing breathing? Sahara's gaze flitted nervously between her cousins.

Naima was completely entranced, while Fanta shrugged in confusion.

"Nenna," Yara said hesitantly, not wanting to disturb her grandmother.

But when Umm Zalabya's eyes finally opened, it was hard for any of them to look away. The clarity and steadiness in her gaze reminded Sahara of Sittu's in her pre-hajj photo. It was like Sahara was seeing Umm Zalabya for the first time. And she wasn't Zalabya's mom, or Yara's grandmother, or even a descendant of the great Husnaya. She was just Samya. But somehow that was more than all those things put together.

She smiled at the children. "Your turn now."

Sahara watched as, one by one, her cousins and Yara closed their eyes. She turned to Umm Zalabya, who was staring intently at her. Sahara had won a lot of staring contests in her life, but she had a feeling this wouldn't be one of them. *Here goes nothing.* She shut her eyes and inhaled.

"Isma'au," Umm Zalabya whispered. "What do you hear?"

The only thing Sahara heard was what she always did when she closed her eyes—her thoughts.

"I hear music," Fanta spat out. "Elton John, I think."

"And I just hear Fanta." Yara giggled.

"Do not fill the silence with your words," the sorceress reminded them.

After a few seconds of quiet, Naima cried, "There's a katkūta in the trees."

"Everyone can hear that bird chirping." Her brother scoffed.

Naima ignored him or maybe didn't even hear him at all. "She's waiting for her mother to come home," she continued, her voice shaking. "She's scared."

Holy smokes. Naima could actually hear what the bird was thinking.

"You can underst—" Yara began.

Umm Zalabya brought her finger to her lips and gently shushed her granddaughter, then turned back to Naima. "Let the bird know her mama is on her way home, and all will be well."

Of course, Naima would ace this lesson on her first try. She was a natural at this kind of stuff. *Listen harder,* Sahara urged herself as a shoulder brushed against hers. "So much dawsha," the sorceress whispered. "Notice the noise and let it move past without reaching for it."

Sahara opened her eyes. "I'm trying," she grumbled. "But it's not working."

"You're trying too hard," Umm Zalabya told her.

Sahara had never heard that before. Wasn't trying a good thing?

"If you have any hope of the wind revealing a message that can help you find your friend, you must not try too hard or too little. The in-between is the perfect space for your mind to receive the hawa."

"Ugh! But how I am supposed to hear what it's trying to tell me? My thoughts keep coming no matter what I do. I can't control them." Sahara began to pace. Everyone else opened their eyes now too.

"It's not about controlling or pushing away. It's about letting go." Umm Zalabya leaned on her cane as she walked over to a steel counter.

Sahara reached into her pocket and rubbed the coin Khaltu had given her. Everyone was telling her how she had to let go, but they weren't the ones trying to keep an amulet safely tucked under their shirts with duct tape so that it wouldn't go nuclear again.

The sorceress returned carrying a wooden bowl. "Pistachios from the Sinai." She plucked one from the bowl and held it up. "If the first pistachio tree didn't surrender its pollen to the wind, we would not have any more of *these* beauties." She dropped a nut into each of their hands. "Enough for today. Tomorrow, we will practice araafat el hawa."

"What's that?" Sahara muttered to Naima.

"Wind divination," her cousin answered excitedly.

"Great," Sahara groaned under her breath. "Another thing I'll suck at."

"Don't talk about my best cousin like that." Naima winked as she cracked open the shell and tossed the pistachio into her mouth. *Best cousin* was a big compliment coming from Naima, who had something like fifteen on her father's side.

Sahara followed suit. The nut's soft-and-creamy sweetness delivered a warm punch to her mouth. "Fine. Maybe seeing in the wind will go better than listening to it."

AFTER THE WALK back in the blaring midday sun, Sahara arrived at her family's building sweaty and tired. She and her cousins quickly swung by the shop for a drink and to check in with Noora, who reported that Khaltu Layla had only called once to see how things were going and was happy to hear that the children were looking in on Umm Zalabya. That wasn't a total lie. They *had* been at Umm Zalabya's.

While Fanta took over for Noora at the shop, Naima headed to the Nassers' apartment again. She'd been spending so much time there lately. How untidy could the prior tenants have left it? Yeesh!

All Sahara could think about was getting upstairs and throwing herself onto the mattress in Naima's room for a break from the heat and some much-needed rest. But as she reached the third floor, she heard the pitter-patter of footsteps above her. They came to a sudden stop, followed by the screeching sound that the chairs at Sittu's dining table sometimes made against the floor when they were slid out. Someone was upstairs. But that made no sense because Amitu was still at the museum, Khaltu Layla hadn't returned from town, and Uncle Gamal was on the road to Jeddah.

What if it was . . . A jolt of adrenaline ratcheted up Sahara's breathing. If Umm Zalabya told her to tune in to her breath now, there would be no way she could keep up with it. Maybe she should get Fanta or the guard stationed outside the shop. No, that would only put them in danger too. *I've gotta do this alone,* she told herself as she tiptoed upstairs. The door to Sittu's apartment was open a tiny bit, but not enough for Sahara to see inside. She extended her trembling hand and pushed the door open.

"Amitu. You almost gave me a heart attack!" Sahara yelled at her aunt, who was sitting at the table with her head down.

"I'm sorry, Susu. I didn't mean to alarm you," she said in a tone that showed less than 1 percent concern for practically scaring Sahara to death. Something was up.

Sahara took a deep breath, trying to calm down. "Shouldn't you be at the museum?"

When Amitu raised her head, her cheeks were wet with tears.

Sahara raced over. "What happened?" she asked, worrying Amitu might have found out about Vicky or, worse, that Fayrouz had struck again.

"I've been fired from the museum," Amitu cried.

Before Sahara could ask what her aunt could've possibly

done to deserve that, Amitu stammered, "It . . . It was stolen. And it's all my fault."

Sahara had no clue what she was talking about. "What was stolen?" she pressed.

Amitu's face crumbled. "The emerald sword."

28

The Last Embrace

966 CE

A year had passed since the hawa twins began training with Aziza. In a few hours, the pilgrims would return to the city once again. With his back against the wall, Marwan agreed to let Hassan take charge of the magic portion of the celebration, despite Aziza's pleas that he wasn't ready.

"I *am* ready." Hassan fumed, marching back and forth through the upstairs hallway that morning. "You'll see." His eyes blazed at Husnaya. "Everyone will. Then there will be no doubt left in Baba's head that he has chosen the wrong son to succeed him."

"You have nothing to prove," Husnaya told her brother. "Rashid may become the khalifa one day, but your training under Aziza has prepared you to be his best adviser."

"I have everything to prove," Hassan blasted. "You wouldn't understand. You've never understood what it's been like to be second best."

Husnaya had always known that being passed up for khalifa had been a great disappointment for Hassan, but perhaps if she'd shown him more understanding, he wouldn't be this bent on proving everyone wrong. She wished she could go back and listen more. But she'd been so busy thinking about her own woes—her desire to be more than just a princess who was content performing the duties expected of her.

Even though Husnaya had promised Aziza she wouldn't do anything to change Hassan's foreboding future, she could still be there for him. And pray that it would be enough to shield him from the darkness looming in the distance.

"I'm sorry, my brother. I know what it's like to feel as if no one understands your sorrow. But I do, and I will. Always." She hugged her brother.

Hassan allowed himself to linger in her arms for a few seconds and then pulled away. "I'd better get back to preparing for this afternoon."

Husnaya watched Hassan disappear down the hallway. Had she known this would be their last embrace, she would've run after him and pulled him close for a little longer.

Instead, Husnaya made for her chamber. The light from the hallway entered the dim room, casting a shadow on the floor of a figure seated on her bed.

Husnaya stepped back. "Who's there?" she cried.

"Settle down, Husnaya. It's only me," Mama reproached.

"Why are you sitting here in the dark?" Husnaya asked, lighting the candle by her bed. Even though it was daytime, the lattice windows let in little light.

"How can you ask me that when you have been lurking

in the shadows for months, defying my wishes?" Dounya's face glowed harshly in the candlelight. "Hassan told me everything."

Betrayal stabbed Husnaya in the chest.

"And I see from your face he wasn't lying."

Husnaya looked away from her mother. "Why would he do this?"

"He was trying to protect you." Mama's voice grew louder. "You are a princess in this court with countless suitors. But no one will marry a royal witch. Curse the day Aziza and her father arrived here looking for work."

A sob rose in Husnaya's throat. "Mama, how could you say that? After all they've done for our family. It's Marwan you should be mad at. He's been lying to you and Baba all these years."

"And what about *you*?" There was a hint of a quiver in her voice. "Have you not deceived us too?"

Husnaya's stomach wrenched with guilt, for she had not been the only one betrayed. But what choice had she had? Mama would have never let her train with Aziza. Tears fell down Husnaya's cheeks. "Have you told Baba?"

Mama shook her head. She cleared her throat, steadying her voice. "Your jidda and I—"

"Jidda knows?"

"Of course. You might think that being a female royal in this court is just about pretty clothes and etiquette, but it is much more than those things. When order in the palace is compromised, it is up to us to restore it. And we *will* restore it." Dounya rose from the bed. "But first, we must see to it that the hajj celebration does not disappoint. We owe the pilgrims that."

Husnaya nodded. She knew how much pride the city took in their returning pilgrims and the chance to celebrate them. She didn't want to spoil that.

"But until then, there will be no more lessons," Mama warned, and then stormed out.

Husnaya muffled her cries with her pillow. She couldn't imagine her life without the magic Aziza had brought into it. And of all the ways she'd worried their secret training could be exposed, never had she imagined it would be at Hassan's hands. The question of why gnawed at her. He had to have known that telling Mama would put an end to their lessons. Unless that was his ultimate goal.

Husnaya stood up. She could spend the next few hours deliberating Hassan's motives or ask him herself, but first, she needed to warn Aziza. She had no idea what Mama had planned when she'd said she would restore order to the palace, but Husnaya wasn't going to wait to find out. Aziza and her father had to leave the court *now*.

Husnaya raced to the servants' quarters, but the maid's room was empty. She headed for the kitchen, where Aziza might be helping her father cook for the celebration.

"Kolu tamam?" Cook asked when Husnaya ran in.

"Yes, I'm just looking for Aziza," she huffed, out of breath.

"It's almost time for her to help me get dressed for the celebration."

"I'm afraid you've just missed her. She's off to the market to pick up some more pistachios. You can never have enough in the baklawa." He laughed. "It's your father's favorite dessert." Cook beamed.

For a split second, Husnaya thought about telling him to get his daughter and run, but when she saw the look of pride on his face, she couldn't take this last moment of triumph from him.

Instead, she turned for the door. "Please send her to my room when she returns."

Anger swelled in Husnaya's chest at all that would be lost because of her brother's betrayal. "Hassan," she growled as she marched to his room.

She didn't bother knocking, throwing the door open. The room was empty. With no Hassan to yell at, the fury at the tip of her tongue had to go somewhere. Husnaya's hand burst forth with a gust that blew Hassan's wardrobe open.

A glint of silver flashed in the corner, followed by a glimmer of green.

Husnaya gasped as her heart pounded in her ears. *No, no, no.*

She inhaled, trying to calm her breathing. But it came out in quick and shallow spurts the way it had when they were younger, and Hassan hid in the wardrobe. Even though she could hear him giggle from inside, her pulse would still race as she tiptoed toward it.

Perhaps, just like back then, she knew what she would find inside if she dared step closer to the truth. The game would end immediately. There would be no going back.

The sound of the musicians tuning their instruments for the procession came through the window. Husnaya breathed in deeply again and crept toward the wardrobe. She pulled away her brother's clothes.

And there it was—the khalifa's emerald sword.

29

The Emerald Sword

It was strange to wipe the tears of the person who had wiped hers from the day they'd started falling. Of course, Sahara couldn't actually remember Amitu wiping them when she was a baby, but somewhere deep inside, she knew Amitu had, which is why her heart broke to see her aunt so distraught. Especially when Sahara knew she hadn't stolen the emerald sword. Her aunt would never steal anything ever.

She wished her dad were here to offer Amitu his hand-kerchief. It was so hard without him. He would know how to make his sister feel better. But since he was far away, it was up to Sahara. She ran to the bathroom, grabbed some tissues, and slid a few before her aunt.

Amitu used one to dry her eyes and another to wipe her nose. "You should've seen the disappointment on Zalabya's face. He gave me this great opportunity, and I let him down."

Sahara couldn't imagine seeing any emotion on Zalabya's face. He always wore that same blank look. "He can't possibly think you stole the sword," Sahara railed, feeling the burn of anger at Yara's dad in her chest.

"It doesn't matter whether I stole it or not. The point is, it's gone, and the theft happened under *my* watch. Zalabya left me in charge when he went to meet with the director of antiquities. And Allah knows how, but somehow, I missed a thief carrying out one of the most valuable swords in all the world." Amitu dropped her head back down on the table.

Sahara remembered the glimmering emerald at the sword's hilt and how her hamsa had vibrated in its presence. In between the thoughts racing in her head was one name—Fayrouz. She didn't know how El Ghoula was connected to the sword or why she'd taken it, but Sahara was sure that when her amulet pulsed like that, Fayrouz had something to do with it.

"Everything's gonna be okay, Amitu. They'll catch the person who stole it, and the sword will be back at the museum." Sahara would make sure of it. She reached for Amitu's hand. "The truth always comes out in the end."

Sahara had learned that the hard way last summer when she'd arrived in Cairo with a necklace she thought was special because her mother had saved it for her, only to learn that it was the key to keeping locked an enchanted lamp her family had been guarding in a secret chamber for over one thousand years. Not to mention discovering that Magda was actually Noora, and Fayrouz, her grandmother's so-called maid, was the real El Ghoula.

Amitu lifted her head. "I suppose the truth does always come out." She dabbed her eyes. "Enough about my problem. How are things with Vicky?"

"Better." Sahara felt a pang of guilt. Less than a minute after touting the power of the truth, she was lying to Amitu's face. "She went to see Yara again," Sahara told her. "If you're feeling okay, I should go and see how she's doing." Again, not a complete lie. She was planning on going over to Umm Zalabya's to find out if Fayrouz had anything to do with the sword's disappearance.

"I'll be fine," Amitu insisted. "Go be with your friend."

If only she could be. Sahara stood up and kissed her aunt's head. As she headed for the door, Amitu said, "I know it's upsetting that Vicky and Yara have been spending so much time together, but it must help to have someone in the same boat."

Sahara spun around. She stared at her aunt. "*What* boat?"

Amitu's eyes went wide. "I . . . I just mean they both don't usually spend their summers in Shobra."

Here's the thing about lying: The better you get at it, the easier it is to spot someone else doing it. Sahara pointed her finger at Amitu. "You knew, didn't you? You knew about the divorce, and you didn't say anything. Why?"

"I'm sorry, Susu. Mr. and Mrs. Miller wanted Vicky to be the one to tell you when she was ready. And I'm guessing by your reaction that she has."

Vicky had, just not in the way Amitu thought she had.

"Yeah," she said as her aunt's words replayed in her head. *It must help to have someone in the same boat.*

For the first time, it dawned on Sahara that maybe Vicky had wanted Yara to hang around because she was going through the same thing—her parents had recently divorced too—and could understand her situation. That made Sahara feel both happy and crappy. Happy that her friend had someone to talk to but crappy that it hadn't been her.

"I wish Vicky would've told me sooner. I may not know what it feels like for your parents to divorce, but I still could've helped. I want to help."

But who was Sahara to criticize her friend when she'd done the same? And while she'd told herself that she kept her family's secret from Vicky to keep her safe, the truth was there was another reason. Sahara wasn't sure Vicky could understand what it was like to be responsible for something as important as the chamber's treasures.

"It's not too late to help Vicky," Amitu told her. It felt good to have her aunt doing the reassuring again. "Now that she's finally talking about what's happening with her family, she might be ready to accept your help."

Sahara nodded as she turned back toward the door, praying it would indeed not be too late.

"Fayrouz," Naima seethed when Sahara was done telling them about the stolen sword.

"I hate the witch too, but you can't blame her every time something bad happens," Fanta huffed at his sister as they climbed the steps to the rooftop. "Are the problems with the economy her doing too?" He scoffed. "It was so much easier when I had my music player. I could turn up the volume and tune out your kalam farigh. Sahara, please talk some sense into her."

"I can't." Sahara bit her lip. "Because I think she's right." She didn't have to be facing Naima to feel the "I told you so" glare she blasted at her brother. "One way or another, we're about to find out."

The late afternoon sun cast a golden light on the garden. The yasmeen glowed around Yara like candles as she sat at the foot of her grandmother's rocking chair, her head resting on her nenna's lap. After everything that had happened, it was nice to see them so at ease with each other.

"Back so soon?" Umm Zalabya looked up at Sahara.

"I know we're early, but something awful has happened." Sahara bent down. "It can't wait until tomorrow."

"I gather you're referring to the disappearance of the sword," the sorceress said.

Naima gasped. "Did you see that in the wind? Are your powers back?"

Umm Zalabya shook her head.

"My father called to tell us what happened." Yara faced Sahara. "He didn't want to let your amitu go, I promise. The director of antiquities insisted he do it since it was stolen under her watch." Yara's voice was filled with the same sincerity as yesterday when she'd asked if she could help find Vicky.

"I believe you." Sahara gave her a soft smile. "And that's not why we're here. I can't shake this feeling that Fayrouz is the one who stole it."

"Because she did," Naima insisted once more, much to her brother's dismay.

"Here we go again." Fanta snorted.

Sahara continued. "When we were at the museum yesterday, Amitu said the sword had belonged to a khalifa who lived in Egypt and Tunisia. But that it had somehow ended up in Baghdad. The same city where Morgana was from and the sorcerer died."

"So what does any of this have to do with Fay—"

Naima stuck her hand in front of her brother's mouth. "Let Sahara finish," she snapped at him.

"Because she's his descendant like we are Morgana's," Sahara explained. "And if the sword belonged to the sorcerer like she believes the lamp did, then why wouldn't she come after that too?"

Fanta pushed his sister's hand away. "I thought you just said it belonged to the khalifa." He rubbed his head in confusion.

"It did. But the sorcerer could've stolen it from the khalifa." Sahara yanked her scrunchie off her wrist and tied up her hair. "Look, I know it's a stretch, but it feels right."

"What do you think?" Yara asked her grandmother.

"I think it's about time our desert rose trusts her feelings." Umm Zalabya grinned like Alice's Cheshire cat.

Yara leaped up and narrowed her eyes at her nenna. "Why didn't you say anything when Baba told you about the sword?"

"I warned Zalabya about the sword's questionable history when he first told me about it last month," the sorceress insisted. "But he wouldn't hear of it. He was set on procuring it. 'Mama, imagine the acclaim it will bring the museum and the visitors it will attract. The more questionable the history, the better,' he said. There was no talking him out of it. But what's done is done. We must concentrate on the now."

"But it's *not* done. Not for me. You put Baba, Sahara's amitu, and everyone else that works at the museum in danger. What if the witch had done something to them?" Yara swung around and hurried for the door.

Sahara started after her. She didn't mean to drive a wedge between Yara and her grandmother, especially now that they were finally getting along.

"Let her be." Umm Zalabya sighed, standing up and resting on her cane. "I will talk to her when she's had a chance to calm down." She walked toward Sahara. "Your mind is full of astute connections, as was your mother's."

Huh? As was your mother's.

"You knew my mom?" Sahara hesitated. "I mean, it makes sense you knew her. You just never mentioned her before."

"I suppose not, but I have thought of her every day since Naima dragged you to my rooftop last year. Amani liked to come here and be with the yasmeen. Even then, the breeze around her was filled with the seeds of hope and belief that would one day grow into you."

Sahara looked at the star-shaped flowers. "I wish I had half of her belief."

"You do. The amulet wouldn't respond to you otherwise. It's just buried underneath all those clever thoughts and rules you've devised for keeping things under control." The sorceress chuckled.

"And what's wrong with control?"

"It's an illusion." Umm Zalabya picked up a jug and began watering her plants. "See you in the morning, children."

Swinging with Mini Magda

Control is an illusion. Umm Zalabya's words swirled around in Sahara's head as she descended the steps. For Sahara, rules and order were something she could count on, not fake like an illusion. That's why she liked to fix things— repairing what was broken was comforting.

Of course, she wanted to be able to let go and lean into whatever magical miracle was supposed to happen. She'd seen plenty of magical miracles last summer. But it was still so hard to surrender to them. Especially now that she was dealing with the fallout of Umm Zalabya's attack, her best friend's kidnapping, and Amitu's firing. All these awful problems led back to one witch. Too bad Sahara couldn't duct-tape El Ghoula to the top of el Borg.

With so many things outside of Sahara's control, she understood why Yara had tried to find a reason for her parents' divorce, even if blaming her grandmother was going about it the wrong way. When there wasn't anything you could do about something complicated like your parents falling out of love, looking for a reason felt like *doing* something. Sahara wished she'd been able to tell Vicky these things. But there was someone she *could* tell.

She came to a halt in between the fourth and fifth floors and turned to Naima. "I'm gonna stop by and see how Yara's doing. She seemed pretty upset."

"Are you sure? Do you want me to come with you?" Naima asked, her voice taking on a protective tone.

"No, it's okay. I won't be long." Sahara started to head up the stairs and then backtracked. In all the times she'd been to Umm Zalabya's building, she'd never actually gone to her apartment.

Naima pointed to the door above them. "We'll wait for you out front. Good luck with Mini Magda." She giggled.

"Right." Sahara laughed half-heartedly as she climbed the steps, unsure if it was a fitting nickname anymore.

When she knocked on the door, Yara cried, "Please go away, Nenna. I don't want to talk now."

"Uh. It's me," Sahara said through the door, rethinking her decision to stop by. What if Yara didn't want to see her?

"Sahara?" Yara's voice was filled with surprise. There was a slight pause followed by the click of the door's lock. Yara appeared on the other side, adjusting her helmet. "Come in," she said, sitting on the porch swing in the middle of her grandmother's living room, which looked like some kind of indoor garden. There were rocking chairs opposite the swing, and lush plants filled each corner. Lit candles of various widths and lengths covered every flat surface illuminating the flowers painted on the walls. Sahara didn't notice a single lamp or overhead light. Did the apartment even have electricity?

"I don't think I've ever sat on one of these *inside*," Sahara remarked, taking a seat next to Yara on the swing.

"It's Nenna's idea of a couch." Yara snorted. "Almost all the furniture in here moves."

"I bet this is nothing like your mother's place." Sahara imagined that Yara's rich mother's apartment was filled with triple the museum-like furniture found in Sittu's Room of Photos. "Do you miss it there?"

"I'm not sure. Since Baba left, it doesn't feel the same." Yara leaned back, rocking the swing.

"No, I guess not." Sahara fingered a loose thread on her shorts. "Do you think Vicky felt like that after her dad moved out?"

Yara stopped the swing with her feet and turned to Sahara. "You know?"

"It was in the letter she started to write me before"— Sahara's breath hitched—"El Ghoula took her. I wish she would've told me when there was something I could do. When she wasn't trapped who knows where." Sahara gave a strong push with her feet, making the swing's swaying start up again, faster this time.

"Vicky wanted so badly to tell you about her parents. She told me so. But every time she tried, the words never came out." Yara lowered her head. "It's hard to say them aloud.

That's why I suggested a letter instead. I'm glad she got around to writing it, but I'm sorry she couldn't finish it." Yara's voice quivered.

Yara had encouraged Vicky to write the note—the possibility had never crossed Sahara's mind. "The letter was your idea?"

"I thought it might be easier than telling you in person."

Sahara's stomach churned with acrid guilt. "Was it my fault she didn't tell me? Did she feel like she couldn't trust me?"

"Tab'an la." Yara shook her head. "She didn't, not because of you but because of *her*. Everyone tells me I had nothing to do with my parents' decision to get divorced, but it doesn't feel that way. It's still happening to me, and it feels like I've done something wrong."

Sahara understood what Yara was saying. Everyone always told her she wasn't responsible for her mother's death, but it was hard not to feel like she was.

"I know it's not Nenna's fault. And maybe not mine either." Yara paused. "If there isn't someone to blame, then what's left to do? Just accept it. But I don't want to accept it. I want things to go back to the way they were."

"Yeah, I know what you mean." Sahara sighed. What good was it having a time-traveling lamp if you couldn't use it to fix the past? *If you do, the consequences are most grave.* Sahara heard Julnar's voice in her head. But what about Vicky's and Yara's parents—weren't their divorces grave enough? Wasn't her mother's death too?

Sahara would never understand magic, but she was certain of one thing. As much as she wished Vicky had turned to her for support, she was grateful her friend *had* someone to turn to. That was more important than anything, even her own feelings of jealousy. Sahara squeezed Yara's shoulder. "I'm glad Vicky had you to talk to."

"Really?" Yara cocked an eyebrow at Sahara.

"Really."

Yara smiled. "She helped me a lot too, you know. Talking to her made me feel like someone else knew what I was going through. That I wasn't alone."

Maybe that's what Vicky had needed to hear from Sahara all along—that she was there for her. Maybe that's what Yara needed to hear now too. What everyone did.

"You're not alone," Sahara said, noticing the silver-and-lapis bracelet around Yara's wrist and feeling silly for ever freaking out about it.

"Neither are you. We'll find Vicky together. Nenna's sorcery may be unusual"—Yara giggled—"but she knows what she's doing."

"Here's to the unusual, then." Sahara raised her hand for a high five.

Yara slapped it, though instead of pulling her hand back, she wrapped her fingers around Sahara's and gave them a light squeeze.

Mini Magda was definitely the wrong nickname for Yara. Everything about Magda had been fake. As Sahara swung back and forth in Umm Zalabya's garden apartment, she found honesty and genuine friendship in the eyes of her former adversary.

LATER THAT NIGHT, Sahara had the familiar dream of her mother in the chamber. Only this time, she caught the deep blue glimmer of the amulet in her mom's hand. She could feel Amani's heart race as the hamsa pulled her toward the curio and the lamp floated out. *Click.* The amulet attached itself to the lid. Seconds later, it clicked again, and the hamsa separated from the lamp. The blue light went out as the lamp clanged to the floor. Confusion seized her mom.

"You shouldn't be here." A familiar woman's voice came from behind Amani, making her jump and jolting Sahara awake.

It wasn't the amulet pulsing against her chest in the silver twilight of the bedroom that woke Sahara, but the pounding of her heart. Her mother had tried to open the lamp but couldn't. And then there was that voice. Sahara knew she'd heard it before but couldn't place it.

Kitmeer leaped down from Naima's bed and circled Sahara, eventually settling beside her. Her breathing calmed as his warm body nestled into hers. And within seconds, she fell back asleep.

31

Zero?

A raafat el hawa and arqam mashura." Umm Zalabya's voice boomed through the rooftop garden the following day. Almaz, curled into a ball on the rocking chair, opened her eyes and lifted her head at the intensity of her owner's voice. Seeing that everything was okay, the cat meowed and went back to sleep.

"With the end of the month only three days away, I need to ensure you are as prepared as possible to face off with El Ghoula," Umm Zalabya continued. "Therefore, I have decided to teach you itnin sorcery tools today." She held up two fingers. "Wind divination *and* enchanted numbers."

Sahara had barely heard the enchanted numbers part because her brain was stuck on *face off with El Ghoula*. She hated the idea of seeing—let alone going head-to-head with—Fayrouz again, but she had to for Vicky.

"We will split into two groups, and I will circle between them. After lunch, you'll switch. Sahara and Yara, over there."

Umm Zalabya gestured to the steel counter at the far end of the garden. "You'll start with araafat el hawa. And Naima and Fanta over here." She pointed to the two rectangular steel planters, which she had covered with wooden planks so they looked like desks, especially with the flipped-over flowerpot stools in front of them. The siblings grumbled their disapproval, quickly biting their tongues at Umm Zalabya's sharp look.

"If you are going to rescue your friend, you must *all* be capable of being partners," the sorceress contended. "We don't know what the witch might throw at you, but the last thing you want is for her to capitalize on your inability to work together."

A week ago, Sahara would've balked at being partnered with Yara, but she was warming up to her *and* her riding helmet. Not many people could pull one off when they weren't on a horse. Sahara didn't skip to the counter, but she didn't trudge either.

Two terra-cotta bowls of sand sat on the table—the grains yellow-gold in the late morning light. Sahara scrunched her brows. What did the sand have to do with divination? She turned to Yara, who, judging by the look on her face, was wondering the same thing.

"Weird, right?" Sahara said under her breath.

"Very," Yara whispered back as the tap of her nenna's cane neared.

"Now"—Umm Zalabya clapped—"yesterday's practice of tuning into the wind will serve as the foundation for harnessing it to make predictions."

Great. Sahara had basically failed yesterday's lesson. There was no way it was going to help her today.

Umm Zalabya grabbed a pile of sand from each bowl and dropped it into their cupped hands. Sahara clenched her fist around the grains so they wouldn't fall out.

"First, connect to your breath." The sorceress closed her eyes and inhaled deeply. The girls did the same. "Move that connection outward. Feel the presence of the wind around you." Umm Zalabya breathed out. "Lean into it. And when you're ready, gently pull it in."

Sahara couldn't believe it, but her whole body slighty tingled. "I feel something!" she cried.

"Me too!" Yara said, equally excited.

"Mumtaz," Umm Zalabya praised.

Training's not gonna be a total dud today. Just as Sahara thought this, the sorceress took hold of her hand with her own. It was firm and rough, probably because of all the years she'd spent working in the dirt. She unfurled Sahara's fingers just as Khaltu Layla had done with the coin. The sand now rested in her open palm. As if in response to being freed from the darkness of Sahara's tight fist, the sand warmed and subtly vibrated, basking in the light of her outstretched palm.

Umm Zalabya's cane tapped toward Yara. Sahara guessed she was adjusting her granddaughter's hold too. A few seconds later, the sorceress said quietly, "Let the hawa flow through you and into your fingers."

Sahara's hand prickled like her foot did when it fell asleep.

"Begin to think of a question whose answer has eluded you," Umm Zalabya added.

All Sahara could think about was the dream she'd had last night of her mother in the chamber. Why did she keep having it?

"Hold that question in your mind," the sorceress directed, her words flowing slow and smooth like syrup. "And when you are ready, release it into the air."

Sahara concentrated. *What are you trying to tell me, Mom?* Then exhaled, letting the question go.

A wave of electricity coursed down Sahara's arms and into her palm. The sand's gentle quiver quickly went into overdrive, and she felt an upward pull in the center of her hand, lightening the weight of the grains. She wasn't sure she was supposed to peek yet, but she did anyway. *Holy moly!* The sand floated up from her palm to the air above it. A giggle—part nerves, part excitement—escaped her lips as the individual grains came together, forming an image as Husnaya's water droplets had done. Nothing nearly as impressive as Morgana's face appeared, though.

"A zero?" Sahara croaked, making the swirl of sand drop into a heap at her feet. After all that, a ridiculous zero. If this were a test, that's exactly what she would've scored.

"How'd you do?" Sahara turned to Yara, totally unprepared

for what she would see. Instead of a circle of nothing, Yara's sand had somehow multiplied, forming a tall, muscular horse with a flowing golden mane and tail.

"Whoa," Sahara let out.

Yara exhaled softly, her wide eyes remaining glued to her vision. Sahara couldn't blame her. It was amazing.

As Umm Zalabya announced there were five more minutes until they broke for lunch, Sahara glanced over at her cousins to see how they were faring. Naima was staring at a paper on her makeshift desk and beaming. She'd probably nailed this lesson too. Fanta, on the other hand, was spitting out numbers, his bandana askew. He looked up at Sahara and mouthed, "Help."

Crap. This afternoon's enchanted *whatever* training would probably go as wrong as, if not worse than, her wind divination disaster.

32

Mustafa Fouad

The line for fool and tameya sandwiches from Samir's stand wrapped around the corner. The savory smell of garlic and cumin mixed with the sweetness of sautéed onions made Sahara's stomach grumble as they waited. She felt a tap from behind.

"You never said what you saw in the sand. Haga gameela?" Yara asked if Sahara had seen anything beautiful.

Embarrassed to tell her what she'd actually seen, Sahara answered, "I don't think I'm very good at your nenna's magic." She was used to picking things up quickly at school. But she was struggling with Umm Zalabya's lessons at a time when much more was on the line than an A in biology.

Naima clicked her tongue disapprovingly at Sahara's self-doubt. "You heard Umm Zalabya. You're just in your head. Stop thinking so much, and you'll get the hang of it. I *know* you will."

But Sahara wasn't so sure. "I wasn't in my head this time."

She huffed. "One minute, the sand was tingling in my hand. The next, nothing." She left out the part about the zero.

"Pfft. It doesn't have to do with that anyway," Fanta griped at his sister. "I wasn't *in my head*, and I still had no idea what Umm Zalabya was talking about with those squares."

"You've got the opposite problem. *You* need to think more," Naima teased.

"Just because you did okay on two lessons doesn't make you master of the wind magic," Fanta railed back.

"What's got you so upset, karate boy?" A familiar voice came from behind.

Mustafa Fouad! Sahara would know that jerk anywhere. He had a knack for showing up at the worst times. She spun around as Mustafa—dripping in gold and name brands—and two of his lapdogs approached, pushing their way through the line.

Mustafa swaggered toward her cousin. "Where are your headphones?" he asked, flicking his finger right by Fanta's ear. "You never go anywhere without your music player."

Fanta's cheeks turned red. Sahara knew her cousin didn't feel like telling this bozo he no longer had them. It was still very much a sore subject. "None of your business." Fanta seethed.

"I hope you didn't lose it." Mustafa feigned sympathy when he clearly had none. "I'd sell you one of mine, but you'd never be able to afford it."

Sahara felt the burn of that insult for her cousin.

"Imshi!" Naima yelled at Mustafa.

"Yeah. Go away!" Sahara shouted.

Mustafa lowered his sunglasses to look at Sahara. "If it isn't Miss New York back in Shobra." He snickered, getting in Sahara's face. It was funny when Uncle Gamal referred to her as that, but it *wasn't* coming from this dodo.

Sahara took two steps back, scrunching her nose. "You stink of cologne, and"—she pointed to the back of the line— "no cutsies."

He opened his mouth, probably to say something scathing, closing it when he spotted Yara standing behind her. He stood up taller, deepening his voice. "You must be Umm Zalabya's granddaughter. I heard you were staying with her this summer. That has to be hard when you're used to the finer things." He strutted, showing off his expensive clothes and the gold watch around his wrist, then gave Yara a smoldering look. "Enchanté. I'm Mustafa. But you probably knew that already."

Gross! Sahara wasn't sure she felt like eating anymore.

Yara shook her head. "Never heard of you."

Sahara liked this girl more and more by the second.

"That's too bad," Mustafa said through gritted teeth, throwing a dirty look at Sahara's cousins, who were busy cracking up. "I wouldn't be laughing if I were you, karate boy," he shot back at Fanta. "There are only a few spots left on the national team, and mine is *guaranteed*."

"Since when does Mustafa practice karate?" Sahara mumbled to Naima.

Naima made no effort to be quiet. "Since his father found out the Junior Karate Tournament was coming to Cairo and hired a big-shot sensei from Tokyo to teach his loser son and his goons. Always taking rich shortcuts." Naima balked. "But you couldn't beat my brother in a dance battle, and you *won't* beat him on the mat."

Fanta flashed a smile at his sister.

"We'll see about that, Na-eee-ma." Mustafa started for the front of the line. "Try and stop me," he called back to Sahara with a disgusting smirk.

Her insides boiled at the idea of this jerk getting to eat before everyone else just because his father was some kind of Shobra mob boss. But before she could show him the back of the line, he circled back to Yara.

"If you get tired of hanging out with this riffraff bunch, you know where to find me."

Yara didn't miss a beat. "Absolutely. If I need anything"— she batted her eyelashes like a maiden in need of saving—"I'll be sure to call for you at the local prison." The crowd erupted into laughter, probably because most of them believed Mustafa's family and their shady money deserved to be behind bars.

Mustafa's eyes narrowed to slits. Sahara could've sworn she saw steam coming out of his ears. He rolled his shoulders back, readying himself to attack.

"I guess the rumors we're right. You're as magnoona as your

grandmother." Mustafa twisted around and swept toward the front of the line.

"Don't call my nenna or me crazy!" Yara's hand flew out, discharging a small burst of wind at the back of his head.

Mustafa must've felt it fluttering through his hair. He turned around, his confusion shifting to laughter at the sight of her outstretched hand. "I told you her family was nuts," Sahara thought she heard him say as he walked away. But she couldn't be sure because she was busy ogling Yara. Even though the hawa that had come from her was minimal, Sahara had only seen two other people wield that kind of power—Husnaya and Fayrouz.

"Oh my God. You can do it too," she whispered to Yara. "Is this the first time it's happened?"

Yara didn't answer, though the way she was looking down at her trembling hand told Sahara it was.

33

An Early Present

966 CE

Husnaya waited in her room for Aziza until she saw Commander Osman riding down the path to the palace steps to announce the arrival of the hajj caravan at the city's gates. She'd have to look for Aziza when the procession ended. After this morning, Husnaya didn't dare test her mother's patience any further, taking her position by Mama and Jidda behind her father, Rashid, and Zain as the musicians played their first chords.

Her eyes darted around the court, searching for any sign of Aziza or Hassan. But still, *nothing.* A soft breeze blew, rustling the palace banners and giving Husnaya an idea.

She closed her eyes and listened for the wind—Aziza's wind. Despite the music, she heard it, blowing under the strumming, tapping, and drumming. It was fiercer than any wind she'd seen Aziza produce, and with it came a warning: *Hassan has stolen the grimoire. You must stop him.*

"Husnaya," her grandmother called, pulling her away from

Aziza's hawa. Jidda pointed to the cavalry. "Can you believe it was a year ago that you awaited my arrival from Mecca?"

Husnaya shook her head. So much had changed since Jidda had returned from her pilgrimage and Husnaya had learned of Marwan's deceit. She'd always thought magic was the answer to all her problems, but it seemed she had more problems now than ever.

Jidda stared past the soldiers. "Time runs faster the older you get. If only we could catch it and ask it to slow down." Sorrow coated her voice and poked at Husnaya's heart.

There was so much of the last year Husnaya wished she could go back and change. She knew if Aziza was here, she would tell her how dangerous it would be to interfere with what had been meant to be. But surely Aziza not being here and Hassan planning who knows what calamity merited interference.

As the first pilgrims came into view, a wind blew from the north. Husnaya's heart dropped to her stomach. She didn't need to look up to know it belonged to her brother. Even his calmest winds carried the whiff of danger.

"Welcome, hajj and hajjas," her brother's voice echoed from the tower. Everyone looked up, breaking out in gasps and applause.

"My son is flying a carpet," the khalifa announced with pride.

How? Her brother had never been successful in enchanting

his carpet. Husnaya raised her head, and that's when she saw it—the maroon-and-gold rug he rode upon now wasn't his. Her body shook with the fierce wind she was holding at bay. Not only had Hassan taken his father's emerald sword and the grimoire, but he'd also stolen Aziza's carpet.

Her brother zipped toward the palace, exhilarating the crowd further. He circled above the procession, finally coming to a stop in front of his family, the carpet hovering a few inches off the ground. Husnaya hadn't realized how tall her brother had gotten over the last year. Even though the rug gave him a slight advantage in height, he was at least a head taller than most of the pilgrims. Respect and excitement filled their unflinching stares at the prince.

"On behalf of the khalifa, I welcome you back home from your pilgrimage," Hassan proclaimed.

While older brother Rashid held back his royal tongue, young Zain did not show the same restraint. "Since when does he speak on Baba's behalf?" he griped.

"You honor us all with your devotion to your faith." Hassan's voice rang with conviction. "And in return for your steadfastness, I promise to protect you and all those living in the khalifa's lands."

The pilgrims and the court bowed their heads to the prince. But Husnaya didn't join their show of reverence. She steeled her chin, sending her own message on the wind to her brother: *Stop this before it's too late.*

Hassan hesitated as her hawa reached him. His eyes softened. Could he be reconsidering what he was about to do? But then he blinked, and his eyes flashed with fire. He swatted her wind like an annoying mosquito.

"It is no secret that enemies near and far threaten my father's rule and your safety," Hassan declared to the crowd. "And while the men of our army have always fought honorably to protect both, it has not been enough to put an end to these pernicious threats."

Husnaya had never seen or heard her brother sound . . . this powerful.

Hassan yanked off the hood of his cloak, baring his hawa mark for all to see. "Over the last year, I have learned all there is about the science of sorcery. My father's sage himself has said he has never witnessed such mastery. Isn't that right, Marwan?"

A confused Marwan nodded. What choice did he have? If he didn't go along with Hassan's display of power, his betrayal would be exposed in front of all.

"In a few days, my sister and I will turn fourteen." His gaze returned to Husnaya, his eyes still fiery. "I can't think of a better time to present her with an early birthday present. One that will protect her and all of you. As only a supreme sorcerer can, I have summoned an afreet."

Nervous murmurs and glances swept through the crowd.

"Do not fear," Hassan assured the people. "The potent beast has succumbed to my control. Under my direction, he will destroy our rivals and ensure our empire's power."

Dread seized Husnaya. This is why he'd stolen the grimoire.

Hassan let out an ear-piercing whistle, louder than any howling wind. And from the tower's gate, a giant, hairy one-eyed afreet exploded through the doors on four burly legs.

Ya Allah! Husnaya froze. She couldn't have run away even if she'd wanted to.

The cavalry's steeds reared up in fright, throwing their riders to the ground. The pilgrims jumped out of the way as the afreet ran toward Hassan. With a flick of her brother's wrist, the salivating creature came to a stop by his side, making everyone sigh in collective relief.

"Behold the gift of my power." Hassan pointed to the fanged beast, then turned to his father. "And the guarantee of your reign."

Husnaya was disgusted when the khalifa bowed his head. She couldn't stay quiet any longer. Just as she opened her mouth to tell her father who had stolen his sword, the afreet pounced, knocking Hassan off the carpet. His blaring growls overtook the air, making everyone scream.

Hassan crawled to his feet. "Don't panic. I shall get him back under my control." He waved his wind in front of the creature, who then lifted one of his clawed limbs and tossed the prince toward the crowd with another thundering roar.

Out of the corner of her eye, Husnaya caught a figure racing toward her. It was Aziza. As much as Husnaya wanted to get to her, she didn't dare move before the terrifying afreet.

Aziza stepped in between the afreet and the court. She

closed her eyes, trying to connect her wind to the creature, but to no avail. She turned to Hassan, who was being helped to his feet by some pilgrims. "You did not follow all the steps of the spell," she railed. "You did not conjure him when the cosmos would've ensured his loyalty. You can't skip steps."

"You were always trying to hold me back. But you can't anymore," Hassan roared back as fiercely as the afreet. "I'll show you the infinity of my power. I summoned this afreet, and I can destroy him." Wind and sand burst out of his hand, hitting the beast. But instead of subduing the creature, Hassan's blast only angered him further. The afreet charged at the court, heading straight for the royal women. The khalifa yelled something to his other sons. Zain bolted for the doors while his father and Rashid hurried toward the women. Mama's and Jidda's eyes were wide with fear.

As her father and older brother jumped in front of them, the khalifa yelled, "Marwan!" The knave was nowhere to be found. Husnaya wanted to do something, but any display of magic would expose her.

In a split second, Aziza leaped onto the carpet and zoomed toward the beast.

"Aziza," the khalifa muttered, seeing her clearly for the first time.

Aziza turned her head and bowed, but as she turned back, the afreet's claws flung her up and back. She hit the palace's brick facade with a thud and fell to the ground.

Husnaya threw her hands up to stifle a scream as the beast dug his claws into the khalifa's chest.

"No!" Rashid stabbed the afreet's foot with his dagger. The creature screeched in pain, then dug his fangs into the prince's neck. Rashid fell to the ground beside his father while the beast thrashed away from the palace and escaped into the woods.

Tears formed in Husnaya's eyes as her mother and grandmother wailed over her father's and brother's still bodies. She ran toward Aziza, hurling her hands over the maid's chest to stop the blood seeping from its clawed wound. "Aziza," Husnaya cried. "You can't leave me."

Aziza lifted her hand and squeezed Husnaya's. "Don't hide . . . like me . . ." She struggled to get the words out. She took one last breath in, then breathed out her last wind— "Show who you are."

Husnaya lifted her burning eyes to the sky, asking Allah to have mercy on all the souls that had been lost today. In the distance, the carpet zipped away from the palace with Hassan aboard, abandoning the palace. Abandoning her.

Enchanted Numbers

Sahara hadn't been able to take her eyes off Yara during lunch. Yara hadn't said a word as they ate. And now that they were back on Umm Zalabya's roof, she remained quiet, staring intently at her hands. There had to be so much going through her head—shock, confusion, fear. All the things Sahara had felt when the amulet pulsed for the first time last summer before she'd found out anything about Morgana's chamber or the hamsa's connection to the lamp. At least Yara had been aware of her family's enchanted history when her wind-shooting power showed up.

"Are you gonna tell your nenna what happened before?" Sahara gestured toward Yara's hand. "She could help you understand it."

"Not now," Yara muttered as Umm Zalabya approached their table.

Sahara couldn't grasp why Yara didn't want her grandmother to know. It's not like the sorceress would be surprised since Yara had obviously inherited the skill from her. Plus,

Umm Zalabya could teach her how to use it against Fayrouz. Sahara would keep Yara's secret for now, but she wasn't sure how long she'd be able to if training didn't start getting them closer to finding Vicky.

"Arqam mashura," Umm Zalabya announced. "The enchanted numbers spell is a hallmark of wind sorcery, based on the principle that there is an underlying code to the cosmos. And when we create magic squares utilizing numbers, with an eye to the harmonious relationship between them, we can tap into that code."

Finally, a concept Sahara could get behind. Coding was right up her alley.

"What does a code have to do with magic?" Yara asked.

"Because once we tap into the code, we can call on the hawa to adjust it," Umm Zalabya explained. "And those adjustments will produce shifts in the physical universe. Changes in what we see around us that were not possible before."

Sahara was no stranger to the cool things codes could do in the realm of computers and robots. She'd spent the whole year learning about and writing her own codes in Robotics Club. But she didn't think Umm Zalabya was referring to the type of coding that could be used to program a robot to perform an iconic dance. "What kinds of changes?" Sahara asked.

"Patience, desert rose. First, let's explore the first part of the spell: the numbers themselves." Umm Zalabya grabbed a sheet of paper from the pile on one of the planter desks and drew a square divided into three rows and three columns. Then she wrote *wind* in the middle of the right column.

Sahara thought about duplicating it in her pyramid pad later, but ever since she'd discovered Vicky's letter with Fayrouz's threat at the bottom, she'd been hesitant to use it.

Umm Zalabya looked up from her paper. "Pay attention to *where* I have written the word *wind*, for how you position the number one in your square designates which of the four cosmic elements you will summon later. I would like you both to draw a square and divide it into nine equal parts as I have done. Since, naturally, we are only concerned with harnessing the wind"—she winked—"you must put the number one here." She pointed to the center of the rightmost column on her square, then handed each of them a piece of paper and a pencil.

Yara and Sahara got right to work. They sat on the garden pot stools and drew their three-by-three squares, then wrote the number one in the spot Umm Zalabya had specified.

"That was easy." Yara smiled. It was good to see her feeling better after being so freaked out earlier.

"For now." Umm Zalabya grinned. "You've placed the first number, but there are eight more. You must now arrange the remaining arqam."

Yara quickly scribbled in the numbers two through eight.

"*Not* arbitrarily," her grandmother urged. "Harmoniously, so they create an enchanted pattern."

Sahara wiggled happily in her chair. She *loved* patterns, especially mathematical ones.

"You want us to do math?" Yara asked as if math on its own wasn't amazing.

"I suppose so," Umm Zalabya said, then walked over to work with Naima and Fanta at the divination station.

As Yara huffed and erased what was on her paper, Sahara began creating a bunch of three-by-three arrangements at the bottom of hers, taking care to leave the number one in the same position. She tried a bunch of combinations: odd numbers in the center squares, even numbers in the corner squares, and vice versa. But nothing amounted to an overall pattern until Sahara started to play with what the numerals added up to. What if she could somehow arrange them so all the rows and columns, even the diagonals, added up to the same sum? Since she was dealing with numbers one to nine, she added all those up to get forty-five. And because this was a three-by-three square, she divided that by three to get fifteen.

After twenty minutes of trying various configurations, she'd finally figured it out. Her foot bounced as she copied the numbers into the original square she'd drawn and cried, "I did it. They all add up to fifteen."

Yara put her pencil down and looked over as Naima and Fanta ran over from their station. They all congratulated Sahara. Umm Zalabya nodded at her square and smiled her full toothless smile, which Sahara was realizing she reserved for happy occasions. "A perfectly harmonious combination," the sorceress praised.

Fanta even asked if he could take her square home to study, which Sahara proudly said yes to. "There's no way you did this when it was our turn," he told his sister, holding up Sahara's paper.

"Of course not," Naima said.

"Then why were you smiling when you were making your square before?" Sahara asked.

"Because it was fun." Naima shrugged. "Anything that has to do with magic is fun."

Sahara didn't agree that anything related to magic was fun, but enchanted numbers definitely were. Though she still didn't get what they had to do with sorcery. "Now can you tell us about those shifts in the universe you brought up before?" she asked Umm Zalabya.

"Certainly." The sorceress slid out a square silver pendant from her galabeya's pocket.

Sahara squinted at the tiny Arabic numerals engraved on it. She studied them for a few seconds, then gasped. "Whoa! The numbers are arranged exactly like I had them on my paper."

"Because yours, too, is a three-by-three square with the number one in the hawa position."

Yara scratched her head. "Then why didn't you just show us the pendant to begin with, instead of having us do all that work, Nenna?"

Umm Zalabya chuckled. "Without the effort, there can be no magic. For the quest for harmony is just as important as the achievement of it."

Fanta held up Sahara's square. "So I can use this to ask for whatever I want?!" he asked, totally missing the sorceress's point.

Umm Zalabya shook her finger. "The enchanted numbers square is not a jinni. And you are not its creator."

I am the creator. Sahara stood up taller.

The sorceress's eyes flitted to Sahara. "And even the creator's work is not done with the arrangement of the numbers. Once you've succeeded in tapping into the cosmic code, it's time to call upon the wind to adjust it in a manner that creates changes in your favor or someone else's."

Umm Zalabya held up the pendant. "After making this square, I summoned the wind with the mystical words, *Arqam mashura, el hawa hakeem,* from an ancient grimoire. Some sorcerers and sorceresses take the extra step of rearranging the numbers when the spell is complete so it cannot be reversed, but that wasn't a concern of mine with this pendant."

Enchanted numbers, wise wind, Sahara repeated in her head.

Meanwhile, Naima spun toward the sorceress. "You have a book of spells!" Her eyes danced with excitement.

Umm Zalabya sighed. "Unfortunately, the grimoire was stolen ages ago. But the great Sitt Husnaya had committed many of the spells to memory, allowing her to pass them down to her descendants. And allowing me to use that of the enchanted numbers to invoke the wind and shift good fortune toward a woman yearning to have a baby."

"Did it work?" Fanta asked.

"Tab'an," Umm Zalabya answered. "You're here, aren't you?"

Fanta's jaw dropped.

"*That* belonged to Mama?" Naima pointed to the pendant. "You made it, called to the wind, and then *boom*, she had Fanta?"

"I think there's more to it than that." Sahara grinned, recalling what she'd learned about babies in health class last semester.

"There *is* more to it," the sorceress asserted. "In addition to the arrangement of the numbers and the words that must be recited, *when* the square is made is just as important. This amulet was forged when Saturn was in a favorable position for fertility."

It was weird to hear another pendant referred to as an amulet.

"By paying attention to the positions of the celestial bodies," Umm Zalabya added, "we can encapsulate their powers into our enchanted numbers squares and ensure the outcomes we desire."

"But how do you know their positions?" Sahara asked. "Do you have a telescope?"

"Better," the sorceress said, removing a gold disc slightly larger than her hand from her pocket and dangling it by the ring affixed to the top.

"An astrolabe," Sahara marveled, turning to Yara. "There's one at your father's museum."

Yara smiled, presumably enjoying Sahara's reference to the museum as her father's.

"This istirlab has been in our family for centuries," Umm Zalabya told her granddaughter, then continued to address all the children. "As wind sorcery is connected to space, we must always strive for harmony with the divine movements of the sun, moon, planets, and stars."

For the next ten minutes, Umm Zalabya showed them how to move the component discs, bars, and rules in tandem with the scales and grids on the front and back. "Not only can we tell where the celestial bodies are now but where they *will be*, allowing us to create spells and amulets like magic squares at the most advantageous times." All that sounded great, but the sorceress blew Sahara's mind when she showed them how to use the artifact to tell time. She couldn't wait to give it a try.

The astrolabe dangling from her finger, Sahara slid the al'idade—a bar on the back—until it lined up with the sun, taking care not to look directly at it. Then she mentally made a note of the sun's altitude. Afterward, she flipped the astrolabe over and moved the rete—the spider-looking outermost circle representing the sky—so the sun's altitude matched what she'd measured. Now that everything was lined up, she moved the rule on the front to the current date and read the time on the outermost scale.

"It's three twenty-four, I think. How do I know if I'm right?" Sahara asked.

Yara pointed to the watch around Sahara's wrist.

Duh! With all the disc shifting and rule sliding, she'd forgotten the handy device around her wrist. It read 3:26. "Not bad. Only two minutes off." Sahara smiled.

Though the afternoon had gone way better than the morning, none of the lessons had been easy or possible without the help of a skilled teacher who'd been trained by her own mentors. Umm Zalabya had learned her sorcery from her ancestors, but what about Fayrouz?

Sahara looked at Umm Zalabya. "On the night El Ghoula returned, you said she was a sorceress who could wield wind magic. But you never said *how* she learned it. Who taught her?"

"Astute question," Umm Zalabya pointed out. "While the secrets of this magic can be passed down from teacher to student—me to you—they can also be inherited. As I've told you before, some are born with the propensity for harnessing its most special powers. Like the women in my family."

"And like Yara and the wind in her hand." The words came out before Sahara could stop them. "Uh. I just mean all this training has come so easily for her."

Sahara did her best to backpedal, but it was too late. Umm Zalabya raised an eyebrow at her granddaughter and asked, "What does Sahara mean?"

"I'm sorry," Sahara mouthed to Yara when the sorceress's back was turned.

"And why is she sorry?" her grandmother prodded.

Crap. Sahara forgot Umm Zalabya had eyes on the back of her head.

"At lunch"—Yara's voice shook—"this terrible boy said something about our family, and it made me really angry. So angry that . . ." She hesitated.

"You felt the air rush into your body and out your palm," Umm Zalabya said softly.

Yara nodded.

"That's amazing!" Naima cried.

Fanta gaped at Yara. "Do you know how lucky you are to have that power?"

"I guess so," Yara said. "For years, I've heard Mama talk about my strange grandmother and all the strange women who came before her. What happened today was scary and confusing, but it also felt right." Yara removed her helmet. On the right side of her head, her hair remained close to the scalp and formed some sort of round golden figure that stood out amidst the rest of her dark tresses.

It looked just like the figure Sahara had seen in the sand. The one she'd mistaken for a zero. But it appeared more like a teardrop than a true circle on Yara's head.

"Is that the letter *hā*?" Fanta asked, craning his neck for a closer look.

Umm Zalabya slid her headscarf back. "The symbol of

the hawa," she said, revealing an identical shape on the right side of her head. They might've spent the afternoon focused on squares, but in the end, the round letter had everyone's attention.

Yara's face fell. "Mama always thought it was ugly, making me cover it since I was little."

Naima's gaze flitted from Umm Zalabya's head to Yara's. "They're beautiful."

Umm Zalabya raised her granddaughter's chin and peered into her eyes. "The letter of the hawa binds you to the gifts of all who came before you. I was worried your powers might lie dormant because of all the time you've spent pushing them away. But I should've trusted that the strength of the legacy you inherited would prevail."

"I was so afraid to be like you because of what Mama said— what other people said." Yara sniffled. "But I'm not anymore."

Umm Zalabya pulled Yara close. A light breeze blew through the garden, picking up the fallen petals of yasmeen and whirling them around their embrace.

35

Spill It

thought our family was amazing because of the chamber. But Fanta's right. Yara's *so* lucky to have inherited such a special power. Do you think she realizes how incredible that is?" Naima asked Sahara as they walked home, the late afternoon adhan echoing from the mosque behind them. Fanta had gone ahead to relieve Noora by four o'clock at the shop. They owed her for all the extra shifts she'd been taking lately on their behalf.

"I don't think Yara knows how to feel yet," Sahara answered. "It's all still new for her." A year had passed since she'd been entrusted with the hamsa, and Sahara was still figuring out what to make of it. She'd always imagined it would be cool to have a superpower like the heroes in the comics, but now she wasn't so sure. Being the wielder of the amulet was lonely.

Even though Sahara shared the duty of protecting the chamber and its treasures with Naima, Khaltu, and Sittu, they'd never felt the amulet's weight around their necks. The only person who could understand was Morgana, and she was one thousand years away. With Fayrouz ready to pounce from a twister of sand at any minute, there was no way Sahara could visit her in the past. At least Yara had Umm Zalabya to talk to.

"I know we promised not to use the lamp, but where would you go if we could?" Sahara asked.

Naima's eyes glimmered at the question. "Since I've already met my heroes, Peri, Julnar, and Husnaya, maybe I'd travel to the early 1900s to meet the writer Kahlil Gibran. His book *The Prophet* is one of my favorites. '. . . love knows not its own depth until the hour of separation.' Have you ever heard a more beautiful line?"

Sahara hadn't. Her lip quivered at the thought of being apart from Vicky. They'd been best friends forever, but it wasn't until Vicky had been kidnapped that Sahara understood what her friend truly meant to her. Life wasn't the same without Vicky. For one thing, it was way less colorful. She had brought a one-of-a-kind neon green brightness to Sahara's life.

"Sahara." Naima nudged her shoulder. "I just asked, what about you? Where would you want to travel to?"

"I'm sorry. I . . . I was deciding on my answer." Sahara could've just told Naima she was thinking of Vicky, but she knew she wouldn't be able to hold back the tears if she started talking about her friend. Luckily, she had a response lined up. It was a no-brainer. "The future," Sahara said without hesitation. "Can you imagine what technology will be like twenty years from now? My robotics teacher said cars will be able to drive themselves."

"No way!"

It always amazed Sahara that Naima could readily accept carpets that zoomed through the sky and magical jinn but questioned technological advances.

Before they turned the corner to Sittu's street, Naima murmured something about having to go back to the Nassers' apartment. *Again?* Unless the Nassers' previous tenants were hard-core partiers that had trashed the place, Sahara couldn't imagine there was anything left for Naima to tidy. Something was up. And the way her cousin was avoiding meeting her eyes confirmed Sahara's suspicions.

She looked at Naima sideways and demanded, "Spill it."

Naima scratched her headscarf. "What does that mean again?"

"It means I know you're hiding something, so tell me what it is."

A grin crept across Naima's face. She grasped Sahara's hand. "Come with me."

TWELVE MINUTES, SEVEN blocks, and six flights of steps later, the girls entered the Nassers' apartment.

Sahara frowned at Naima. "You brought me all this way"— she sucked in air—"to see an empty apart—"

Meow.

"What was that?" Sahara hurried toward the bedroom.

"They were already here when I showed up three days ago," Naima spewed as Sahara swung the door open.

"Kittens!" Sahara cried. "I should be asking what the heck you were thinking, but I can't. They're *so* cute." She bent down to the floor and caressed the three kittens lying on a folded blanket on the tile floor. They were so fluffy. "Where did they even come from?"

Naima lifted her hand to her heart. "I swear I didn't bring them. I found the qutat inside the apartment when Noora first sent me to clean up. I'm not sure how they got in or how long they've been here, but there hasn't been any sign of their mother. That's why I keep coming by. Someone has to take care of them."

Sahara couldn't blame Naima for wanting to help. Who knows what would've happened to the kittens if her cousin hadn't shown up? "Do you think the previous tenants left them behind?"

Naima shrugged as she snuck a peek at a cardboard box in the corner of the room. "Good girls," Naima praised the kittens. "You're learning to use your litter box."

"Wait. How do you know they're girls?"

"Don't tell me I have to explain the difference between boys and girls." Naima snorted as she headed out of the room.

"Right," Sahara giggled. "Where are you going now?"

"To the kitchen. I'll be right back."

Sahara sat cross-legged on the floor. She was glad the cats had their blanket because the tiles underneath her were hard. *Definitely a present from Naima,* Sahara thought as the kittens hopped into her lap.

"No wonder Naima's been spending so much time here," she cooed, peering into their blue eyes. "Look at your little paws and your little ears." One of the kittens rolled onto her back. Sahara wasn't sure if, like Kitmeer, that meant she wanted a belly rub. She hardly knew anything about cats and had never played with a kitten before.

"You're lucky Naima found you," Sahara whispered as her cousin returned, clutching three baby bottles.

"Milk?" Sahara asked.

"Kitten formula," Naima said, shaking the bottles.

She spent the next few minutes showing Sahara how Kitmeer's veterinarian had taught her to position the kittens on their bellies and hold their heads to feed them. As wild as it was for Naima to be harboring orphaned kittens, at least she'd consulted a vet.

"Do they have names?" Sahara asked.

"Tab'an. Meet Peri, Julnar, and Husnaya." Naima beamed.

"You're kidding."

"No. They're the perfect names. I found the qutat the same day we met the magical trio."

Their training with Umm Zalabya had been filled with ups and downs. Regardless of its outcome, Sahara had seen her share of the magical. But as the kitten in her lap began sucking, her tiny ears wiggling, Sahara couldn't imagine anything more extraordinary. She rubbed her shoulder against Naima's and smiled. "You were right about their names. They're perfect."

So Far, So Good

Sahara lay in bed for another hour, trying to fall asleep. In the midst of all that kitty cuteness, it had totally slipped her mind to tell Naima about what her wind had drawn in the sand. She'd asked it what her mother was trying to tell her, and it had shown her the letter *hā*. The same letter Yara and Umm Zalabya were born with on their heads. There had to be a connection between the hawa symbol and Sahara's dreams of her mom.

After a few frustrating minutes of listening to the sound of Naima's and Kitmeer's steady breathing while sleep evaded her, an idea thumped Sahara on the head. *The spyglass!* Its power to show what one desired to see could be the key to discovering the connection. Technically, she'd only promised to stay away from the lamp, not the rest of the treasures. And with the hamsa in check, securely taped to her shirt, what could go wrong?

Sahara's stomach flip-flopped the way it had when Amitu was on that "our family must eat healthier" kick and Sahara snuck into the kitchen at night for Fruity Pebbles, telling herself it was okay since there was *fruit* in the name. She'd had one spoonful before she thought she heard her aunt's footsteps and scrambled back to bed. But tonight, the fervor of her curiosity shoved the fear of getting caught out of the way.

Sahara needed to know what the hawa symbol had to do with her dreams since they were her mom's way of showing her things she needed to see, like the vial of spring water that would end up waking everyone up from the sharbat curse. If her mother was trying to communicate something that Sahara didn't understand yet—something that could help her find Vicky—then the spyglass could reveal it. And with only two days left to get Vicky back before Noora told Khaltu and Amitu she was missing, Sahara had to act now.

She rolled off her mattress as quietly as she could, but Kitmeer still heard her. He lifted his head. "Go back to sleep," Sahara whispered, shooting a glance at her cousin, who, luckily, was still sound asleep. Even though Naima would kill her for going to the chamber without her, it was risky enough without another person involved.

Sahara opened the door just enough to slither through. She could've kissed Khaltu right now as she entered the partially lit living room. With Uncle Gamal away, her aunt had insisted on leaving one of the table lamps on. "The apartment feels dark enough without him," she'd said.

Sahara tiptoed toward Khaltu Layla and Uncle Gamal's bedroom. She'd never had to be the one to sneak in and grab

Khaltu's keys from her purse before, but without Naima, it was her or no one.

She scrunched her face and turned the knob, praying the door wouldn't creak as she lightly pushed it open. *Phew!* Sahara mentally thanked the Rocket Chemical Company of San Diego, the inventors of WD-40 lubricant, for the door's smooth-moving hinges as she peeked inside the dark room. Her aunt's snores rattled into her ear. Clearly, Khaltu had inherited the skill from Sittu. But at least the noise would disguise any sound Sahara made.

She'd never actually been inside this bedroom before, though she'd seen it from the hallway and knew that the dresser where Khaltu kept her purse was on the right side, across from the bed. Sahara crept toward it, squinting in the moonlight until she made out the dark rectangular shape of her aunt's black purse. She undid the zipper slowly and then combed through its contents. Seconds later, her fingers met the cold metal of Khaltu's keys. *Please don't jingle. Please don't jingle,* she said over and over in her head as she carefully pulled them out of her aunt's bag. *Crap!* They'd jingled.

Khaltu let out a snort while she turned to her other side. Sahara braced herself for her aunt's wrath. Instead, the steady *zzz*'s of her snores returned. Sahara didn't waste any more time. She zipped toward the door, slipped through, shut it, then hurried out of the apartment in record time. Once outside, she let out the breath she'd been holding since she'd entered Khaltu's bedroom.

Hopefully, the second half of this escapade would be easier than the first. Her heart pounded like a heavyweight boxer at a punching bag as she made her way down the steps into the empty street, which glowed with the golden lights of the mosque across the way. The sweet smell of incense entered her nose. Maybe it was coming from the mosque or one of the apartments above. She'd better hurry before whoever was burning it showed up. Sahara unlocked the metal gate with the small brass key she'd seen her cousins use many times. As quietly as she could manage, she lifted the gate, crawled under, then lowered it back down.

Relax, she urged herself as she squinted again—no way was she turning on the overhead lights—and grabbed a lantern from one of the shelves behind the counter. She turned the switch to low mode and used the soft beam to see as she rotated the dials of the padlock to her mother's name. *A-M-A-N-I.* Sahara touched the amulet through her shirt. This duct tape was a miracle because she was minutes away from the chamber, and the hamsa was completely still.

Inhaling deeply, she opened the door to the refrigerator and crept inside. She turned her lantern to high, then crawled down the tunnel into the chamber, giving herself a mental pat on the back. *So far, so good.* She hurled that sentiment at her shaking hands. There was no need to be nervous. She'd be in and out of the chamber before anyone knew it, *and* with the information she had come for to boot.

Sahara quickly descended the rope ladder onto the stone

ground. And that's when she felt it. First, a soft pulse, then the warm glow. She reached under her collar and pressed the tape to her shirt. "The spyglass, not the lamp," she repeated over and over, faster and faster. But the amulet didn't hear her, or it purposely ignored her. Within seconds, the chamber turned sapphire blue as the hamsa tugged her toward the curio. The tape held, but it didn't matter. With a sizzle, the blaring light of the hamsa burned a hole through her shirt. Sahara tried to stuff the amulet back in, but it was too hot to touch.

No, no, no! This was exactly what was *not* supposed to happen. There was no emergency backup remote to help her fix this. The necklace stretched toward the hovering lamp, jamming itself onto the lid with a loud click. Sahara felt herself spinning away from the chamber. And then it stopped.

Sahara twisted back, falling to the chamber floor with a thud. The lamp rolled onto the carpet as the sickeningly sweet smell of incense smothered her.

"All this time, the lamp's been right under my nose," a voice slithered.

The familiar threatening tone sent shivers down Sahara's spine. She was afraid to turn and look, but she did.

El Ghoula stood at the bottom of the ladder, a sinister smile peeking through the hood of her gray cloak. Her face appeared harder, more angular than Sahara had remembered. The amulet's deep blue light only accentuated the coldness in her eyes and the dark veins bulging through her skin. The last time Sahara had seen her looking this . . . this scary was on the tower when Fayrouz was desperately trying to unlock the lamp. Vicky must be terrified.

"What have you done with my friend?" Sahara cried.

But the witch didn't answer her question. "The lamp's been right under my nose," El Ghoula repeated. "Behind an old refrigerator door *you* forgot to close." She sneered.

What were you thinking?! Sahara railed in her head. There'd be plenty of time later to beat herself up about her horrible mistake but not now. Now she had to make sure she locked the lamp. Her eyes darted to the ground, but before she had a chance to grab it, Fayrouz's wind sucked the lamp straight into her slithery grasp.

"No!" Sahara screamed and leaped for her. She had to get the amulet back on that lid. Only by the time she'd made it to the other side of the chamber, El Ghoula was gone in her cyclone of sand. Sahara flew past the spot where Fayrouz had been, hitting her head against the rocks of the chamber wall. The world went dark.

You Shouldn't Be Here

"Y ou shouldn't be here."

Sahara blinked her eyes open. At first, she only caught the glow of the chamber's flickering lanterns. Then, the hazy silhouette of a woman. The words must've come from her. Sahara wasn't sure if she was dreaming. As she lifted her head, a sharp sensation threatened to knock her out cold again.

"Easy, my desert rose," Umm Zalabya said, slowly helping Sahara sit up.

Sahara winced at the burning ache coming from her head. She raised her hand to it, relieved to see very little blood on her fingers when she brought them back down. As the pain subsided, the memories returned. Sahara cried out. "Fayrouz . . . she . . . she has the lamp."

"I know," the sorceress said, not sounding the least bit shocked.

"It wasn't locked," Sahara blurted, but Umm Zalabya still didn't flinch. "Wait. How are you even here? And why don't you look surprised?" Confusion gave way to a fury that blazed through the chamber. "You knew, didn't you? You knew El Ghoula was going to get it. And you did nothing to stop it!" Sahara yelled. "So much for not having your powers."

"I *don't* have my powers," Umm Zalabya asserted. "That is not a matter I would ever lie about. But you're right. I did know. I foresaw it before Fayrouz attacked me."

"Then why did you say nothing before... before I wound up here?" Sahara looked around at the pictures of her ancestors, and a terrible shame overtook her. The anger she had hurled at Umm Zalabya ricocheted back in her direction. "No, no, no!" Sahara's voice grew louder with every denial. "El Ghoula knows where the chamber is, and it's all my fault!"

Not only did the witch have the unlocked lamp, but everything that Sahara's family had worked so hard to protect had been compromised tonight because of her.

Umm Zalabya pressed her lips together. "It certainly does look grim."

"How could you say that now? You had the power to stop this. To warn me that this would happen if I came here, but you said nothing."

"Because it wasn't my place to stop you. It is never the seer's place to try to undo what was written from the beginning."

"So this is Allah's will again." Sahara snorted, leaning on the wall to stand. Her legs wobbled as she walked away from Umm Zalabya. "I don't think so. This was the will of a nasty witch and a seer who didn't have the guts to tell me the truth."

"And what about you? What is your role in all this? Did

you not come here after we warned you to stay away from the lamp?"

As much as the words stung, Umm Zalabya only said what Sahara felt. "This is my fault . . . I know. I thought I could come down here without having anything to do with the lamp. But I couldn't. I wasn't strong enough."

"Yet," Umm Zalabya said softly. "Not strong enough yet." Her voice rose with conviction. "This is not about fault but responsibility. This is your mistake to own. Had I steered you away from it, you wouldn't be able to do what comes next."

"What's that?" Sahara sniffled.

"Rescue your friend and get back the lamp." Umm Zalabya smiled.

"But couldn't I have saved Vicky without this happening? That's why you're training us, isn't it?"

"Certainly," Umm Zalabya answered. "But who's to say the blows you've taken tonight aren't equally important? True sorcery isn't just about following steps. You're not baking a cake. You're harnessing the magic of the wind. And you can't learn to ride the hawa's gentle breeze until you find your way home after being swept away and knocked down by its fierce gusts."

No kidding. Sahara had definitely been clobbered by some ferocious winds tonight.

"Those blows are not for the faint-hearted." Umm Zalabya's eyes darted from the hole the hamsa had burned through

Sahara's shirt to the scrape on her head. "But necessary, for life ebbs and flows between fortune and misfortune. The latter, though often harrowing, leaves us with an unwavering gratitude, ready to spill out of us when the light of fortune shines on us again. Our mistakes, if we allow them, can fortify us. Both in here"—the sorceress pointed to her head, then to her heart—"and in *here.*"

Sahara raised her hand to her own heart. "It's the here part I still have trouble with. I thought I was getting better at it after last summer. But when things spin out of control"—Sahara pointed to her head—"here feels safe. I can come up with a plan and carry it out."

"And how did that work out tonight?"

Talk about kicking someone when they're down. "Ouch." Sahara winced. "I already said it was my fault."

"That's not what I meant. Last year, you were able to lock the lamp in the face of a powerful witch because you leaned into your heart. But that is a choice you must make every day—in the big moments, like at the top of the tower, and the little moments, like a talk with a friend."

"I'm trying . . . I tried." Sahara hesitated. "It's just so hard. The amulet and the lamp are impossible to keep apart."

Umm Zalabya held up a finger, signaling Sahara to wait. She walked over to the curio and removed the spyglass, then held it up to Sahara's eye. "Look," the sorceress commanded.

Sahara pressed her eye to the glass. At first, all she saw was a magnified version of the curio's brass handle.

"Ask it what you came down here to discover," Umm Zalabya advised.

Sahara nodded and then mouthed, "What do you want me to know, Mom?" Within seconds, her mother came into view with the amulet in her hand.

Sapphire blue shrouded the chamber as the hamsa pulled Amani toward the lamp. Strangely, the light fizzled out at the last minute. The lamp clanged to the carpet in the darkness.

"You shouldn't be here." A woman's voice echoed behind Amani.

As the torches in the chamber flickered on one by one, Amani swung around. "Umm Zalabya," she cried, racing to pick up the lamp and put it back in the curio. "I'm relieved it's you, but how did you know about this place when I didn't?"

"I take it your mother is unaware you're here." The sorceress's deep voice may have been the same, but there were way fewer lines on her face.

"Yes, but I . . . I had to come. I know the fortune teller at Khan el Khalili said this was meant for my daughter." Amani held up the amulet. "But it started shaking in the night and pulling me down to the shop, to the old refrigerator Baba bought. I used Mama's key, the one she and only Layla have, to get in." Amani scanned the room, her mouth agape. "Ya Allah! What is this place, and what is this lamp?" she marveled.

"What does your heart tell you?" Umm Zalabya smiled softly.

"Magic," Amani said with the same wondrous tone Sahara

had heard Naima use countless times. "Like in Baba's stories." She spun her head toward the curio. "Does the lamp have a jinni inside?"

Umm Zalabya paused before she responded. "Its magic is extremely potent, which is why the hamsa you hold—an amulet meant for your daughter—must keep it locked. In the wrong hands, its consequences could be disastrous." She pointed to the lamp. "The sorcery inside must not be unleashed again."

A bell seemed to go off in Amani's head. "It wasn't *always* locked, then?"

"I'm afraid not."

Amani stared at Umm Zalabya's somber face. "So whatever's in there is dangerous—khatir enough to need to stay locked with this." She held up the hamsa. "And yet you want me to pass it on to my daughter? To put her at risk? Why didn't you tell me this when I came to see you after the market?"

"Because despite the peril, it is her destiny. One day, when the moon and Saturn align, the two that must not join will become one, unlocking what has been hidden in the dark. And it will be your daughter who will stand between us and that darkness. You must make sure she gets it."

"That's why its glow went out." Amani's face fell. "It isn't meant for me."

Umm Zalabya raised her chin. "While that may be true, do not underestimate your role. For the love that you felt after the fortune teller gave it to you—the love and certainty I saw in your eyes when you showed it to me and said it was for your daughter—they will light the sky ablaze one day."

Amani cocked an eyebrow at the sorceress. "How do you know all of this? Have you foreseen it?"

"We all have our parts to play," Umm Zalabya answered. "Generations of your family have kept the lamp safe in this chamber, guided in their duty by generations of mine. We are connected." She waved a finger from herself to Amani. "That's how I knew you were here."

Amani's cheeks grew red. "Why didn't Mama tell me about this place? How could she keep a secret like this?"

"Because keeping it secret until the next generation is ready to receive it has been the legacy of all these women around you." Umm Zalabya walked over to the paintings and stopped at one of a young woman with raven hair peeking out from under a violet headscarf. "Meet Morgana. It all began with her."

"Morgana?" Amani hurried over to the seer's side and studied the portrait. "The only Morgana I know of is the one from the story of Ali Baba—" She stopped, then gasped. "If that lamp is real, then she could've been too." Amani covered her mouth, stifling an excited giggle. "Are you saying my family is descended from *her*? Everyone talks about Ali Baba, but I know from Baba's stories that Morgana was the real hero. She saved him from the thieves."

"I have been saying that for years." Umm Zalabya chuckled.

"So if my family's legacy started with Morgana, whose did yours begin with?"

"Sitt Husnaya." Umm Zalabya beamed.

Amani's eyes bulged. "She was real too?" she asked, then raced over to a small sack on the ground by the chamber's entry, noticing the rope ladder for the first time. She shook her head. "There's a sillim? I nearly killed myself jumping down."

"I would've told you if you'd asked." Umm Zalabya shrugged.

Amani mumbled a few choice words under her breath as she pulled out the leather journal from her sack. "I've always had a theory about Sitt Husnaya and the awful sorcerer who terrorized Ala el-Din to get his wicked hands on the lamp." She rummaged through the pages. "Layla says my idea is ridiculous, but Baba thinks I might be right." Amani stopped at a section in the middle of the journal. "Sitt Husnaya was born in North Africa. So was the evil sorcerer." She pointed to the bottom of the page. "And in each of their tales, they're both described as possessing great magic. Tab'an, she used hers for good and he for evil. But when I listen to their stories, though they have nothing to do with each other, my heart clenches in a similar way. I swear they're connected."

Umm Zalabya waved the notion off. "Husnaya was never married."

"Not as husband and wife." A smile crept over Amani's face. "As brother and sister. Because the khalifa wasn't only Husnaya's father, but the sorcerer's too." She paused and took a deep breath, then came back with "And that would mean the sorcerer was also alive!"

"You are very clever. Let's hope your daughter is the same but asks fewer questions." Umm Zalabya winked.

Amani shut the journal and peered at the sorceress. "You promise you will help me keep her safe?"

Umm Zalabya brought her hands to her head and bowed. "I swear."

The spyglass went black.

"No, wait. Not yet. It wasn't finished," Sahara protested as Umm Zalabya lowered the glass from her eye.

"It's not a movie." The sorceress snorted. "I wanted you to see that you are not the only one who has fallen victim to the magnetism between the amulet and the lamp."

"I guess not." Sahara tightened her ponytail and thought about what else she'd witnessed in the spyglass. "My mother was right about Husnaya and the sorcerer—Fayrouz's ancestor, that is."

Umm Zalabya nodded. "Amani was an expert at listening with her heart. That's how she detected the connection that lay hidden underneath her baba's words."

"A connection she clearly wanted me to know," Sahara said. "She's been trying to show me the moment she asked you about it, but I kept waking up from the dream before she had the chance. Which means it's gotta be important. *Why*, though?" She paced around the chamber, her mind buzzing. "If your ancestor and Fayrouz's were brother and sister, that means . . ." Sahara stopped dead in her tracks, the realization hitting her in her chest like a high-speed baseball. *Oh no.* "That means you and El Ghoula are related."

Umm Zalabya pursed her lips. "I'm afraid so."

"I should've seen it sooner." Sahara slapped her thigh. "No wonder Fayrouz can blast wind out of her hand." The letter *hā* flashed in her head, clicking more pieces into place. "And that's why my wind showed me the hawa symbol during divination practice." Sahara had only seen the shape on Umm Zalabya's and Yara's heads, but she was now certain El Ghoula also had it. Her gaze flitted to Umm Zalabya's hair, mostly concealed by her headscarf. "Fayrouz was born with the *hā* mark too, wasn't she?"

"All the children of the wind—the descendants of Sitt Husnaya and her brother Hassan—are," Umm Zalabya replied simply.

Hassan. Sahara had never considered that the wicked sorcerer had once had a name.

Umm Zalabya edged closer to Sahara. "There is a silver lining here."

Sahara had always thought of herself as more of a glass-half-full-than-empty person, but she was failing to see the bright side of this situation. "What could be good about you and Fayrouz being from the same family?"

"Nothing," Umm Zalabya said, but then her mouth curled into an unexpected smile. "Up until now. For the origins of the magic I have shared with you over the last few days and

El Ghoula's are the same. While Husnaya and the sorcerer followed two very different paths, their foundations were rooted in the same principles of hawa sorcery. All this is to reiterate what I told you when we started train . . ."

A light bulb went off in Sahara's head. "You've been teaching us the only magic that can beat Fayrouz—her own. That's what my mom was trying to tell me." Tears welled in Sahara's eyes, blurring her vision. Once again, her mother was bolstering her with the conviction she needed to take on Fayrouz.

"Precisely." The sorceress gave a definitive nod.

Sahara prayed that between her mom's faith, Umm Zalabya's lessons, and Yara's newfound power, they could defeat El Ghoula. "Does Yara know you both are related to Fayrouz?"

"For years, the relationship between Husnaya and the sorcerer has remained a secret few have known about in my family. My ancestors didn't exactly want the knowledge of how their cherished magic had been dangerously exploited for vile self-serving purposes—by one of the children of the wind, nonetheless—to get out. But if I am to send you into battle, I must arm you with the greatest weapon—the truth. I told Yara earlier."

"How did she take it?" Sahara asked.

"She grew up hearing these stories. I think deep down she always knew."

"You mean in here"—Sahara pointed to her heart, then her head—"before here." She smiled at Umm Zalabya and walked over to Morgana's portrait, noticing the silver chain around her neck for the first time. "I wish I could talk to her. I don't think anybody else knows how I feel."

Umm Zalabya squeezed her shoulder. "Your duty as the amulet wielder is unique, but you are *not* alone. We all have our individual roles to play in this life, and it is natural to feel isolated by them. Ironically, it is the universality of this loneliness that connects us. Not one of the women who have come before you hasn't felt it. The same will be true for those who come after you."

"I just wish there was a way for me to wield the amulet without it wielding me," Sahara groaned. "I hate not being able to stop the hamsa and lamp from coming together."

"Your duty is not the whole of who you are," Umm Zalabya asserted. "It's important, but it is a drop compared to the ocean of your spirit. The less you let your responsibility *define you*, and the more you *define it*, the more you can fulfill it." The sorceress stopped, then came back with gusto. "Now, what's next, my desert rose? And please don't tell me it's another question."

"Nope." Sahara grinned and hurried toward the ladder. "A plan."

Sitt Husnaya

966 CE

As the last pilgrims exited the palace gates with their heads down, Husnaya climbed to the top of her oak tree. No one would be sent looking for her this evening. Mama and Jidda had retired to their chambers, sick with grief. The army was out scouring the woods for the afreet, who hadn't been seen since he'd disappeared this afternoon. And Hassan was gone.

Tears dripped from Husnaya's eyes, making small puddles on the branch's leaves below her. She yearned for the days when she and Hassan had climbed their trees together and named what they saw in the clouds. Sometimes the two trees' limbs were so intertwined they looked like one.

Husnaya had no idea where Hassan had gone or if he would ever return, but she was certain of one thing. They would never be able to stare innocently at the clouds again. Just as she thought this, a warm wind circulated around her and then inside her. She let it travel through her hands and toward the sky, where it began to shape the clouds into a vision of the future. Before she could make it out, a movement at the base of the tree made her jump.

"Husnaya," Zain called.

"Up here." Husnaya climbed down, meeting her brother on one of the middle branches.

His usual sly look had been wiped away by all he'd seen today and replaced with sorrow. She yearned to erase it from his face.

Zain lifted his thumb to his lips, then quickly dropped it.

"It's all right. I won't tell Mama."

He shook his head. "The future khalifa can't suck his thumb."

Ya Allah. Zain was right. With the khalifa and his heir dead, and Hassan missing, Zain would have to assume the throne at the age of ten.

"I'm scared, Husnaya." His voice shook.

"Me too." Husnaya wished she had something more encouraging to say. She took hold of her brother's hand and said what it had been too late to say to Hassan. "But you are not alone. And neither am I, because I have you."

He flashed a smile.

"And I know you won't let anything happen to our city."

"How do you know that?" he asked.

"Because I have seen it in the wind." She pointed to the pink-and-violet dusk sky. "See that boy with a crown stretching high into the heavens?"

"Is that me?"

Husnaya nodded. "You will make Baba proud."

"And is that you on a horse next to me?"

"I believe it is."

"I'm glad I never told Mama that Aziza was training you and Hassan."

"You knew?"

"I know everything that happens in my palace," he said, deepening his voice to sound older.

Despite her grief, a chuckle escaped Husnaya's lips.

He tapped her head with his hand. "I dub thee Sitt Husnaya, the greatest sorceress in all the land."

The words pierced through her heart.

Zain continued, "Do you pledge to be my supreme adviser and stand by my side as we protect the people of our city?"

"I do." Husnaya bowed her head to the future khalifa. "But won't Mama be upset with you? She doesn't want me to practice magic."

"All must yield to the khalifa's authority." He stuck his tongue out. "Even mothers." He turned to take one more look at the clouds before sliding down the tree.

As the future khalifa ran toward the palace, Husnaya stared at the setting sun and inhaled. A gentle air with an underlying hint of hope flowed through her. It was true that today had been horrific. If she'd seen it in the winds a year ago, she would've done anything to change it. But if it hadn't happened, Zain wouldn't have become who he was meant to be, and neither would she. She could finally show her sorcery.

Because her brother and their city needed it more than they needed outdated traditions.

She let the breeze flow out of her hand and hoped it reached Aziza, telling her she had not died in vain. All her sacrifices had been for a reason. And Husnaya would spend the rest of her life honoring all Aziza had stood for.

But first, she had to get out of this tree. There was an afreet to capture. And there was no way she'd be able to catch him on the speed of her two legs alone. She'd take her carpet if it weren't so slow. Though even if she managed to get it to move faster, she needed something sturdier. Something the beast couldn't fling with a swipe of his hand.

Husnaya lifted her gaze to the image in the sky. The answer had been there all along. "Almaz," Husnaya blew into the air.

The tree's trunk vibrated, its leaves and branches quivering as flashes of silver zipped through the underbrush. Husnaya's heart pounded faster and faster. The beat of the horse's hooves grew closer and closer.

Husnaya didn't know what would happen next, but she made a last promise to Aziza. *No more hiding.*

When the hisana's silver tail swished under the tree, Husnaya slid down into the open. She kissed Almaz's head.

"It's time we get you a saddle."

PART FOUR
You Are Not Alone

39

Vicky's Song

Sahara let out a quiet sigh of relief when she returned upstairs to find Khaltu and Naima still asleep. She glanced at her watch—3:03 a.m. As exhausted as she was, there was no way she'd be able to settle down with her mind racing between her catastrophic run-in with Fayrouz, seeing her mother in the spyglass, and Umm Zalabya's mic-drop revelation about her family's ties.

She threw on a new shirt, grabbed her backpack, and headed to Fanta's room. As Sahara peeked at the stars through the balcony's open shutters, she thought about how her dad and Amitu often said she reminded them of her mother. She had seen that for herself tonight. Sahara smiled, remembering all the curious questions Amani had asked Umm Zalabya, many of which she would've asked herself. Since the day she'd learned about the chamber, she'd always suspected her mom had known about it. Though, she hadn't guessed that her mother had also opened the jewelry box. No wonder there was a drawing of the hamsa in the journal with the prophecy underneath.

So much had happened before Sahara was even born that was responsible for where she was today. So many women had gotten her here. Umm Zalabya was right—she'd never been alone. And neither was Vicky.

Despite the unfortunate turn tonight's events had taken, Sahara had come back from the chamber with an empowered resolve. She removed the pyramid pad from her backpack and turned to Vicky's letter, tearing off El Ghoula's nasty scribbles at the bottom. This was her notebook, and she would no longer allow Fayrouz to keep her from using it. It was time to plan *Operation: Rescue Vicky*.

Sahara flipped to a clean page and jotted down the five steps: Figure out where Fayrouz was hiding Vicky, get there fast, free her, locate the lamp and lock it, and get out alive. The success of the last three hinged on one major unknown— would Fayrouz be there and get in their way? With the unlocked lamp in her possession, El Ghoula didn't have to wait for the moonless night. She could already be anywhere in time right now, so Sahara had to act fast. But not alone.

This wouldn't be a solo mission. Sahara couldn't—didn't want to—do this on her own. Even though she'd summoned the trio and agreed to the hawa training, she wasn't sure she'd ever truly accepted help. She'd gone through the motions of asking for it, but all the while, she'd pushed it away. If the operation stood a chance, she'd need her cousins and Yara on the ground with her and the backing of the army of brave women who'd come before her. Not to mention Peri and Julnar, who had promised to stay close. And, of course, Umm Zalabya would be watching and guiding from her rooftop garden.

Sahara took a deep breath and shut her eyes. A soft breeze touched her cheek. She brought her hands to the middle of her forehead as she'd seen both Umm Zalabya and Husnaya do. Channeling Sittu's stillness, Sahara listened to the wind. And with it came a voice. *Vicky's.* She was singing, but there was something else. Something behind her friend's song. Sahara let the sound settle into the space between her thoughts. *Hoot, hoot, hoot.*

40

Good News, Bad News

The sun's upper rim had barely reached the horizon as Sahara gathered her cousins and Yara—who she was happy to find without her helmet—and headed to the garden, where Umm Zalabya was already waiting.

"What was so important that you woke me up and dragged me across Shobra?" Fanta grumbled, rubbing his eyes.

Sahara walked in circles, barely able to contain the jolt of energy she had gotten when she'd discovered where her best friend was. "Trust me. You're gonna wanna hear what I have to say. I'll start with the good news first. I know where Fayrouz is keeping Vicky!"

"That's amazing!" Naima clapped her brother on the back. "Are you awake now?"

Fanta was speechless, but any hint of exhaustion had left his face.

"Izay?" Yara leaned in closer. "How did you figure it out?'

"I was looking out the balcony, tuning in to the wind." Sahara shot a smile at Umm Zalabya. "And then I heard her singing that 'On My Own' song she always listens to. But there was another sound too." Sahara cupped her hands around her mouth. *"Hoot, hoot."*

"An owl?" Yara asked. "And then what?"

"More owls." Sahara smirked.

Yara cocked her head, clearly confused by what Sahara was getting at.

"It wasn't the sound of just one or two owls," Sahara explained. "It was the sound of *a lot* of them together, just like the night at—"

"El Muizz Street!" Yara spat out.

"Remember that abandoned old mansion? Bayt Sss-oool-taaan," Sahara said in the same creepy way Fanta had after dinner at Khalid's Café.

Naima screwed up her face. "Tab'an, El Ghoula would make that decrepit house her lair." She made for the door. "Yalla. We have to get there."

"Slow down." Fanta grabbed the hood of her sweatshirt and pulled her back, then turned to Sahara. "What's the bad news?"

Sahara's stomach twisted into a double knot. She looked to Umm Zalabya, who gave her an encouraging nod. It was time to own what had happened earlier tonight. "I snuck into the chamber, and my amulet went cuckoo again and unlocked the lamp; then Fayrouz came in because I forgot to close the talaga, and now the witch has the unlocked lamp and Vicky," she blurted, not stopping for air.

There was silence as they processed everything she'd said.

Fanta was the first to speak. "The super tape didn't hold?" he asked.

"It held, all right. But the hamsa burned a hole right through my other shirt to get to the lamp."

Sahara was waiting for Naima to chastise Fanta and her about their duct tape shenanigans. Instead, she just muttered, "El Ghoula knows where the chamber is."

"I'm so sorry." Sahara's voice cracked.

"*I'm* the one that should be sorry." Naima ran over and hugged her. "Did Fayrouz do that to your head?" she asked, not waiting for an answer. "I should've been there with you. I've seen the way the amulet pulls you to the lamp. It's not your fault."

Sahara's heart smiled at her cousin's understanding. "Thank you for saying that, but it was my fault. My *mistake*," she corrected, glancing at Umm Zalabya. "And now all that's left—"

"Is we fix it together." Yara laid her hand over Sahara's.

"Good, because I can't do it alone."

"Of course not. You'd be lost without me," Fanta teased, placing his fingers atop Yara's. His sister quickly joined in on the fun.

"A hand sandwich." Sahara giggled, then mouthed, "Thank you," to Umm Zalabya, who was busy looking up at the sky, but Sahara knew she'd seen it anyway.

The sorceress smiled her toothless smile as she bowed her head.

Sahara could've basked in this much-needed support all day. But they didn't have all day. "Naima's right. We have to get to Vicky now. There's no time to wake Noora, so we'll need another cover."

"Nenna can do it, right?" Yara asked, gazing imploringly at her grandmother.

But Umm Zalabya was already on board. "Tab'an. I'll call Layla and Malak later and tell them I invited you over for an early breakfast. And there's no need to worry about Zalabya. He has been practically sleeping at the museum since the sword disappeared."

The sword! Sahara always suspected Fayrouz had stolen it, but now it was more than a hunch. Husnaya and the sorcerer had *both* been the khalifa's children, which meant the sorcerer had means of getting hold of the emerald sword and taking it to Baghdad. And El Ghoula had reclaimed it on his behalf one thousand years later. Sahara would have to run her theory by Umm Zalabya later, but for now, she headed for the door.

"Where are you going? We don't have a car, and no taxis are running this early," Fanta yelled from behind.

"No, but we have something better." Naima's voice bubbled with excitement.

Fanta shook his head and groaned, "Not again. Besides, I

thought Fayrouz had blocked us from using the treasures to find her location."

Sahara turned on her heel. "She did. But now that we know the location, we can get there," she told him, turning her attention to Yara. "How do you feel about carpets that fly?"

"The faster, the better." Yara beamed.

Yara had already proven to be pretty cool. But Yara without her helmet, the hawa symbol on her head out in the open—*amazing.*

WITH THE CHAMBER compromised, Sahara refused to leave any of the treasures behind. Even though Fayrouz already had the lamp and didn't seem to know about the rest, Sahara wasn't taking any chances. *Better safe than sorry.* She raced to the curio and packed the spyglass and the healing vial in her backpack before she joined her cousins and Yara on the rug.

"Take us to Bayt Sultan," Naima told the carpet, then snapped.

The rug remained glued to the floor. Naima snapped again—but still, nothing. She even howled at it like Kitmeer had done, earning her confused looks from her brother and Yara, but zero reaction from the carpet.

"I thought you said this would work," Fanta whispered to Sahara.

Sahara's shoulders slumped with doubt until she remembered that the Sultans weren't the first owners of the mansion.

It had originally belonged to a Turkish family for many years. She turned to Yara. "Do you remember the name of the family that first owned the mansion?"

Yara scratched her head. "I think it was Aydin. Why?"

"Maybe our ancient carpet only knows the house by its ancient name." Sahara grinned.

Naima looked back. "That's genius," she praised, then turned to the carpet and commanded, "Take us to Bayt Aydin!"

As Naima's snap echoed through the chamber, the rug rumbled underneath them. Sahara let out a relieved breath, sucking another one in quickly as the carpet reared back and then took off with a jolt. They zipped through the tunnel, twisting and turning at lightning speed. When they got to the talaga, they shrank to a fraction of their size and made it past the shop's gate, only to return to normal as the carpet catapulted into the sky.

Sahara peeked at Yara during the latter. She'd expected to see a look of exhilaration, possibly fear, on Yara's face. But her eyes were soft, and her lips were parted into a gentle smile.

The carpet zoomed past Shobra and over the 6th of October Bridge, reaching the round towers of Bab el-Futuh in less than a minute.

"I see it!" Naima pointed to the mansion, which didn't look any less ominous in the early hours of morning than it had at night. It might not have been as massive as the museum, but its eerily looming presence stood out among the other homes on the street.

The carpet descended toward the courtyard, suddenly jerking back as if it had crashed into something.

"It can't land," Fanta yelled.

Sahara looked around in case she'd missed some tall fortress. But there was nothing.

"There must be some invisible barrier around it—" Naima started as the carpet tried to land again. Whatever was blocking them pushed back harder this time, catapulting Fanta off the rug and plummeting him toward the mansion's gates.

"Fantaaaa!"

41

Chess Hopping

Every one of the trillions of cells in Sahara's body screamed as Fanta dove to the ground. Her terror was echoed in Naima's shrill cry. Sahara covered her eyes, unable to tolerate the inevitable. Naima and Yara must have done the same, for there was a second of silence before Fanta's body should've hit the wall surrounding the mansion. Only there was no thud. When Sahara lowered her hands, she couldn't believe what she saw. Fanta was hovering about five feet above the entry gate.

"Ya Allah," Naima cried.

Sahara's gaze darted from Fanta to Yara, whose fanned-out hand was aimed at her cousin, its wind vibrating with a subtle whoosh. She'd saved Fanta. Sahara watched in awe as Yara curved her hand down, guiding the hawa to lay Fanta gently on the ground.

Naima must've then directed the carpet to land by the entry because it turned away from the courtyard and floated down to the sidewalk. She ran off. "Ahmed, are you all right?"

He flipped onto his back, his face pale. "Was I flying?" he asked.

His sister sighed in relief. "You could say that. Yara's hawa was your wings."

Fanta sat up and smiled at Yara, his face regaining some of its color. "Alhamdulillah for the hawa."

But Yara hadn't heard him. Her eyes were fixed on her shaking hand. Sahara squeezed it gently and brought it down to Yara's side. "You're okay. Better than okay. Thanks to you, Fanta isn't hurt."

Yara blinked several times, then nodded, slowly recognizing that she was all right. They all were, thanks to her.

Naima helped her brother to his feet. "What now?" she asked as Sahara jumped off the carpet. After Fanta's close call with gravity, there was no way she was risking getting back on. The carpet was no match for whatever convoluted no-fly-zone spell Fayrouz had cast on the mansion. When Yara hopped off, Sahara turned to the rug. "Don't go too far. We'll need you to get out of here when it's time to return home."

As their ride flew away, Sahara approached the iron gate. She had no idea if it was locked. "We'll just have to try the old-fashioned way." She shrugged, giving it a shove. It opened with a squeak. Sahara wasted no time. She slid inside and hurried toward the courtyard. Less than ten feet in, she tripped at the foot of a stone path.

Yara gestured to a loose stepping stone, the likely culprit, and the ones around it. "They're higher than all the others."

Sahara bent down, counting a total of nine large raised pavers, each engraved with a faded figure.

"Do you see something?" Naima asked.

"Numbers, I think." Sahara headed back to the wall and hoisted herself up. From this vantage point, she saw that the elevated stones formed a three-by-three grid. And she had a feeling that was by design. She jumped down and raced over to the start of the path, reaching her fingers into the courtyard. The air pulsed back, stopping her hand from going any farther. "I knew it! It's some sort of giant magic square."

"But aren't those only supposed to be on pendants like the one Umm Zalabya made Mama?" Fanta asked.

"They can be on anything"—Naima stared down at the ground—"as long as they're made correctly and at the right astrological time."

"And this one was made to create an invisible barricade," Sahara said. "One that wouldn't let the carpet in up there and won't let us in down here either."

Sahara crouched down again, squinting to make out the numbers. "The arqam are not arranged correctly. This row"—she pointed to the closest one—"adds up to eleven when it should add up to fifteen." Sahara remembered what Umm Zalabya had said about some sorcerers scrambling the numbers in the square so their spells couldn't be reversed. "Fayrouz must have mixed them up to throw us off. If we can get them back in the right order, maybe we can summon the wind with the words Umm Zalabya taught us to reverse El

Ghoula's magic"—Sahara crossed her fingers—"and bring down the barrier."

"But how do we get the numbers back in the right order?" Yara paused to scan the square. There was a slight quiver in her voice when she spoke again. "And what happens if we don't do it right?"

Yara had a point. Maybe they should plot it out on paper first and make all their mistakes where there were no consequences other than losing time. Sahara yanked the pad out of her backpack and began scribbling down the current configuration of the squares. "The number one isn't in the position of the wind. It should go where the three is." She pointed to the stone in the center of the third column. "Now I just have to remember where the other eight numbers go." Sahara wished she had memorized the square she'd made yesterday.

"That should be easy," Fanta remarked, making the three girls shoot confused stares in his direction. "I know I didn't get all the math stuff, but when I was looking at Sahara's square last night, I noticed something."

"Bit harag? *You* studied Sahara's square?" Naima asked, in complete shock.

"I'm not joking," he answered his sister. "The way the numbers were ordered made me think of the chess moves I use to beat Khalu Omar." He grinned.

"Fanta Saeed, you're full of surprises." Sahara kissed her cousin's cheek, making him go from grinning to full-on beaming.

"Don't let it get to your head." His sister gave him a playful shove, but Sahara could tell from the smile on her face that she was impressed.

Sahara passed the pad to Fanta. "I'll move the number one to the hawa position, and then you tell me where the others go."

Fanta nodded as she lifted the first stone. It was heavy, quicksand heavy.

Everyone ran over to help, but it was no use. The pavers weighed a ton.

"There's gotta be another way." Sahara huffed. As she eyed the square, an idea came to her. "What if it's me that should be moving, not the stones?" So instead of trying to carry number one to where it was supposed to go, Sahara hopped there. In a flash, the number three transformed into a one.

"It's working!" Yara and Naima cheered as Sahara jumped to number two.

Fanta peered at the paper. "Now move like a knight—take one step up and two to the right. That's where itnin should go."

Sahara had played so much hopscotch in elementary school that she had no problem bouncing around the square as Fanta directed her to move the way different chess pieces did. One hop at a time, the square came together until only the seven and nine had to swap places. Sahara took a deep breath as she made her final leap. It had worked. *Phew!* Now that all the numbers were in the right place, it was time for the last step.

Fanta raised his hand toward the courtyard, but Naima

heaved it back. "Not yet," Naima railed. "She still has to say the mystical words."

Sahara closed her eyes and tuned out everything but the breath entering and leaving her nose. Slowly, she shifted her attention to the air around her and whispered to the hawa, "Arqam mashura, el hawa hakeem. Take down El Ghoula's barricade."

Within seconds, the stepping stones lowered underneath her, settling into the rest of the path, as an audible zap sounded around them.

She turned to Fanta. "Now."

Fanta nodded his understanding and threw a karate chop over the once loose pavers. "It's down." He smiled.

Yes! Math had never looked so good.

Naima and Yara high-fived each other, then ran over to Sahara.

"You did it." Yara clapped.

"Of course she did. My best cousin can do anything." Naima winked.

Sahara's eyes flitted around her *Operation: Rescue Vicky* team. "*We* did it," she told them, doing Vicky's signature moonwalk-robot happy dance in her head.

"What are we waiting for?" Sahara raced through the courtyard. Its stiff trees and shrubs seemed to let down their guard, swaying with the breeze that blew through them. As she sprinted around the empty fountain, out of nowhere, it rumbled and began spurting water. Seconds later, the gate leading to the front door swung open. On its own.

Sahara walked through cautiously, coming to a stop before the tall arched wooden doors. She had no idea what was on the other side, but as long as there was a strong chance that Vicky was there, she had to enter. Her hands shaking, she pushed open the door and tiptoed in. Once everyone had made it through, a gust came from behind, nearly knocking them down and blasting the door shut. The lattice windows on the inside were boarded up, swallowing any light trying to enter and leaving the children in complete darkness.

42

Peri's Candle

Trying to find Vicky in this creepy old mansion was going to be challenging enough, but trying to find her in this creepy old mansion in the *dark* would be next to impossible.

Sahara jumped as something slid across her leg. She stifled a scream.

"What was that?" she whispered, even though it was pointless. With the way that door had slammed, if El Ghoula was home, she already knew they were here.

"Sorry, Sahara. It was just me," Naima muttered back. "I was reaching into my pocket."

"For what?" Fanta asked under his breath.

"For my flashlight." Naima clicked its button, but nothing happened. *Click, click, click.* No light.

In case you ever find yourself in the dark. "Peri's candle," Sahara remembered. She'd put it in her backpack after they'd returned from the past. She reached into the front pocket, pawing through until she felt the smooth wax of the candle.

The moment she drew it out into the open, a mini flame flickered on. It barely lit Fanta's frown.

"How is that little shamea going to help us find our way around this huge—" Fanta started.

One by one, each of the countless tapered candles in the house began to burn. Though most were partially melted, together, their glow illuminated every inch of the large, empty hall the children stood in. Not to mention all the dust in the corners and cobwebs on the ceiling.

"You were saying?" Naima shot her brother her very practiced "I told you so" look.

Yara sighed in relief. "I'm so glad you remembered to bring that."

"Peri gave it to us in case we found ourselves in the dark, and I never ignore anything that begins with 'in case.'" Sahara grinned. "Now we just have to figure out where to start." She circled her finger around the endless number of closed doors above them when she heard the front door creak open. Her heart caught in her throat.

"Who's . . . who's there?" Yara sputtered, not daring to look.

Sahara's entire body went full-on wobble like a giant gummy bear trying to walk. She grabbed on to Naima to steady herself, then very slowly turned around.

"I knew I'd find you here."

"Baba?" Yara spun toward the door and asked, her voice drenched with panic and confusion. "What are you doing here?"

"I should ask you the same thing," he answered in his infamous monotone.

Yara's eyes darted between Sahara and her cousins, pleading for help.

Sahara didn't hesitate. It was sad how easily lying came for her these days. She'd commit to quitting *after* they found Vicky. For now, she put on a fake smile and said, "I can explain. Ever since Amitu pointed out this place, I've been dying—"

"I should ask you the same thing," Yara's father repeated.

"Baba, you just said—"

"I should ask you the same thing . . . I should ask you the same thing . . . I should ask you the same thing," he continued in the same strange automated tone.

"What's the matter with him?" Yara cried.

"He's glitching." Sahara approached him slowly, sliding behind him. A red glow pulsed in the middle of his back. "Er. I don't think this is your father," Sahara said as the light flashed on and off even faster, until it finally went out.

Zzzzp! Zzzzp!

Yara's father, or whatever was supposed to be him, fell to the floor and shook. Orange sparks flew out of him, followed by a thick red smoke. It enveloped his body until Sahara could no longer see him.

"Baba!" Yara ran toward him. Her movement dispersed the cloud, revealing an empty spot where her father had been. "Where did he go?" she screamed, patting the floor frantically.

Sahara and her cousins hurried over and knelt beside her.

"Did you hear what Sahara said?" Naima spoke softly. "That *wasn't* your father."

Yara lifted her head. "What?" she asked, wiping her nose with the back of her hand.

"That wasn't your father," Fanta repeated gently.

Yara looked toward Sahara.

Sahara pressed her lips together and shook her head. "Definitely not your dad. That was some kind of cursed droid created by Fayrouz's sorcery. Maybe he was connected to the barrier around the mansion, and when we disarmed it by fixing the magic square, he . . . he malfunctioned."

"Then where is Baba? The real one?"

"I'm guessing somewhere in here," Sahara said, looking around. "I wouldn't put it past El Ghoula to have kidnapped him too."

"El Ghoula." Naima and Fanta seethed simultaneously.

"So if we find Vicky, we can find Baba?" Yara sniffled.

"I think so," Sahara answered, jumping to her feet. "There's no sense in tiptoeing around. If the witch didn't know we arrived before, she does now. That's if she's even here."

Sahara rubbed the hamsa. "The amulet isn't shaking or pulling, which tells me neither Fayrouz nor the lamp is nearby." Sahara wasn't sure which was worse—having to face off with El Ghoula or knowing the witch was away, traveling through time to bring back a dangerous jinniya.

After searching several dusty empty rooms with no sign of Vicky, Sahara turned the knob to the door at the end of the hall.

"Ya Allah. A library!" Naima marveled at the towering shelves of leather-bound books that lined the entire perimeter of the room.

As much as Sahara knew Naima could stay here for hours—maybe days—going through all the books, they had to keep moving. Sahara gestured for them to head out. They still had another level of the mansion left to check.

"Fine," Naima groaned. "But if we have time, I'm coming back for that one." She shot a woeful glance at the thick book lying on the circular table in the middle of the library.

"We're here on a rescue mission, not to pillage the place." Her brother scoffed as Sahara raced up the curving staircase. Despite being short on breath, a shock wave of adrenaline powered her legs. Yara's father and Vicky had to be on this floor. Sahara zipped from empty room to empty room until she reached the fortieth door in the house. In so many of her mother's folktales, the fortieth room was the one filled with all the treasures and jewels. She twisted the doorknob, one jewel—beginning with *V* and ending with *Y*—on her mind.

"Sahara!" Vicky yelled, but not in an "I'm so relieved to see you" way.

Sahara followed her friend's gaze to the ceiling. Her heart nearly stopped. It had been a "Run. There's a monster" yell.

43

The Afreet

All the times Sahara had thought about rescuing Vicky, she never imagined coming face-to-face with the hideous creature hanging above her. Actual fire blazed out of his eyes as he stared at Sahara like she was breakfast. Saliva dripped from a mouth full of rotten teeth and knifelike fangs. Long, yellow-brown claws ripped into the ceiling, keeping him mounted upside down and giving Sahara a clear view of the oozing warts and blisters on his bald head.

"Is Baba in there?" she heard Yara cry out as she approached from behind.

Before her cousins or Yara reached the door, Sahara threw out her arms, blocking their entrance. It only took a second for them to realize why.

"An afreet." Yara's voice shook, giving words to the gasps coming from Sahara's cousins.

Sahara nodded, swallowing her words in case talking agitated the rust-colored beast. Her stare flitted to Vicky, who cowered in the corner. "Go," she mouthed to Sahara. But the look of resignation in Vicky's eyes only steeled Sahara's determination. There was no way she was leaving her friend to fend for herself against this awful monster.

"I'm not going anywhere without you," Sahara told her.

And though she kept her voice down, the afreet clearly didn't like what she had to say. He let out an earsplitting screech that Sahara was surprised didn't shatter the grimy glass candelabra hanging from the ceiling. If its flames—presumably an aftereffect of Peri's enchanted candle—had hit the floor, they would've set the room on fire.

He followed up his banshee scream by flicking out the most frighteningly massive tongue Sahara had ever seen. A few inches longer and its curled end would have surely smacked her on the head. Sahara's legs nearly gave out underneath her. Meanwhile, Yara and her cousins trembled behind her as the afreet sucked his tongue back into his mouth with a slurp.

"I-don't-think-any-of-us-are-leaving," Fanta muttered.

"He's . . . he's really scary . . ." Naima hesitated. Oddly, when she spoke again, her voice was steadier. "But what if he's scared of us?"

Sahara rotated her neck slowly to look back at Naima. Hopefully, it had been slow enough for the afreet to miss. Unlike the wild fear she saw in Fanta's and Yara's eyes, there was something more than fright in Naima's—sympathy, perhaps.

"Remember what Yara said about the man who used to live here and how he turned into a monster?" Naima mouthed the last word. "What if that's him? Maybe I can talk to him through the wind." Her eyes now asked the question, *Can I do this?*

Sahara gave one careful nod. If anyone could communicate with the beast, it was Naima. She held her breath as Naima stepped forward. The afreet cocked his head, staring strangely back at her.

"Naima, no!" Vicky cried.

"It's all ri—" Naima broke off.

The beast dropped from the ceiling with a thud, landing on all four of his hulky legs.

Yara and Fanta shrieked, but Sahara's scream got stuck in her throat like it did in her nightmares sometimes. Still, Naima didn't move. She raised her hand cautiously toward the afreet. It had barely risen an inch when he pounced, snapping wildly at her with his mouth. She fell back.

"Naimaaa!" Fanta screamed.

Just as the beast swiped his claws at Naima, something small barreled toward him, whacking him in the head. The afreet roared, spinning toward the source of the offending blast—Vicky. He slunk down and crept toward her, ready to strike.

Sahara shut her eyes, unable to look. Her mind raced like a flip-book of images, searching for something that could help them if it wasn't already too late. *The orphanage.* A little boy with dimples cupped his hands and whispered a secret Sahara couldn't make out. She strained to hear him as he spoke again.

"Afreets love stories. But it has to be a story about when they were good so they'll turn back to that."

She opened her eyes and sucked in air as if she'd been holding her breath underwater for the last minute. The afreet was inches away from Vicky, who was curled into a ball. Sahara's eyes searched for Naima. She was still on her back.

"Naima," she called out to her cousin.

The afreet swung his head toward Sahara and snarled, but she yelled out to her cousin over him. "You have to remind him of his life before all of this."

Naima warily propped herself onto her elbows. The beast twisted away from Vicky and crawled in her direction. She looked up at him, her eyes wide. "Your . . . your name used to be Fareed Sultan."

The afreet shook his head vigorously, but when he stopped, the fire in his eyes went out, revealing a pair of dark brown eyes.

Encouraged by this transformation for the better, Naima continued. "You fell in love and got married. You were happy. So happy."

As the beast shrank back, Naima stood up slowly. Very slowly. "But sometimes bad things happen." Naima's voice broke. Large tears fell from the afreet's eyes. "I'm . . . I'm so sorry. But your wife died."

The afreet fell to his knees. He let out a piercing wail, one Sahara's own grief immediately recognized. Loss's ballad sounds hauntingly the same no matter who sings it—human or beast. Sahara's heart wrenched as Naima extended her hand out once more.

"No!" Fanta cried from behind, but this time the afreet stretched his head toward Naima's fingers. His eyes softened.

"You don't have to live like this anymore," Naima told him. "It's not too late. You were good and loved. And you still can be."

Maybe Sahara was hallucinating, but she thought she felt the entire house exhale. And as that breath traveled through the remote parts of the house that hadn't seen the light of day in so long, it carried a message from Naima's hand to the heart of the afreet.

You are not alone.

Sahara glanced at Vicky. From the way tears fell down her best friend's face, Sahara could tell she'd heard it too.

The afreet began to pace around, suddenly seeming unsettled and preoccupied. Naima backed up toward Sahara as her pendant pulsed wildly, blue beams bursting forth from her chest. The house shook, rattling the shutters. Sahara turned to Naima and spoke quickly. "There's a room at the top. I saw it the other night. Take Fanta and Yara and go find her father."

Naima whipped around and grabbed her brother and Yara just as the glass candelabra clinked so loudly that Sahara worried it might crash down onto Vicky's head.

"Run over to me," Sahara yelled, but Vicky was frozen.

The shutters burst open, unleashing sunlight into the room. The afreet leaped back up to the ceiling as a cyclone of wind and sand whirled steps away from him, growing and growing in intensity—an intensity Sahara had only experienced once before.

Sahara raced for Vicky, dragging her to the other side. "Hang on to something," she yelled as the twister spun more viciously. Vicky grabbed the door. Sahara grabbed Vicky. They clasped hands, digging their heels into the ground like in a game of tug-of-war. But the more they bore down, the more the wind roared.

"This isn't working. Stop fighting it. Lean into it instead," Sahara shouted.

As their grips relaxed, the whirlwind of sand slowed until it came to a stop, leaving behind in its wake an ominous figure cloaked from head to toe in gray. Eyes peering out, glowing black like obsidian. So cold and hard they could only belong to one person.

El Ghoula.

Sahara's limbs went heavy. It was impossible to move. Time, motion, everything slowed down. Blood rushed through her ears, making it hard to hear Vicky. Though she thought she might have heard a scream followed by the words: *the witch*.

Dizziness quickly set in. In between the spots swimming in her eyes, Sahara caught a glimpse of the lamp dangling from one sleeve of El Ghoula's cloak and the golden apple peeking out of the other.

A tidal wave of devastation washed over Sahara. They'd been too late. Fayrouz could've already used the apple to heal the evil Jauhara and gotten the ring that would allow her to unleash the worst kind of jinn in the world.

But before Sahara's vision went black, a familiar hand, Vicky's, squeezed hers. How many times had the girls intertwined their fingers to celebrate their greatest joys or get through their worst troubles, even when they couldn't admit them to each other? There was still so much left to experience together. And nobody, especially not El Ghoula, was going to get in the way of that.

Sahara clenched Vicky's hand, allowing her friend to pull her out of this nightmare. As she took a deep breath, she opened her eyes, her senses snapping into high gear. Sahara stepped forward and looked Fayrouz dead in the eye.

"What did you do?" she growled at the witch.

"Me?" A surprised look overtook El Ghoula's face. "This is all *your* fault," she seethed. "Ever since you showed up, nothing has gone as it should."

Sahara knew the frustration of thwarted plans better than anyone, and she saw its sting in Fayrouz's eyes. *Yes!* Fayrouz may have had two of the enchanted treasures, but she had not accomplished what she'd set out to do with them.

El Ghoula looked down at the lamp and hissed, "You'd better work next time or else."

It started to shake. As the witch shoved the apple into her cloak and clutched the lamp's handle with both hands, Sahara spotted the emerald sword hanging from her belt. She'd been right.

"I knew you stole the sword!" she shouted. "Because of you, Amitu got fired."

"Because of you, Amitu got fired," Fayrouz repeated, mocking her. "And Sittu can't come home. Boo-hoo. Enough whining," Fayrouz railed. "I only took what was mine."

Sahara should've known the witch was responsible for the winds that had kept her grandmother stranded. "Naima was right. Everything bad that happens is because of y—" Sahara jerked forward.

The hamsa dragged her toward the lamp. The lamp dragged El Ghoula toward the hamsa.

"Sahara!" Vicky cried.

Sahara looked back. "It's okay. I promise." With the lamp already unlocked, this could only mean one thing. She turned toward Fayrouz and smiled. "It won't work. No. Matter. What." The pendant drove itself into the indent on the lid and twisted. *Click.* Sahara had never been so happy to hear that sound.

"It's over, Fayrouz. Give me the lamp," she demanded, then turned to Vicky. "Go find the others. I'll be all right."

"You didn't leave me, and I won't leave you." Vicky grabbed her hand again.

There was still a part of Sahara that wanted to shove Vicky out of the room to shield her from Fayrouz's wrath. But since when had pushing her friend away to protect her ever worked? She needed her. They needed each other. Sahara nodded and held on tightly to her friend's hand.

The afreet watched warily from the ceiling as Fayrouz strode toward the girls. Once again, the hamsa pulsed. *No!* Sahara thought as it tugged toward the lamp again.

"You can't control it, can you?" Fayrouz snickered, then threw her head back and let out a menacing laugh. Her hood had slipped back just enough to reveal the edge of the letter *hā* on her scalp.

If Sahara hadn't been busy wrestling with her amulet, she would've yelled, *Aha!* When she finally managed to force the pendant under her shirt, it popped right back out.

"It's meant for me." El Ghoula stared at the floating pendant yanking Sahara by the neck. "It has always been meant for me." Her eyes suddenly grew very faraway.

Your duty is not the whole of who you are. Umm Zalabya's words came rushing back as Sahara watched Fayrouz lose herself to what she had been told she was supposed to be. She looked back at Vicky, who hung on with all her might, not to the prophesied one, but to her best friend. Sahara was more than the girl who'd inherited the amulet. As she submitted to the depth of all she was and would be, the hamsa settled down. Within seconds, it was back against her chest.

"Hand over my family's lamp. You will never use it again," Sahara declared.

"You wretched girl." Fayrouz sneered. She turned to the afreet and murmured something that sent him diving off the ceiling. He swung his sharp limbs in the air and screeched. Whatever El Ghoula had said to him had made him really angry. Fayrouz raised her hand, commanding the wind around her.

"I don't know what your family's lamp does, but we can't let her escape with it," Vicky yelled.

Sahara would have a lot of explaining to do when they got out of here. "She won't," Sahara shouted back, jerking her head toward the window where Naima, Fanta, Yara, and the real Zalabya hovered outside on the magic carpet.

"You are good, Fareed Sultan," Naima reminded the afreet.

The beast gazed at Naima and bowed his head, then bounded for Fayrouz, knocking the lamp out of her hands. It clanged to the floor.

"No, you fool!" El Ghoula roared at the beast. The black glow in her eyes blazed as she removed the sword and heaved it into the afreet's stomach. A gurgle escaped his mouth when Fayrouz yanked the blade out. He fell backward, and his body went still.

"Fareed!" Naima screamed.

Just as Sahara was about to make a run for the lamp, it zoomed past her and into Yara's outstretched hand.

Fayrouz glared at the hawa symbol on Yara's head and then let out a piercing wail—not of grief, but rage—summoning a twister that broke through the foundation of the house, spiraling up and up until it crashed against the ceiling, smashing the candelabra and sending flames shooting down to the ground. The candles throughout the house must've fallen over too, because smoke billowed in through the hallway.

"We've gotta get out of here," Sahara yelled to Vicky between coughs, throwing one last glance at the golden sphere in Fayrouz's grasp. As much as she wanted to get Morgana's apple back, she knew there wasn't enough time. She grabbed Vicky and bolted toward the window. Yara's dad and Fanta pulled them onto the carpet.

As the rug zipped into the sky, El Ghoula's twister exploded through the roof, the old mansion collapsing into a fiery mess in its wake.

44

He's Gone

966 CE

As the sun gave way to the night's moonless sky, Husnaya raced through the garden to the front of the palace, where an officer arrived, panting. His eyes quivered wildly as he looked toward the soldier stationed at the entry.

"The afreet"—he sucked in air—"is out of the woods. He's headed straight for the city!"

"You must lead him away from our people and back toward the palace." A voice came from the steps.

Husnaya turned to find Zain. An irritated Marwan stood at his side.

"But, my prince, the palace will be ruined," Marwan urged heavily. "All that your father has worked for will be ruined."

"Mind yourself, Marwan." Mama strode through the doors. "He is soon to be your khalifa."

Jidda followed her. "Palaces can be rebuilt. But lives cannot be restored."

Husnaya stepped out of the shadows astride Almaz. "Zain is right. We should lead him back here."

Mama and Jidda looked up, their eyes flashing their surprise.

"And do what with him?" Marwan blasted.

"Lure him into the dungeons," Husnaya shot back. "If we use the steps in your study, we can get him in there quickly."

Marwan's eyes narrowed into angry slits.

"You heard the princess," Mama told the officers. "Lead him here, and we will trap him in the dungeons." She turned to her daughter. And for the first time, Husnaya saw something gentle and warm in her mother's eyes. Love, perhaps. "May Allah protect you, binti."

Husnaya bowed her head, then steered her horse toward the city. As Almaz galloped away, Husnaya could hear her mother command the soldiers to station men at the northern gate. If they were going to trap the afreet, they had to ensure all the entrances could be locked.

Husnaya was taken aback. Not just by how bold her mother was in the face of danger, but by her surprising support. The latter lit a fire within Husnaya. "Faster," she ordered Almaz, who gladly obliged.

In a matter of minutes, they raced past the mosque at the city's border. All around Husnaya, citizens screamed as the beast's roar infiltrated every inch of their home.

"It's coming from over there," Husnaya yelled to Almaz over their cries, steering her west. They reached the market just as the afreet was about to pounce on a mother and her two young children.

Husnaya had to get the afreet's attention. She thrust out her hand, delivering a gust of air that knocked him back into a fruit stand. He leaped to his feet, shaking the ground and screeching with anger.

Almaz reared up and neighed back at him. "Come and get us," Husnaya cried, riding past the afreet and toward the palace. The angry beast shrieked. But judging by the pounding coming from behind, he had shifted direction.

"It's working," Husnaya shouted to Almaz. She turned back for a peek at the afreet whose limbs stretched long, gaining on them with each stride. "Run as fast as you can, Almaz. I'll slow him down."

Husnaya channeled the wind into her hand, blasting it at the creature. He roared wildly against it, clawing at its invisible power as they reached the palace.

The afreet had been so distracted by the gusting wind he'd ignored the officers. The sound of the gates clanging shut bolstered Husnaya. She rode on, envisioning the relief she would feel when the dungeon doors finally locked behind the afreet. And then a blaring whistle came from the middle of the grounds at the edge of the garden, stopping both Almaz and the afreet in their tracks. Had Hassan come back to help?

"You have been a nasty thorn in my side all year." Marwan slithered out from behind one of the trees. "You may think I'm a fraud, but I learned a thing or two from your dear, dead Aziza."

Husnaya balled her fists.

"Unlike your fool of a brother, I pay attention," Marwan sneered.

Husnaya caught a flash of something gold in his hand. The beast slithered to Marwan's side and whined. "Spells must be cast at opportune times, amulets forged from the fire when the moon is missing from the sky, like tonight, to ensure their power." He twisted the scepter in his hand, and the afreet fell to his side, writhing in pain.

"You're hurting him," Husnaya cried. As much damage as the beast had done today, she couldn't bear to see him suffer.

"This is why girls should stay out of the affairs of men. They aren't brave enough to do what is necessary when the time is right."

He reached for something from behind. "You may have thought I was finished, but when I return to the palace with the carcass of the afreet, I will be back in the good graces of your family—what's left of it." A menacing smile took over his face as he raised a spear above his head and aimed for the beast.

"No!" Husnaya blasted her wind at him, knocking the spear out of his hand.

Marwan howled and foamed at the mouth. It was hard to tell the difference between him and the afreet. He charged at Almaz, making her rear up. Husnaya grabbed the reins, but they slipped out of her hands as she fell back onto the ground.

"Go and get help," Husnaya yelled to her horse before Marwan grabbed her wrists.

"I will end you tonight and blame it on the beast," he growled. "And no one will be the wiser."

Husnaya might not have been able to summon the wind with her hands restrained, but she could sense something was traveling against it.

"Unhand my sister, you devil," Hassan shouted, zipping toward them on the carpet. Marwan shifted his vicious gaze to her brother, giving her enough time to knee him in the stomach and knock the wind out of him. He fell back with a groan.

She ran over to Hassan. "You came back."

"I had to." His voice shook. "It was all my fault."

"Of course it was," Marwan hissed, struggling to get to his feet. "You've always been impulsive and petulant. Not fit for a khalifa."

Fire blazed in Hassan's eyes.

"Ignore him," Husnaya beseeched, but it was too late.

Hassan hurled himself at Marwan, knocking him back down to the ground. The cursed former sage grabbed her brother's throat and squeezed.

"Hassan," Husnaya screamed, hurrying toward them. A flash of emerald ripped through the air as Hassan yanked the sword from his belt and thrust it with all his might at his adversary's chest. Marwan fell over instantly.

Husnaya turned to her brother. A dark terror replaced the

burning rage in his eyes as he stood over Marwan. Hassan stared at the dead disgraced sage the same way he had stared at the lark's nest he'd accidentally knocked out of his tree when he was a young boy.

Then the afreet groaned. "He's alive." Husnaya ran over and put her hand on the beast's head. A breeze left her fingers, sweeping across his body. He let out a whine and stumbled to his feet. *It's over,* she told him through the wind. *Go back to where you came from.* The afreet sprang into the air and flew high into the sky, past the stars.

When she could no longer see him, Husnaya turned back to her brother. His eyes were filled with tears. "You saved him, and I . . ." He looked back at Marwan's body, unable to say the words.

In the distance, Husnaya heard Zain, Mama, and Jidda calling her name.

"They're looking for you." Hassan returned his sword to his sheath.

"For us," Husnaya said.

"How I wish that were true," he whispered as Almaz galloped through the trees, whinnying at Husnaya.

"It's all right." Husnaya brushed her hand along the horse's nose and then spun toward her brother. The carpet floated by Hassan's side.

"Don't go," Husnaya cried.

"Aziza would want you to make sure it gets to its *next rightful owner,*" he said, using the maid's words.

"It will," Husnaya promised.

"Good. I have no need for it anymore."

"Does that mean you'll stay?" Her voice rose with hope.

"I can't." Hassan raised his hands and circled his wrists. Wind twisted around his body, pulling the dry leaves and earth from the ground. It rotated faster and faster. Husnaya tried to slow it down with her hawa, but it was no use. She had never been able to control Hassan's winds. The quicker his whirlwind spun, the more he faded.

By the time Zain reached her, Hassan had completely disappeared. Zain's eyes darted to Marwan's body. "What happened? Are you all right?" he asked, throwing his arms around her. Mama and Jidda joined their embrace.

"The afreet?" Mama asked, her eyes searching the grounds.

There was so much Husnaya had to tell them, but all she could manage to get out were two words.

"He's gone."

PART FIVE
A New Start

45

No More Secrets

Fire truck sirens rang in the distance as the carpet zoomed away from the burning mansion. No one said a word for the next few minutes. They just silently leaned against each other. But as they whizzed toward the sparkling Nile, Naima signaled to a glimmering figure hovering above the water. One with arms and legs. And a face. The figure smiled and waved a hand at them before it zipped into the sky.

"It's him," Naima cried. "He's returning to his wife."

They watched Fareed Sultan, the man, not the afreet, soar out of view. Seconds later, a wind swept through the carpet, leaving behind a message: *Thank you.*

Hope filled Sahara's heart for the first time in days. She leaned into Vicky, who looked equally excited and nauseated, just like on all those school fair rides.

"We're almost there," she whispered to her as the carpet tilted down toward Umm Zalabya's building. Naima had directed the rug to the rooftop since landing there would be less conspicuous than in front of their building. The streets had begun to wake with the recent rising of the sun.

In the garden, the smell of the yasmeen's nighttime bloom lingered on their dewy petals as Sahara helped Vicky off the carpet. When they'd all gotten down, Yara introduced her father to her friends.

"Amani's daughter." The real Zalabya smiled, approaching Sahara. "Same eyes and same courage," he said, making Sahara beam. She loved Omni, but she'd take this version of Yara's father any day over El Ghoula's bewitched bot.

"Why have you been hiding this amazingness"—Vicky pointed to Yara's head—"under your helmet?"

"I was hiding from myself," Yara answered, her eyes shining with newfound confidence. "But not anymore."

Zalabya proudly eyed his daughter. "I never told you, but you inherited the hawa symbol from your nenna and all the women—"

"Who came before her," Yara finished for him, smiling at her father, who looked perplexed by her sudden knowledge. "There's a lot to tell you, Baba. Nenna's been training us."

As Yara filled her dad in on all that had happened while he was Fayrouz's prisoner, Vicky walked over to Umm Zalabya's empty rocking chair and leaned on the back of it.

Sahara joined her. "Happy to be back on the ground?"

"Happy to be back with you." Vicky looped her arm through Sahara's.

"How about a walk around the roof?" Sahara asked. "I've got a ton to tell you."

"Me too," Vicky said as they took their first steps together. For the next ten minutes, they unloaded the secrets they'd held so close to themselves and far away from each other all year. And though the circumstances of the stories they shared with one another couldn't have been any different, Sahara got exactly how Vicky had felt this year when she said things like, "I know I should've told you, but I wasn't sure you'd understand," or "I didn't know how to act. I've never been through anything like this before," and especially, "I felt so alone."

When they finally came to a stop, Vicky flung her arms around Sahara. "I was so worried I'd never see you again." Her voice broke.

"Me too." Sahara sniffled. "But that would be impossible. We're connected. For life. So whatever happens, I'll find you and you'll find me. Okay?"

"Okay," Vicky answered, then let go and held out her pinkie. "No more secrets."

"No more secrets," Sahara repeated, curling her finger around her friend's.

Vicky, who had kept her cool as Sahara had told her all about Morgana's legacy, now let her excitement fly free. "A magical chamber, seriously!" She grabbed Sahara's shoulders and jumped up and down. "Your family is way cooler than mine."

"The Millers are pretty cool too."

Vicky's face turned serious. "Even now?"

Sahara would tell Vicky later what Umm Zalabya had said about how the mistakes we make and the blows we take make us stronger, but for now, she just answered, "*Especially* now. Even though your brothers' room still smells like dirty socks."

Vicky giggled as Sahara playfully pushed her shoulder. "But there's still one thing you haven't told me." Sahara grinned.

"There's nothing else. I swear." Vicky's hand flew up to her heart.

"I'm talking about the thing you flung at the afreet's head to get him away from Naima. What was that?"

Vicky looked down regretfully at her wrist. "My bracelet from the market."

"Oh no. At least it made for an amazing slingshot. Besides, we still have mine and Yara's. We can share them."

"Since when are you okay with sharing anything with Yara?" Vicky snorted.

"Since she helped my best friend through a hard time." Sahara smiled at Yara, who was still speaking to her father. "She's pretty awesome."

"Talking about me?" Naima asked, sliding in between them.

"Of course," Sahara told her as she spotted her other cousin standing alone at the end of the roof. "Is Fanta okay?"

"He'll be fine," Naima groaned. "We make it back home alive with our family's lamp, and all he can think of is how long it's going to take him to earn enough money for another music player."

"I have an idea." Vicky strolled over to Fanta.

Sahara and Naima eavesdropped, but it was hard to hear from so far away. Though Sahara was able to catch Vicky saying something about having an extra music player back home. Fanta's face lit up like a neon sign.

Naima watched with a silly grin on her face.

"Don't even say it. They're just friends," Sahara insisted.

"Tab'an. Very close friends," Naima teased as the roof door opened.

One by one, Umm Zalabya, Amitu, Noora, Khalu Omar, Khaltu Layla, and Uncle Gamal poured out, flooding them with questions about their whereabouts.

Kitmeer charged through last, nearly knocking all the grown-ups down to get to Naima.

"I missed you too," Naima cooed as he jumped up and placed his front paws on her shoulder like he, too, was giving her a hug.

Sahara looked to Umm Zalabya, who was supposed to be their cover. The sorceress shrugged and turned toward the door. "I tried, but there's no hiding anything from her."

Sittu, still dressed in her white hajj clothes, stepped out onto the garden. A soft breeze rippled through the hem of her abaya and the tail of her headscarf. Simultaneously, the morning sun cast a warm glow over her face as her round brown eyes sparkled with specks of gold and her lips curled into a gentle smile. Dad and Amitu often told Sahara stories from the Koran about angels. She'd always had a hard time picturing them until today.

"Sittu!" Sahara cried, racing over to her grandmother's side.

As Sittu pulled her close, Sahara settled into the embrace she'd longed for since arriving in Cairo.

46

Double Trouble

"W ill you never learn?" Sittu chuckled, her chest shaking with laughter against Sahara's head. *Best feeling ever.*

"Enough with the lovey-dovey." Uncle Gamal snorted. "Now tell us il lihassal?"

Sahara treaded forward apprehensively, readying herself to take responsibility for what had happened. But before she opened her mouth to speak, her cousins, Vicky, and Yara hurried over, defending her on each side like a fleet of ships.

Bolstered by their support, Sahara rolled her shoulders back and started, "So you know that creepy mansion by Khalid's Café." And as best as she could, she recounted what the grownups had missed, her team of reinforcements filling in any gaps. Interestingly, neither she nor her cousins mentioned anything about the lamp's real power. And even though Sahara had promised Vicky no more secrets, it was the one piece of information she hadn't shared with her. Maybe because it didn't matter anyway since there was no way Sahara was unlocking that lamp ever again. Or maybe because Husnaya had warned about divulging its time-travel powers. Either way, the truth would remain hidden between Sahara, her cousins, and the magical trio for now.

"We only lied to protect you," Fanta added for good measure as the grown-ups descended upon the children.

In between a barrage of hugs, conflicting sentiments flew out of the adults' mouths: "How could you be so reckless?" "Alhamdulillah, you're safe." "Never do this again!" "What would we do without you?"

When everyone calmed down, Sahara turned to Sittu and Khaltu. "I'm so sorry about the chamber." That had been the hardest part to admit to. "It meant so much to our family, and now . . ." Sahara choked back tears.

Sittu caressed Sahara's cheek. "There's more to a magic chamber than walls and enchanted items. It's the promise to protect it that keeps it alive."

"And that has *never* been compromised," Khaltu Layla added softly.

"We will continue Morgana's mission. Just from a temporary base," Sittu declared.

"Mama, don't tell me you're thinking about Khaltu Zahra's. You haven't spoken to your sister in years."

"Well, then she'll be surprised to see us all. I'm a hajja now. It's time to let go of grudges," Sittu told her daughter, then turned to Umm Zalabya. "You and your family must come too, Samya. We cannot leave you when your powers haven't returned."

"That is kind of you, but something tells me they're almost back." Umm Zalabya smiled at her hand.

"What about the shop?" Naima asked.

"I can watch it while you're gone," Noora answered. "Allah knows I've been practically living there since I had to cover all the shifts you missed while training to save the world with your cousin. And Omar can't leave his patients or his boys."

"Are you sure?" Khaltu Layla asked.

"We'll be fine, my sister. There's no need to worry," Omar assured her.

"Morsy won't leave them alone," Uncle Gamal added.

"Unless fatteh's involved." Fanta snickered, making Sahara laugh.

Naima approached her mother. "I think I should stay and help Noora with the shop."

"Help her or the qutat you've been tending to in the Nassers' apartment?"

Naima's eyes widened. "You knew?"

"I didn't until this morning when I brought the Nassers' new tenant over. Could you imagine my surprise as I opened the door and found the box of kittens? You're lucky he's a retired tailor who lives on his own and loves cats. He'll take good care of them while we're gone." She squeezed her daughter's shoulder.

"One hour to get your things together," Sittu announced, heading for the door. "We have a long drive ahead of us."

Sahara had no idea where Sittu's sister lived. "Where are we going exactly?" she asked Naima.

"The Red Sea. Pack a bathing suit." Her cousin winked.

As Naima followed Sittu and her mother out the door, Amitu excused herself from the discussion she'd been having with Yara and her father and rushed over to Sahara and Vicky.

Tears fell down her cheeks. "Thank God you're all right. I promised your parents that I would watch over you. If anything had happened to either of you, I don't know what I would have done."

"We're okay, Amitu. Look, not a scratch." Sahara spun around slowly.

"What about that one?" Amitu pointed to the cut on Sahara's head.

"Except that one," Sahara said, then switched the subject. "So now that Yara's father knows the truth about Fayrouz stealing the sword, will he give you your internship back?"

"It turns out he wasn't even the one who offered it to me. Fayrouz had kidnapped him by then and must have had the fake Zalabya make the call to offer it to me."

"Ugh!" Sahara clenched her fists. "Probably to get us here before the end of the month. I'm sorry, Amitu."

"There's no need. Zalabya says the internship is mine whenever we return from the Red Sea."

"That's a relief. But speaking of the Red Sea, we should let

Dad know where we're going before he arrives here in nine days and freaks out."

"Good idea, Susu," Amitu told her, then turned to Vicky. "I'd understand after everything that's happened if you wanted to go home instead of coming with us. It wouldn't be any trouble. My friend works for the airline and can fly back with you."

"Are you kidding?" Vicky blurted. "I can't leave now. Not when the fun is just getting started." Her eyes flitted to Fanta, then back to Sahara and Amitu. Sahara pretended not to notice. "I love the beach." Vicky danced, shimmying her shoulders.

"We'd better get packing, then." Amitu signaled for the door.

"Be right there," Sahara said, then leaned toward Vicky.

"Are you sure? Wherever I go these days, trouble seems to follow."

A mischievous smile flickered across Vicky's face. "What's better than trouble?" she asked, striking a superhero pose.

Sahara puffed out her chest. "Double trouble!"

And for the first time in several months, the girls shared a long-overdue belly laugh.

A New Khalifa

966 CE

A week after the most significant loss the city had seen, rebuilding began with the coronation of the new khalifa. Imam Abdallah stood before a kneeling Zain. He placed the gold khalifa's crown on Zain's head. "May Allah bless you as he has blessed the great rulers who have come before you and will come after you."

As Zain stood up, the large crown slipped over his eyes. He quickly slid it back up, letting out a laugh that made everyone, even Husnaya, smile. Since Hassan had disappeared into a twister of wind, Husnaya wasn't sure she'd ever smile again.

"Though my father's crown may be too big for my head, I promise you I will grow into it and be as just and generous a khalifa as he was," Zain declared to the crowd. His eyes darted over to Husnaya. "My first official decree is to appoint my brave and honorable sister as my supreme adviser." All eyes turned to Husnaya. She had no idea her brother was planning on announcing her position today.

He gestured for her to join him.

"Today is about you," she said under her breath as she climbed the steps.

"It wouldn't be without you." He winked, flashing a new sword presented to him by Commander Osman for Zain's courageous and wise leadership in the face of the dangerous afreet and the treacherous Marwan.

Husnaya brought her hands, adorned with leather cuffs, to her head and bowed. She'd found Aziza's bracelets on her dressing table, along with an early birthday note from her the night she'd died. *Kol sana winty tayiba, habibti Husnaya. As you prepare to turn fourteen, it's time these became yours,* it read.

She smiled at Aziza's gift as the new khalifa raised his steel blade over her head. "Sitt Husnaya, I declare you principal sage and sorceress supreme of my empire. May your wisdom and benevolent magic guide me and all of us for years to come."

Husnaya couldn't believe these grown-up words were coming out of the mouth of the same boy who had stuck his tongue out at her last week. But then again, she was not the same. And neither was the city they both had vowed to protect today.

As Husnaya raised her head, Mama and Jidda joined them at the top of the steps. They placed yasmeen garlands over their necks.

"Sitt Husnaya." Jidda smiled at her granddaughter. "It has a nice ring to it. Don't you think, Dounya?"

"It certainly does." Mama turned to Husnaya and bowed her head. "We may choose to execute our royal duties differently, but we both strive for the security and happiness of our family and the people we serve. Without your courage, our city would have fallen. For that, I will be forever grateful." She peered into Husnaya's eyes. "You will always be my princess, but your brother and our people need—deserve—a sorceress supreme."

Husnaya kissed her mother's hand. She wished Aziza could be here to see this. But her heart warmed as Cook joined the court in throwing petals at her and her brother's feet. Mama had agreed to let him stay in honor of Aziza's bravery. For the first time in days, the air wafted with the sweet scent of hope.

Though Hassan never returned home, once a year on their birthday, Husnaya would wake to a burst of wind. Hassan's wind. She'd rush out of bed, hoping to catch it. But it was gone before she reached the window. Only his message lingered.

"Forgive me."

She was never quite sure if he was asking for forgiveness for the things he had done or would do. Either way, she always gave it to him.

The Next Adventure

The Saeedmobile pulled away from the shop a little after lunch, with Noora and Khalu Omar waving and praying for their safe travels, while a vigilant Morsy scanned the passersby. Yara and Umm Zalabya had stopped by while the girls were finishing packing to say goodbye and deliver good news.

"Nenna's powers are back!" Yara said, bouncing on the bed. "Show them," she told her grandmother, who smiled her toothless smile. The sorceress raised her hand, sending a soft breeze through the room that blew Sahara's curls away from her face. With it came a reminder: *If you need us, look to the moon.*

As they turned onto the 6th of October Bridge, Sahara held her backpack close—the vial, spyglass, Peri's candle, and the lamp secured inside. The hamsa gently tugged beneath her shirt. There would always be a pull between her amulet and the lamp, but as long as Sahara didn't allow her duty to overtake her whole being, she could control it. As for the magic carpet, it lay rolled up across all three rows of the van. Uncle

Gamal had initially suggested tying it to the roof but quickly took back the idea when Khaltu Layla shot him a look that brimmed with *Are you kidding?*

Not more than a minute onto the bridge, Naima yelled, "Wait. We have to go back. We forgot the paintings of the women in the chamber."

"Don't worry," Sittu said, craning her neck to see Naima. "They'll find their way to us. Remember it was not by our hands that they got to the chamber. And it will not be by our hands that they'll follow. But I am certain they will."

Naima nestled into Kitmeer, worry draining from her face. Her eyes danced with ideas, presumably of how the portraits would magically get to them.

Sahara pressed the hamsa to her chest, feeling the presence of all the ancestors accompanying them on their journey, as they had for the last thousand years. And though the moon wasn't visible, she was sure Umm Zalabya, Peri, Julnar, and Husnaya were there too—rolling along with them to the next adventure.

◇—○—◇

Author's Note

Letting go and leaving room for the unexpected are themes that consistently run through the pages of the Daughters of the Lamp series. Admittedly, I don't always greet the unexpected with open arms (remind you of anyone whose name begins with *S* and ends in *A*?). But I'm learning to accept that change, whether it shows up as a tiny ripple or a giant wave. It is unavoidable and, if I allow it to, often leaves me better than it found me. In 2017, I experienced a tidal-wave change when my family and I moved across the country. It was hard not to feel sad about all we were leaving behind. There were lots of tears and many days that left me wondering if things would ever be the same.

And they *weren't* ever the same. Since my previous plans no longer fit the current situation, I had to ask, "What now?" and sit in the uncomfortable "I don't know" space. But the more I did, the less uncomfortable it became. My *what now* turned into *what if* and *how about*, eventually leading to "How about I try to write a novel?" Sahara and her world were born from that question.

Writing has always been my go-to for self-expression. From a young age, when I couldn't figure something out, I would put my thoughts down on paper. So it makes sense that years later, when so much was uncertain in my life, I would turn to writing again. Though I would never have had the courage to dream I could write a novel if I hadn't had childhood teachers who celebrated my skills and if I hadn't grown up with my father's two published engineering manuals as mainstays on our living room bookshelf. It still amazes me that my dad, whose first language wasn't English, wrote and got two books published in America. Immigrant parents are incredible!

Back to the *what ifs* and *how abouts*. Once I'd figured out I wanted to write a novel, I had to decide what type of story and whose story to tell. The answer to the latter came quickly. As a mom and teacher, I was eager to share what I had learned from my daughters and students and the perspective I'd gained from my personal childhood experiences. Additionally, the books that impacted me the most were those I had read when I was young. Only, I often wished that the characters in those stories looked and sounded more like me and the people around me. Sahara developed from that wish.

I spent over six months researching Arabic folklore, asking my parents to recount stories they remembered from their childhoods in Egypt and reading published adaptations of them. Many of the anecdotes my mom and dad told me were variations of tales from *One Thousand and One Nights*.

I also encountered versions of them in the stellar compilation *Folktales of Egypt*, edited by Hasan M. El-Shamy.

Though the research phase was long and tedious, there were light bulb moments like the day I re-read the story "Ali Baba and the Forty Thieves." The character of Morgana, Ali Baba's servant, popped off the page, captivating me with all the witty ways she repeatedly saved Ali Baba from the thieves seeking to punish him for infiltrating their secret chamber. After discovering Morgana, I searched other tales for heroines who were courageous, wise, tenacious, and resilient. Women who left me wondering what if they were known for more than their beauty or lack of it (I encountered some hideous ogresses during research) and for more than their relationships to the male leads? What would those stories look like? That's when the series really started to take shape for me.

Now I just had to write the first book. Easier said than done. I knew nothing about crafting a novel. At forty-one, I was a beginner again, attending workshops online, studying craft books, and making new writing friends. I also read countless novels by other middle grade authors to learn what elements like story structure and deep point of view looked like in action.

It took two years to complete the initial draft of *Daughters of the Lamp* and one to get what I read on paper to match what I envisioned in my head. I found help with the second part in the form of input from dedicated critique partners and an exceptional mentor. Though, receiving feedback presented another challenge—accepting it. I'm not going to pretend it was easy, especially not with something I'd poured so much time, energy, and myself into. It still isn't. But it *is* necessary.

Everything I learned from writing the first book in the Daughters of the Lamp series informed how I crafted this second installment. I wouldn't say writing *Children of the Wind* has been easier, but it has been different because I now have a toolbox and a solid support system, which includes wonderful family and friends, an encouraging writing community, a rockstar agent, and a brilliant editor.

In many respects, this series is a tribute to the ancestors whose shoulders I stand on—the women, in particular. Both those I never got a chance to meet, whose stories have been overshadowed or lost, and those I grew up surrounded by. They blazed trails so I could have opportunities and choices they didn't have. And their fierce, savvy, and generous spirits made them the perfect muses for the heroines who grace my pages.

Nothing I've ever written or will write is going to be perfect. I'm not sure anything is. But I hope it will be honest. I hope it gives us a place to get knocked down by the waves of change and get back up together. I hope it shows that although life can be challenging and messy, it can also be joyful and beautiful. Especially when we let go of what we've determined should be and open ourselves to the possibility of what could be by venturing into the uncomfortable but transformative space of *what ifs* and *how abouts*.

That's where the magic happens.